Y0-CCB-118

"AN ABSOLUTE ROMP . . .

Written in lighthearted prose that will leave you smiling when it doesn't make you laugh out loud. A standing ovation for Maestro Levin is definitely in order."

West Coast Review of Books

"Thoroughly entertaining . . . Levin has a sharp wit. . . . [His] funny story is filled with more colorful characters than you can shake a baton at."

The Orlando Sentinel

"This hilarious portrait of classical music performance . . . keeps the reader smiling to the end."

Times Record (Wichita Falls)

"Clever dialogue, memorable characters . . . Levin is at his best in this finely tuned comic tale."

Library Journal

"Light and always enjoyable comedy . . . A well-orchestrated work indeed."

The Kirkus Reviews

Also by Michael Levin:

JOURNEY TO TRADITION (nonfiction)
THE SOCRATIC METHOD*

Published by Ivy Books

SETTLING THE SCORE

Michael Levin

IVY BOOKS • NEW YORK

Ivy Books
Published by Ballantine Books
Copyright © 1989 by Michael Graubart Levin

All rights reserved under International and Pan-American
Copyright Conventions, including the right of reproduction in
whole or in part in any form. Published in the United States by
Ballantine Books, a division of Random House, Inc., New
York, and simultaneously in Canada by Random House of
Canada Limited, Toronto.

*This book is a work of fiction. Names, characters, places and
incidents are either the product of the author's imagination or
are used fictitiously. Any resemblance to actual events or lo-
cales or persons, living or dead, is entirely coincidental.*

Library of Congress Catalog Card Number: 88-33660

ISBN 0-8041-0632-0

This edition pubished by arrangement with Simon and
Schuster, Inc.

Manufactured in the United States of America

First Ballantine Books Edition: October 1990

For my mother, Jenny Graubart

"I have written the most wonderful Missa [Mass]. . . ."
—W. A. Mozart,
undated letter to his publisher

THURSDAY MORNING

ONE

All right, all right. Let's get started, ladies and gentlemen. Come on. Find your seats." Donald Bright, baton in hand, perched himself on his conductor's stool in front of the chorus and clapped his hands to bring his troops to order. Years of experience had taught Donald that the best way to get everyone seated and to begin a rehearsal was to start them singing and save the speeches and criticism for later.

Donald considered himself a great motivator. He excelled at giving preconcert pep talks. He could make singers believe that the future of the Western world depended solely on how well they sang. Donald saw himself as the Knute Rockne of classical music. Like all great motivators, though, Donald knew that timing was everything. Donald had one large problem when it came to talking with his chorus. He often had trouble keeping his mouth shut.

"From the Gloria, ladies and gentlemen," said Donald. "Two measures before you come in. Do you have the place, James?"

James Carver, the accompanist, his lengthy frame folded beneath the piano, nodded quickly. James knew all of Donald's routines. James, in fact, knew virtually everything there was to know about Donald.

"All right, let's go," Donald said, his hands poised in front of him at shoulder height. His hands moved quickly to the sides, then up, and then down, as he called out, "Three and four and Gloria"

The chorus attacked with something less than full voice. Half the singers were still flipping through their scores, looking for the right page, and a dozen or so were still finding their seats. Within a few moments, all were singing loudly, and to Donald's ear, joyously. The volume of the sound was overwhelming.

Donald conducted vigorously, his entrances and cutoffs precise and firm. He bounced slightly on his seat as he led the group. His eyes were not on the score, or even on the singers, but were focused instead, somehow, on the sound itself. He seemed to be looking slightly above the chorus as though the sound were visible and hovering over their heads. He was listening to all four parts— soprano, alto, tenor, and bass—at once. Veteran Donald-watchers in the chorus thought he had not looked as spirited in months. After allowing the chorus a few minutes of energetic singing, he brought them to a halt merely by dropping his hands.

"All right. All right. That was good. You sounded *wonderful* at yesterday's rehearsal, ladies and gentlemen. I was delighted with you. Even the *sopranos* sounded wonderful."

The chorus laughed. Donald's war with the soprano section went back years. He would accuse them of attempting to outsing each other and the rest of the chorus. The key to choral singing was blending, not standing out, he would tell them. They would respond by singing even louder.

"I don't think Donald likes women," one of the sopranos, Alison Gardiner, whispered to her neighbor, Corinne Gates.

"He likes women just fine," Corinne whispered back. "He just likes men more."

Donald gave a quick glance toward the soprano section. He expected silence when he spoke. "Seriously," he told his singers, "I was thrilled yesterday morning. You all know how much this piece means to me. And it meant the world to me to hear you sing it with the orchestra. It's not every chorus that gets to make musical history. You should be proud of yourselves."

The chorus buzzed with self-congratulation. The idea of making musical history outweighed the inconvenience of three straight weekday morning rehearsals. Half of the singers were professional musicians with flexible schedules. The rest were teachers, bankers, lawyers, retirees, working and nonworking mothers, a car salesman, two intensely competitive astrologers, and a handful of the musically inclined idle rich. The members of the chorus who worked full time had to take vacation time, call in sick, or sneak away to attend the morning rehearsals. All considered the sacrifice worthwhile.

Today's rehearsal schedule was the same as the previous day's, calling for separate choral and orchestral rehearsals at 9 A.M., followed by a joint session at 10 on the Carnegie Hall stage. Tomorrow, the day of the performance, there would be a single joint rehearsal at 10 A.M. and a warm-up call at 7 in the evening, an hour before the concert.

"But you shouldn't be *that* proud of yourselves," Donald was saying. "We've got a lot of work to do and we've got very little time left before the performance. Just over twenty-four hours, ladies and gentlemen, and I understand that some of you want to see your spouses and children between now and then."

Again the chorus responded with laughter.

"So let's work smart, all right? By the way, are any of our trial lawyers present?"

Half a dozen hands went up.

"It's too bad Mozart's no longer with us," Donald said. "Otherwise he might hire some of you. To sue Andrew Barnes for malpractice."

The chorus laughed again. For weeks, Donald had been criticizing Andrew Baker Barnes, the guest conductor. It never surprised Donald that the chorus laughed at all of his jokes. After all, Donald alone decided who sang with the group and who did not. He accepted, on average, only one singer in ten who auditioned, and every member had to reaudition annually. This practice cemented Donald's grip on their attention.

"Just some minor things that I shouldn't have to be saying the day before a performance," Donald said, getting down to business. "First. Your Latin. It's *awful*. Gloria. Your vowels sound like mush. Make them as bright as possible. Glow-ria. Like Glowworm. And stay on the vowel all the way through the beat. The 'r' sound that follows is an ugly sound. 'R' always sounds ugly, and if you rush to it you'll ruin the sound. Let's hear it. Just speak it for now. Glow-ri-ah.''

"Glow-ri-ah," the chorus repeated.

"Een egg-shell-sis Deh-oh," Donald continued.

"Een egg-shell-sis Deh-oh," the chorus repeated.

"Good," said Donald. "I know that some of you have sung with other choruses 'egg-*che*lsis' or '*ex*-chelsis' or something entirely different. But *I* always ask for *egg-shell*-sis and I know and you know that it will sound much better if we all do it the same way. Once more: Glow-ri-ah een egg-shell-sis Deh-oh.''

"Glow-ri-ah een eggshellsis Deh-oh.''

"Good. Good. Moving on. Measure thirty-two. Find the place quickly. We've got a lot to cover. You completely ignored the dynamics," said Donald, referring to the markings in the score that indicate changes in volume. "*I* know why you ignored them. It's because Maestro Barnes ignored them. Ladies and gentlemen, whenever you have a choice of ignoring what's written and ignoring Barnes, please ignore Barnes. All right?''

James, the accompanist, stiffened as the chorus laughed at the criticism of the guest conductor. He wished Donald could be more discreet about his feelings toward Barnes.

"I shouldn't have to explain what I'm talking about," said Donald, chiding the chorus. "Dynamics, basically, means singing loud or soft. Shouldn't you know that by now? And one way to indicate them is with letters in the score.''

In the soprano section, Alison leaned toward Corinne. "I hate when he does that," Alison whispered.

"Does what?'' Corinne whispered back, eyeing Donald and hoping that he did not notice their conversation.

"You know," whispered Alison. "Lecture us. Whenever he gets pissed off, we're back in Music Theory 101.''

Donald glanced in their direction and went on. "A lower-case *p* just above a line of music," he told his singers, "means *piano*, which means 'soft.' An *f* means *forte*, or 'loud.' Two *f*'s means *very* loud. Triple *forte* means, well, wake the dead. Or the subscribers sound asleep in row Z.''

The singers laughed again. They understood that Donald simply wanted them to live up to his high expectations for them.

"Conversely," Donald continued, "*pp—pianissimo—* means *very* softly, and three *p*'s is so soft that only the angels, and the front six rows, can hear. If Maestro Barnes can get this chorus to sing *that* softly, *pianississimo*, it's called—he'll have done something *I* never could. This group knows only two dynamic levels. Sing your bloody head off, and sing even louder."

The chorus responded again with laughter.

"You think I'm kidding. Seriously. Look at your scores, ladies and gentlemen. Measure thirty-two. If you'll notice, there's a *pp* over the *laudamus te*. 'We praise you.' Sing it softly. Then *benedicimus te*. 'We bless you.' That has one *p*. Sing it slightly less softly. Let the intensity grow naturally and build into *adoramus te*. 'We worship you.' And then finally *fortissimo—glorificamus te!* 'We glorify you!' *Mean* it! Mean it when you sing it! Let it build! Let it *mean* something to you! Focus your attention on what you're doing, and it will mean something to the *audience*. Okay?

"Also, please. I don't expect you all to be Latin scholars but this is hardly the first time you've sung a Latin mass. What does *te* mean? It means 'you.' It means God. I don't care how you feel about God. I don't care if you're Roman Catholic or Hare Krishna. When you're onstage, you're conveying the *composer*'s ideas about God. Even if *you* haven't got any. Make *te* mean something. Don't just let it get swallowed up because you're getting ready for the next line of music. Make the whole line flow and make it beautiful. Right there. Measure thirty-two. Ready? *AND!*"

"*Laudamus te, benedicimus te . . .*" the chorus sang, and Donald noted with satisfaction the difference in volume on each successive phrase.

"That's it," he said, waving his baton sharply to cut them off. "Moving on. Measure sixty. '*Propter magnam gloriam tuam.*' Now when you sang that onstage you gave each syllable e-qual em-pha-sis. Imagine how silly it would sound if you did that when you *spoke*. It sounds just as silly when you sing. You'd sound like one of those talking computers in the movies. 'Good morning, Hal,' " he said in a mock-metallic voice. "Is that what you want to sound like? Anyone listening who knows anything about music will just laugh at us. And the audience tomorrow night will know plenty about music, I assure you, *Pro*pter *ma*gnam *glo*riam *tu*am, not whatever *you* were saying. For Your Great Glory. When you sing it, *mean* it. Let's go. Two beats before measure sixty. James, give me a D and an F-sharp."

Again Donald held his hands out at shoulder height, but this time as he indicated the tempo he kept his eyes on the chorus.

"*Pro*pter *ma*gnam *glo*riam *tu*am," they sang.

Donald cut them off.

"Excellent," he said. "Measure seventy-two. Actually, before we get to that, I just want to say a few words about the piece."

Members of the chorus, sensing a speech coming on, settled back in their folding chairs. A few of the women took out their needlepoint or knitting. On the surface, the singers all seemed to get along well with each other. In fact, the chorus had been divided into two camps as a result of a lengthy, bitter argument at a postconcert party five years earlier.

The dispute centered on whether the song "Happy Birthday" was in the key of F or D. One of the tenors had just turned thirty, but his birthday celebration, coinciding with a chorus party, dissolved into acrimony. No one would sing "Happy Birthday" until a key could be agreed upon. The people who believed it was in F themselves disagreed over whether the first note of the piece was F or C. Key of F people barely even spoke to Key of D people. Newcomers to the chorus would find themselves asked in what key *they* thought "Happy Birthday" should be sung. To their surprise, depending on their answer, half of the members of the group would treat them warmly and the other half would ignore them completely.

"You know what this piece means to me," Donald was saying. "I've already told you the story of how I found it. Many of you know how hard I've worked editing the score and preparing it for these performances. For me, being a part of these concerts is the greatest experience of my entire career. I wonder whether anything else I ever do will even come close. And I want all of you to feel the same way.

"I want you to know I got *chills* yesterday, listening to you sing. You all know how proud I am of you, and how excited I was when I found the score. Because I knew then that you, and no other chorus, would perform the premiere. So if I seem a little more testy than usual—"

Donald was interrupted by knowing laughter. He feigned surprise, smiled, and grew serious again.

"All right. I'm always testy. But if I'm even more of a perfectionist—okay, a pain in the ass—than usual—I hope you understand why. It's because I want you to be as good as you possibly can. And believe me, ladies and gentlemen, you can be *quite* good.

"I don't think it's ever proper to criticize a fellow musician behind his back. I shouldn't say what I'm about to say, but I just can't help myself. I've known Andy Barnes since graduate school. We were classmates at the Manhattan Conservatory."

Donald paused. The room was still. He opened his mouth to speak, but he stopped himself. He looked slowly around the room and looked down at his score. "Never mind," he said finally. "There's no point in getting into it now."

He checked his watch and looked at his singers again. "It's nine-fifteen, folks. Let's try to make good use of the time. Measure seventy-two. Let's go on."

TWO

Years and years earlier, Donald Bright had been the sort of musical child prodigy who gives the term "genius" a bad name. A thoroughly arrogant adolescent, Donald at twelve could outplay virtually any grown-up on his chosen instrument, or, more accurately, the instrument his parents chose for him, the violin. He looked with disdain on anyone who was not his match in talent. Few were, so he sneered at the world. At first, the world did not sneer back. The young Donald played recitals throughout the country to packed houses, breathtaking reviews, and the sort of career predictions reserved for only one child in a generation. He was written up in *Newsweek* and *Time*. "He is a genius," scholars, critics, and the world declared. Donald listened and agreed.

His childhood, therefore, was far from normal. He began violin at five and practiced seven hours a day under the watchful eye of his mother, a promising opera singer whose own career had ended when she learned she was carrying Donald. The boy seldom played with other children—he and his mother considered it a waste of time. He gave his first recital at age seven for family, his parents' friends, and his mother's talent agent. His first public performance followed a year later. From ages eight to twelve, Donald rarely saw a toy or game, a classroom, or another child his own age. He was touring and receiving increasingly important bookings until, finally, at age twelve, he was performing violin concertos with some of the leading orchestras in the nation. His earnings supported his entire family: his father, who quit his job as a payroll accountant and became the boy's booking agent when the family had tired of paying commissions; his mother, his first and only violin teacher and also his private tutor; and his brother, Sam, who at eight possessed as much raw talent as did Donald, although he refused to practice.

All this glory came at a high price. Deprived of even the semblance of a normal adolescence, and accustomed to being the center of attention in his family, in rehearsal and performance, and at postconcert receptions in his honor, the young Donald became moody, petulant, short-tempered, and occasionally foul-mouthed (he picked up swear words from the stagehands). He was a terror to those conductors whose misfortune it became to conduct him. He took direction badly. As often as not, he ignored conductors, steamrolling past them in concert, doing things his own way. Eventually word about the difficult young virtuoso made its way along the classical-music grapevine. Orchestras refused to play with him; conductors turned down concerts at which the young Donald was scheduled to appear. Bookings dried up. Donald's budding career was over.

Donald's parents reacted by abandoning interest in him, turning their attention instead to his younger brother, Sam. Unlike Donald, Sam was gentle, pleasant, and unremarkable on the violin. The world embraced Sam nonetheless when the boys' parents first presented him in a solo Carnegie Hall recital. Donald unknowingly underwrote Sam's debut: his parents tapped Donald's earnings to pay for the rental of Carnegie Hall and for a massive publicity campaign on young Sam's behalf. The investment paid off. Good-natured Sam was launched on a career that rivaled Donald's despite his inability to play as well as Donald. No one minded; he was such a pleasure to conduct or to accompany that he could almost have played out of tune and he still would have won the hearts of the audience. The boys' parents dumped Donald in a rigid, expensive New England boarding school and went off to tour with Sam. They rarely called or visited. When summers came, they enrolled him in summer school.

Donald's world had collapsed. No longer the center of attention, he sulked. He made no friends. He became a discipline problem. He was unused to classes and fell far behind his classmates academically; his grades were poor. He refused to go near the violin. Besides, his parents had given his beautiful Amati to Sam. Donald's arrogance now became a cover for the sense of confusion and abandonment he carried with him. Most of his teachers liked him as little as did his fellow students.

Most, but not all, of his teachers felt that way. An instructor in English, a Mr. Pirante, who alone among the faculty had seen the young Donald perform in concert, made of Donald a "project." Slowly, over the course of several semesters, this Mr. Pirante drew Donald out of his shell, taught him study habits, upbraided him for his occasional rudeness, and even got him to play on a borrowed violin. Mr. Pirante played the piano. The two would perform duets, but never for an audience. Mr. Pirante, in short, humanized Donald. For the first time, Donald found himself able to make friends. Mr. Pirante's own friendship, though, like everything else in Donald's life, came at a price. He regularly sodomized the boy and threatened him with expulsion if he reported it. Donald would never have reported it. Mr. Pirante's advances constituted the first affection Donald had ever regularly received.

By the time Donald was graduated from prep school, he was an A student, awkward socially but no longer quite so arrogant, an applicant to the leading music conservatories in the country, and thoroughly confused as to his sexual identity. His parting with Mr. Pirante was a tearful one, at least on Donald's part. Unbeknownst to Donald, Mr. Pirante had found himself a new, introverted twelve-year-old to encourage. Neither of Donald's parents, who had divorced after a bitter dispute over their sons' concert earnings, attended Donald's graduation.

Donald, who never saw a nickel of his earnings as a child prodigy, enrolled at the Manhattan Conservatory of Music in New York City. He studied conducting—Mr. Pirante had suggested it. His vast talent reasserted itself. His arrogance did not. Donald, for the first time in his life, found himself liked by the majority of his fellow students. He won a string of conducting prizes. Women asked him out on dates. Some of the male students invited him for quiet assignations in the dorm. Whatever the offer, Donald usually went along. It passed the time.

Donald essentially kept his sadness to himself. He never spoke about the past. His conducting professor, Albert Nouse, took him aside and told him that a great career was his, if he wanted it. Donald wanted it, although he was not sure why. Perhaps he wanted to prove his parents, who had lost faith in him, wrong. He received his bachelor's and his master's degrees from the conservatory. He won his first conducting job as assistant to the world-renowned conductor of the New York Symphony Chorus, Philip Popham. All those who thought they knew Donald thought Donald was on his way.

THREE

Donald's conducting career had gathered momentum under circumstances of which he was not particularly proud. Philip Popham had hired Donald for two reasons: first, Donald's brilliant record at the conservatory, and second, Donald's attractiveness—brown, troubled eyes, curly hair, a healthy if unathletic body. Donald parried Popham's advances—he knew how, by now—but after only a week with the chorus, Donald was dismayed to learn that Popham expected him to do something unmentioned in Donald's formal job description.

As disillusioning as this may sound to lovers of fine music, Donald was expected to procure for Popham—to hire prostitutes, one of each sex, in New York and in every city when the chorus and orchestra took to the road. Cash for this purpose was siphoned quietly from the New York Symphony Foundation, a nonprofit organization supported by private donations and large corporations.

The donors thought they were supporting the arts. The arts they were supporting were probably not the ones they had in mind.

Symphony management knew of and tolerated Popham's deviancies because he was such a good choral conductor. Many music critics, in fact, considered him the leading Brahms interpreter of his generation. They often wrote of him as a likely candidate to replace Ugo Barelli, the New York Symphony's chief conductor, upon Barelli's retirement. Barelli did not intend to retire, though. Ugo claimed that he wanted to die with his baton in his hand. Popham often said this would be perfectly fine with him.

Barelli, like many orchestra conductors, considered choral conductors second-class citizens on the podium. The roots of this prejudice are obscure, but it is fairly deep-seated in the music world. Barelli, an unsubtle sort of man, called chorus conductors "zookeepers." In his thick Sardinian accent, the word sounded like "zucchinis." Philip Popham did not like to be called a zucchini by *anyone*, Ugo Barelli least of all. An uneasy truce existed between Popham and Barelli until Popham was forced to resign, suddenly and in disgrace, during Donald's first summer with the chorus. Donald was inadvertently the cause of Popham's firing.

Two people, a man and a woman, stole Popham's car, which was parked outside a Detroit hotel three blocks from where the chorus was staying. The Symphony orchestra and chorus were on their summer tour. The thieves found a briefcase in Popham's trunk containing eighty thousand dollars in payroll checks for the Symphony. The cheks were cashed and the money was never recovered. People connected with the Symphony thought it wrong to fire someone over something not entirely his own fault. People who were even better connected knew that there was more to the story.

Philip Popham, the great Brahms expert, had been lying in an oversized hot tub enjoying the services of his two twenty-year-old prostitutes, one male and one female, for whose services Donald had been unhappily obliged to arrange. After Popham fell into a highly satisfied slumber, the youthful professionals rifled his wallet, found the garage claim check, pretended to be Mr.

and Mrs. Popham, and removed the briefcase (and the rest of Popham's luggage, including his formal concert wear) from the trunk of his car. They even tipped the parking attendant with a pair of tickets to that night's Symphony concert. The tickets also came from Popham's wallet.

The car was found six months later at the bottom of the Detroit River. The prostitutes had cashed the checks, split the proceeds, and disappeared. How they knew to find the checks in Popham's trunk remained, for most people, the unanswered question. The answer was that they overheard a telephone conversation between Donald and Popham in which Donald advised the conductor to get the checks out of his trunk before he went to the hotel room for his encounter in the hot tub. Popham failed to take this advice, however, and the checks were lost.

Symphony insiders partial to Popham blamed Donald and said that Donald had deliberately set Popham up. This was not true, but rumors take on lives of their own. The version of the story blaming Donald found a place in the official backstage mythology of the Symphony. Most people accepted it as fact. Even some people auditioning for the chorus had heard, from friends in the group, of the Popham affair. Their friends encouraged them not to make jokes around Donald concerning prostitution, stolen cars, payroll checks, or the city of Detroit. Such topics were not likely to surface in choral auditions, but forewarned was forearmed.

Donald hated that people believed he sabotaged Popham's career. It frustrated him to think that there was nothing he could do to convince them otherwise. Even after all these years, though, Donald often asked himself why he had made the fateful telephone call to Popham in the presence of the prostitutes. Perhaps, on some murky level of his subconscious, he really intended to get Popham in trouble. Donald was never able to shake this question from his mind. Procuring for an autocratic bisexual choral conductor on the outs with Ugo, Donald believed, was no way to get his own great career off the ground, but he did not want to think that he acted deliberately to get Popham fired.

Ugo Barelli fired Popham before the chorus and orchestra even left Detroit and he installed Donald as acting choral conductor. Donald's interim position became permanent with the passage of time—Ugo never got around to interviewing other candidates or officially giving Donald the job. Choral conducting did not really matter to Ugo. Thirteen years later, though, Popham was leading the glee club at an obscure religious college in the Pacific Northwest. The New York Symphony Chorus still belonged to Donald.

Like Popham before him, Donald viewed choral conducting as a way station to something he considered even more important—leading an orchestra of his own. Donald knew, though, that virtually every first-rate orchestra conductor shared Barelli's idea about dying with baton in hand. Donald therefore considered himself trapped, along with hundreds if not thousands of other aspiring conductors, in something he called the "funnel"—a vast talent pool of men and women searching for ways to distinguish themselves from their peers and achieve a little stardom of their own. His classmates, who tried to support themselves conducting "downtown" orchestras of lawyers and accountants, church groups, children's ensembles, and college students, were among those trapped in that funnel.

Donald was luckier than most of them, of course. His salary was relatively high for a professional musician. His position in New York guaranteed him a lot of visibility. He had escaped the ignominy of some young conductors of small-city orchestras, who actually earned less than the janitors of their concert halls. Donald might not have had an orchestra of his own, but at least he was not starving.

Not everything went Donald's way during his years with the chorus. His emotional life remained unfulfilling and unfulfilled. His professional life included some disappointments as well. Another rumor about Donald began to circulate, to the effect that he had quit his performing career at age twelve because he had developed a severe case of stage fright. This was not true, of course, but Donald was hardly about to counter the rumor by explaining how his parents had abandoned him in favor of his younger brother. He therefore gained an unfair reputation for doing a good job in rehearsals (this much was true), but when it came to performances, people told each other, *Donald couldn't hack it*.

The three New York Symphony concerts he was permitted to conduct over his years with the chorus only served to add to the veracity of the rumor. The first time he conducted, he was given inadequate rehearsal time for a premier of a complex, nonrhythmic, atonal, eighty-four-minute piece scored for an enormous orchestra and taped sound effects. It fell apart in performance, and people backstage gave each other knowing glances. Donald's fault, they told each other, although it was not Donald's fault. No one could have made that performance come out right.

Donald's second concert, ironically enough, involved a bitchy eighteen-year-old cello soloist who refused to take orders from any conductor, especially one as young and relatively unproven as Donald. Another disaster; more undeserved blame for Donald. By the time of Donald's third, and, it seemed, last chance to salvage his reputation and his career, he felt so much pressure to succeed that he developed a case of stage fright such as the music world had seldom seen. He came down with diarrhea, laryngitis, rashes, a high fever—and when he went on stage to conduct, he knew, and so did everyone in the orchestra, that the concert would be an utter disaster. It was. Donald was never asked to conduct again.

The experience was so humiliating for Donald that he took a leave of absence from his chorus and went to Vienna, to hide. The ostensible purpose of this sabbatical trip was to study the music of Franz Schubert. While he was in Vienna, though, a small miracle happened. Donald became the beneficiary of luck that was wholly good. While going through packets of Schubert's letters, Donald came upon a score of a Mass that he had never heard. The handwriting on the score, Donald knew instantly, belonged to Mozart. The Mass had been hidden away for two hundred years. Donald's cry of recognition could be heard a block away.

Donald was certain that Providence had sent him this Mass as an opportunity to redeem himself. He would conduct the premiere, do a magnificent job, lay to rest

the rumors about his inability to perform—and then some
fine orchestra, somewhere on the face of the globe, would
offer him the post of chief conductor. For the first time
in his life, Donald believed that in the Mass he had found
something that no one could possibly take away from
him.

But he was wrong.

FOUR

Shortly after the conclusion of the choral rehearsal, the
guest conductor, Andrew Baker Barnes, stood in the
harsh glare of television lights at the podium on the Carnegie Hall stage. He was smoothing the pages of the Mozart score on his music stand. He stole a glance at the
unruly orchestra running through the last of its warm-
ups, scales, and trills. Some motion in the large chorus
behind the orchestra caught his eye, and he scanned the
singers' expressions for a sign of warmth: a smile, an
upturned face, anything. Those few singers not talking
or studying their scores returned the conductor's gaze
with a look of polite curiosity.

Barnes turned for a moment to face the cameras ready
to record the rehearsal. He looked around the nearly
empty hall, its tiers and boxes seeming to stretch back
forever. He peered at the last row of the highest balcony
and remembered sitting there once for a concert with the
same New York Symphony Orchestra now seated before
him. He remembered watching Leonard Bernstein conduct Gershwin's *Rhapsody in Blue* from the piano. *My
God*, Andrew thought. *I'm standing where Bernstein
stood. God help me.*

Barnes then began to wonder why he was thinking

about Leonard Bernstein and not about the Mass he was about to conduct. He knew, though, that he often had trouble concentrating, sometimes even during performances. Once, he was leading a huge orchestra and chorus in the "Ode to Joy" when he caught himself trying to recall how many shirts he had dropped off at the dry cleaner that morning and whether he remembered to ask for extra starch. Conducting is a lot like sex, he decided: if your mind wanders, don't tell anyone.

Andrew glanced at the side of the stage and noticed that the patrolman assigned to guard him, Officer Caruso, was watching him intently. Officer Caruso was twenty-three and in his first year on the force. Guarding Barnes was his first important assignment. Not that arresting muggers and turnstile jumpers on the IRT wasn't important, of course, but working in Carnegie Hall had a little more class. The patrolman had been at the conductor's side since his arrival from London two days earlier. Officer Caruso was planning to repanel his den with the overtime pay he had been racking up. Other police officers had been wandering through Carnegie Hall for days and several were backstage this morning—Barnes required a lot of guarding.

Twelve rows from the stage sat Donald and James, his accompanist. Donald sat low in his chair, his arms folded, his mouth set in a deep frown, his eyes fixed on Andrew Barnes. Donald's conductor's score lay unopened in his lap. Onstage, Barnes took a handkerchief out of his pocket and mopped his brow.

"He doesn't look too confident up there," James observed.

Donald nodded. "He has no right to be confident," he said. "He may be the least qualified conductor who ever stepped on that stage."

Andrew Barnes in fact did not feel confident, although his situation was enviable. For thirteen years music director—principal conductor—of London's Royal Symphonic Society, he had come back to the United States to make his debut as guest conductor of the New York Symphony Orchestra. The Symphony had engaged him to conduct three performances of the Mass in F Major by Wolfgang Amadeus Mozart. The Public Broadcasting

System was even preparing a documentary on "The Making of the Mass." This explained the unusual presence of television cameras at a rehearsal.

(The narrator of the special would be the highly popular Charlie Churchill, a two-hundred-fifty-pound former weatherman and, more recently, public television's arbiter of what was new and important in America. Charlie, who confessed to knowing almost nothing about classical music, would not arrive until tomorrow, though. The program would be edited over the weekend and presented nationwide the following Tuesday evening, introducing America both to Barnes and to the Mass. Purists were horrified at the thought of a nonmusician doing a special on the Mass, but for Barnes, an unknown in the United States, Churchill's imprimatur was a public relations coup.)

Although Andrew would conduct the concert, Donald expected to play a large role in Charlie Churchill's special. After all, Donald had found the Mass. Mozart himself acknowledged the existence of the Mass in an undated letter to his publisher: "I have written the most wonderful Missa only this month. It contains a cadenza [brief solo section] for oboe unlike anything I have done before. It is for B, the young woman who plays oboe so well in my chamber orchestra. I will send it to you for printing shortly."

No Mass in F ever appeared at the publishers. Musicologists subsequently identified "B." as Beatrice Hofsteder, a student of Mozart's who, evidence suggests, refused Mozart's attentions and was unmoved by his composing a Mass in her honor. ("This man Wolfgang writes nice music," she wrote a friend, "but he *talks* so much.") After she refused to sleep with the composer, who was then twenty-two, he withdrew the Mass from his orchestra and hid it away. No record of its performance survived, and the score itself was thought lost until Donald unearthed it. Andrew Baker Barnes, therefore, was about to do something that no one had done for two hundred years. He would conduct the world premiere of a composition by Mozart.

From his twelfth-row seat, Donald continued to stare at Barnes's back. "You know, it should have been me up there," he said to James, who responded with a look of sympathy. Donald had been making similar comments for the past six months, ever since he learned that Barnes and not he would conduct the premiere. James always responded with the same look of sympathy. James prided himself on giving good sympathy.

At the podium, Andrew looked around the orchestra again. "You bastards had better pay attention this time," he murmured. Then he remembered that a technician had clipped a microphone to his shirtfront. "I mean, this is just the finest orchestra I've ever had the privilege to conduct," he added, just loud enough so that the microphone could pick it up.

Barnes rapped his baton against his music stand, but the orchestra ignored him and continued to warm up. Barnes should have known that rapping his baton for attention was a display of bad form bordering on amateurism. Although movie scenes of orchestra rehearsals invariably show the conductor tapping away for silence, professional musicians consider it insulting and a breach of musical etiquette. Barnes, unaware, mopped his brow again and rapped the baton a few more times. He would have done anything to get their attention.

"I'm sure the orchestra would much rather be playing for you," James whispered to Donald, trying to make him feel better. James knew, though, that nothing could make Donald feel better short of Andrew's being struck by lightning.

Onstage, Andrew Barnes, through a combination of rapping, throat clearing, and imploring glances, at last won silence from the orchestra. He addressed them briefly.

"Good morning, ladies and gentlemen," he began. "It's an honor for me to lead you. As I told you yesterday, this is my first time as a guest conductor of the famous New York Symphony Orchestra"—Barnes chose not to mention that this was his first guest-conducting job *anywhere*—"and I've been looking forward to these concerts for quite some time. It's an honor for all of us to do Mozart's work. Shall we begin?"

Barnes motioned with his right hand for the chorus to

rise. They stood, shuffling their scores open to the first page.

"From the top, ladies and gentlemen," said Barnes, lifting his baton and holding it for a long moment between his hands, which were clasped penitentially before him.

"Is he going to pray or conduct?" Donald whispered.

"I don't know," James whispered back. "Maybe that's his style."

At length Barnes drew his hands apart and with a graceful upward and then downward motion of the baton and his right hand he commanded the orchestra to begin. The strings—the violins, violas, cellos, and basses, began the slow, stately Kyrie Eleison, the first movement of the Mass. They were joined moments later by the woodwinds—the oboes, the bassoons, and the clarinets. Barnes conducted smoothly with barely perceptible motions of his hand. He was known for an unaffected style. He was not one for leaping around the podium in transports of musical ecstasy, but he could be fairly dramatic in his movements once he got going. He held the baton lightly against his open palm, a palm that seemed to caress and shape the sound as it passed him on its way to the vast hall.

With an upward sweep of his left hand Barnes indicated a crescendo, a gradual increase in volume. The orchestra obliged and the music grew louder and more complex. Then, at the top of the controlled, shimmering sound Barnes looked to the thirty basses in the chorus. Suddenly he gave an imploring signal with the baton and gave their entrance cue—flicking his index and middle fingers off his thumb—with his left hand, and in the bass section, there was a tremendous rush of air as the singers all took breath.

The basses responded with power and control and exploded as one man the "K" at the beginning of the phrase "Kyrie Eleison," placing it at the precise moment that Barnes flicked his fingers across his thumb. They sang their line, an echo of the first notes of the piece, and now Barnes turned his attention to the tenors and gave them their cue. They came in with an equally percussive "K" on "Kyrie," their notes echoing the line of music that the woodwinds had just finished. Moments later Barnes added the altos—the women whose voices were the lowest. They repeated the line of music the basses sang. Finally came the sopranos' entrance. They repeated the tenor line. At last all the elements of the piece were in place and the sound of orchestra and voices filled the hall.

Watching from the side of the stage, Officer Caruso took off his cap and scratched his head. His cap, like the rest of his uniform, was practically brand-new and was slightly too large for his body. He had barely met the minimum qualifying standards for height and weight. At five feet nine and one hundred forty-five pounds, he was not exactly the imposing force that elicits the respect and fear of potential wrongdoers. His baby face and ill-fitting uniform only made him look smaller and less authoritative. His enthusiasm for his job more than compensated for his distinctly un-coplike appearance. Officer Caruso thought that the orchestra was not watching Barnes carefully enough. This bothered him.

Donald Bright also thought that the orchestra was not paying much attention to Barnes, but he did not care. He sat low in his seat, his eyes closed, a slight smile on his lips. "Not even Andy Barnes can screw this up," he said softly.

By now Barnes's gestures had grown in size as the volume of sound increased. He continued to beat time with his right hand and give editorial directions—louder, softer, not so much clarinet, a little more cello—with his left. The chorus, divided in four parts—soprano, alto, tenor, and bass—repeated the phrase "Kyrie Eleison" in a variety of ways, their eyes fixed not on Barnes's expressive direction but on their own scores. At length Barnes gave the chorus their last out-cue, a semicircular motion with his left hand in the course of which his middle finger and thumb met. The chorus stood silent. Some of them turned back a few pages in their scores and penciled in some performance notes that had come to them while they were singing. The orchestra played on.

The mood of the piece changed now. The music was softer, more intimate, almost pleading in tone. The soprano soloist rose from her metal folding chair a few feet from the podium, and at Barnes's cue—a slight toss of his head—she sang "Christe Eleison"—"Christ, have mercy"—again and again, accompanied by the orchestra and, after a while, by the chorus. Barnes failed to cue the basses for their entrance this time. Half came in anyway and half came in a few beats late. Barnes, conscious of his error, gave clearer directions to the tenors, altos, and sopranos at their respective entrances.

"Just get to the end of the movement," Donald implored.

"Huh?" James said.

"I'll explain later. I just want him to go through the whole movement once without stopping."

"Did you hear a mistake?" James asked.

"I'll explain later."

Andrew Barnes was also intent on finishing the movement. The Christe Eleison section, with its interplay between soprano soloist and full chorus, ended. The orchestra returned now to the slower pace and more majestic sound of the opening section. Failing to give the basses their cue for the "Christe Eleison" was a small thing. By the time of the second orchestra rehearsal, a chorus should not expect the conductor to provide every cue and cutoff. Accomplished singers should know these things simply by looking at their scores. The lapse rattled Barnes nevertheless. He was perspiring freely now and he grabbed at his handkerchief and wiped his brow, conducting all the while. Instead of thinking about Mozart, Barnes was recalling his personal record for sweat stains—all the way down to his elbows. For this reason, he usually wore white shirts to rehearsals.

Moments later, the handkerchief still in his hand, he failed to cue either the sopranos or the altos to begin the final Kyrie Eleison section. The chorus, in brief disarray, managed somehow to pull itself together and the end of the movement was as stirring and graceful as its beginning.

"Well, I'm wrong," Donald told James with an air of wonder. "He *did* find a way to screw it up."

"To no one's surprise," said James, glancing at Donald. Donald was thirty-eight. His curly dark hair, flecked in places with gray, had begun ever so slightly to recede.

He tended to overeat, especially on those nights when, after eight weeks of rehearsals, he turned the chorus over to Ugo Barelli for the last few rehearsals prior to concerts in which the chorus would perform. On those days, Donald suffered from a form of separation trauma. He assumed that mothers felt the same way on the first day their children went to school. Those were the times when he was most likely to spend the evening within cruising distance of his refrigerator. He could go through a pint or more of ice cream at a sitting. Donald often joked that he would write the ultimate self-help best-seller: *Solving All of Life's Problems Through Food.*

"Why were you so worried about him stopping?" James asked. "Conductors always stop during rehearsals."

Donald made a face. "A typical Andrew Barnes rehearsal involves a lot of Andrew Barnes talking and very little music. He'd rather tell stories than conduct. It's not that he's lazy. He just doesn't know what to listen for. Like the second violins at measure one thirty-eight, did you hear them?"

James, whose ear was keen, had not heard them. He was in awe of Donald's ability to hear every note played or sung onstage. Donald could absorb a musical score in the time it took most people to study a train schedule.

At the podium, Barnes mopped his brow again. The orchestra and the more musically astute members of the chorus could sense his discomfort. "*Bravo*, ladies and gentlemen," he was saying. "*Bravi tutti*. Janet, your solo was marvelous. Don't change a thing. Now, chorus—"

Janet Ikovic, twenty-four years old, strikingly attractive, and about to make her own debut with the New York Symphony, gave Barnes a puzzled look. She knew that her solo had *not* been marvelous and that if she took his advice and changed nothing, she would never be invited back to sing with the Symphony. Most soloists spare their voices in rehearsals, and rightly so. Their voices are their livelihoods and it is pointless to waste a "money note"— say, the high C on which their reputation is based—on an empty hall. According to opera legend, Enrico Caruso (no relation to Officer Caruso) was the last singer to practice and to sing in rehearsals at full voice. Mere mortals cannot afford to do such things.

Janet had given a relaxed, professional reading of her part, but she had hardly sung it the way she would in concert. Did Barnes really want her not to change a thing? She seated herself, shaking her head slowly. She had heard the rumors that Barnes was a nice guy but a hack as a conductor. Maybe there was something to those rumors, she thought. At least he did not try to rush her through her part, as so many conductors did. That was a plus. As she sat down in her folding chair, though, she felt a slight tightening in her throat. *Not now*, she thought. *I can't get a sore throat now.*

Paul Martland, the tall, stoic New Englander who would sing the tenor solos in the Gloria, Credo, and Agnus Dei movements, was seated next to Janet Ikovic. He glanced appreciatively at Janet and wondered whether she was staying in his hotel.

Barnes, meanwhile, was addressing the chorus. "You've just *got* to watch your entrances. I'm not kidding around, folks. If you don't come in where you're supposed to, the whole thing will fall apart. Okay? Are you with me?"

In the twelfth row, Donald was disgusted. "I can't believe he's blaming them," he told James. "It was his own fault, screwing up those entrance cues, and he knows it. Or he *should* know it, anyway."

Andrew Barnes continued to address the performers. "Failing to come in can be a disaster," he said. "This reminds me of a performance—" and now he rested his baton on his score.

Donald finished his sentence for him—"of the Leonore Overture Number Two of Beethoven."

"—of the Leonore Overture Number Two of Beethoven."

"How'd you know that?" James asked.

"I've worked with him in London," said Donald. "He never changes."

"It was an evening performance in Central Park. Bruno Walter was conducting the New York Philharmonic."

Some of the musicians, sensing a long story, put their instruments down on the floor or on their laps. A few

moved the Mozart score a bit on their music stands, un-
covering copies of *Time* or *People* magazine, and surrep-
titiously began to read. The second trombonist, Alvin
"the Chipmunk" Reischel, a short, wiry man with unusually large front teeth, ran a betting pool for the benefit
of his fellow musicians. He pushed his music score out
of the way and glanced at his copy of the *Racing Form*.

"Now, in this overture," Barnes was saying, without
the full attention of the orchestra and chorus, "Beethoven wanted to demonstrate the approach of the city counselor. Normally, to get that effect, you place a trumpeter
backstage when you perform the piece. The conductor
cues someone standing at the edge of the stage and this
person cues the trumpeter. A minute later, the conductor
cues the trumpeter himself, who by now should be standing at the edge of the stage, where his prompter had
stood. And then, the third time, a minute later, the trumpeter walks onstage, and he plays, and the illusion of the
great city counselor's approach is complete."

One by one, and then in small groups, the chorus
members were seating themselves.

"Just shut up and conduct the Gloria," Donald murmured, referring to the second movement of the Mass.

"Now, for this Central Park performance," Barnes
continued, "Walter placed the trumpeter in the bushes to
the left of the bandshell. At the appropriate moment he
signaled the go-between, who turned and signaled the
trumpeter.

"And *nothing happened*." Barnes paused for effect.
"Walter went purple with rage. There was *silence* where
there should have been trumpet calls. A minute later into
the piece Walter signals again. By now the trumpeter
should be at the edge of the stage. Again—*nothing*. Walter is seething. He's conducting away"—Barnes gave a
comic impression of Walter conducting despite his an-
ger—"and all he can think of is how he is going to ruin
the career of the man who embarrassed him so."

At this, even the orchestra players reading *Time* and
People looked up. Alvin Reischel looked up from his
Racing Form.

"The piece ends and Walter rushes offstage and finds
the poor trumpeter. 'You!' he cries, grabbing him by the

lapels. 'I am mortified by you! You have made a fool of me! You're finished, do you understand? You will never work again!'

" 'M-may I just explain?' said the trumpeter. 'I was positioned—I was ready—I heard the opening notes of the piece, and I saw my cue to play. And just as I lifted the trumpet to my lips I felt a hand clap me on the shoulder.

" 'I turned to look. It was a police officer. And he said, "Okay, buddy. In case you didn't know it, there's a concert going on over there. And if you blow one note on that thing—" ' "

"I'm going to run you in!" Donald whispered.

" ' "I'm going to run you in!" ' " roared Andrew Baker Barnes.

Barnes smiled broadly, acknowledging the laughter of the chorus and orchestra.

"You've heard this story before?" James asked.

"Only every time he conducts," said Donald.

At the podium, Barnes seemed relieved, calmer, and for the first time, in control. *At least they're in a better mood now,* he told himself. *Maybe this won't be the nightmare I thought it would be.*

"I know there are a lot of police here in the hall," Andrew told the performers. "I know it's a distraction for you. It's a distraction for *me*, believe me. But please watch my cues anyway. It's the only way we can get this piece off the ground."

Andrew Baker Barnes lifted his baton again, turned a page in his score, and addressed the orchestra and chorus with an air of efficiency and confidence heretofore absent.

"Let's take the Gloria, ladies and gentlemen," he said. His baton was poised. "Ready?"

FIVE

Halfway through the rehearsal, Donald had heard as many Andrew Barnes stories as he could handle. Donald never enjoyed watching joint chorus-orchestra rehearsals, but this morning he found himself hating it more than usual. Watching the police officers comb the hall as part of the security arrangements for Barnes reminded Donald of his role as unofficial understudy. Everyone knew that if Barnes withdrew, only Donald was familiar enough with the score of the Mass to conduct the premiere.

This slim chance to conduct the piece he had discovered, and edited, and loved as much as if *he* and not Mozart had composed it, aroused in Donald a host of conflicting emotions. Donald wanted Andrew to withdraw so that he, Donald, could conduct the Mass. He wanted nothing to happen to Andrew, so that he, Donald, would not risk disgracing himself on the podium a fourth time. Donald wanted to be an international conducting star, as Andrew seemed destined to become. At the same time, he wanted only to be left alone with his chorus, who loved him, respected him, feared him, and never expected him to conduct them in concert. Donald never had problems in rehearsals. In a concert, though, he might freeze again. Suddenly he felt the need for fresh air. He really felt the need for a drink, but Donald considered it a point of honor not to touch alcohol before noon no matter how desperate, miserable, and rotten he felt.

"Take over for me," he told James, handing over his conductor's score. "I need a break."

James accepted the score without a word. After three

years of working closely with Donald, he knew his moods better than anyone at Carnegie Hall. He did not need to be told what Donald felt as he watched Andrew conduct the Mass. Donald took a last look at Barnes onstage and left the auditorium. He headed for the main entrance to the hall on West Fifty-seventh Street.

Donald's main chance to replace Andrew in the premiere of the Mass had its roots in a series of events that had taken place in London the previous spring. Andrew had conducted four benefit concerts for a Palestinian refugee organization based in London. The concerts drew full houses to Royal Albert Hall on successive Monday nights. Andrew's involvement aroused the ire of another pro-Palestinian group whose tactics and philosophy differed from those of the group sponsoring the concerts. The other group began to agitate for Barnes's dismissal from the R.S.S. and otherwise disturbed him with death threats and picketing outside his conducting engagements.

The London branch of a radical Jewish organization, equally displeased by Barnes's affiliation with the Palestinians, also sought his removal from his post. This group tried to institute a boycott of the orchestra by Jewish subscribers and showed up at his appearances with picket signs, once going so far as to pelt the conductor with eggs. The irony of Palestinian and Jewish groups competing in their efforts to harass and discredit the conductor did not go unnoticed. "In three thousand strife-torn years," the *Times* of London editorialized wryly, "the only thing the Arabs and the Jews have managed to agree upon is Andrew Baker Barnes."

On several occasions, Barnes had received death threats only hours before a concert. Management of his London orchestra decided to replace him at the last minute with another conductor rather than risk his life and let him perform. News of these unscheduled absences quickly made the rounds in the music world, and speculation abounded among those connected with the New York Symphony as to whether Barnes's life might be in danger in New York. James opened Donald's score and waited patiently for Andrew Barnes at the podium to begin again.

* * *

At the side of the stage, Officer Caruso also felt like stretching his legs. He headed for the stage door at the West Fifty-sixth Street entrance to the hall. There stood Tommy, the stage-door guard. Tommy, well past seventy, had been the stage-door guard for as long as anyone could remember. He had the face of a benevolent gargoyle on an Irish cathedral, if there were such things. He was one of the world's leading experts on Manhattan parking regulations.

"How ya doin'," Officer Caruso said to Tommy, trying to be friendly.

"How come you got so many cops in there?" Tommy asked, his tone suspicious.

"What, are you kidding?" asked Officer Caruso. "You got a lot of crazy people that want to kill your conductor."

"Yeah, well, how come you need those mental detectors. We never needed 'em before." Tommy resented the presence of police inside Carnegie Hall. For half a century, he had provided all the security that was necessary. Now, all of a sudden, they needed cops. Tommy didn't understand.

Mental detectors? Officer Caruso thought.

"Whaddya think?" Tommy asked. "The terrorists are gonna come in throwing Mazeltov cocktails? Is that it?"

Officer Caruso leaned forward, trying to smell Tommy's breath.

"You know," Tommy added, as if it settled the matter, "it'll cut into ticket sales if people don't think it's safe to go to a concert. They'll see all you cops around, they'll turn around and go home and listen to the phonograph." Tommy took a proprietary interest in the box-office affairs of the Symphony, even though to him all the music sounded the same.

"Look, I'm just a patrolman," said Officer Caruso, weary of the conversation. "You got a problem, talk to my sergeant."

"That's a good idea. I know this place like the back of my hand. Well, have a nice day, now," said Tommy, who made it a rule to tell everyone, friend or foe, to have a nice day.

Officer Caruso reentered the hall and forgot about Tommy. He was halfway down the corridor that linked the stage door to the left-hand side of the auditorium when he saw one of the ushers stopping to say hello to Donald. The usher looked to be about eighteen years old. He wore a name badge that said "Eric."

"Good morning, Maestro."

"Hmm? Oh. Morning."

"Isn't it *incredible*?" the usher asked Donald. Like many of the younger ushers, he studied at the Manhattan Conservatory of Music, which Donald had attended. "A premiere of a Mozart piece! It's just too bad that *you* can't conduct it. After all, it *is* your piece."

"Well, I don't know about that," Donald said modestly.

"We all wish *you* were conducting and not Barnes," the usher added. "That's what everybody's saying at the conservatory."

"Thanks," said Donald, surprised and flattered. The comment lifted his spirits. *I've never seen him before,* thought Donald. *He must be new.* He gave the usher a nod, made a mental note to remember his name, and headed back into the auditorium. Donald liked ushers.

Officer Caruso wondered why people wanted Donald, and not Andrew, to conduct the Mass. He knew nothing of Donald's role in discovering and editing the piece. With Andrew onstage, the patrolman was free to explore the area backstage at Carnegie Hall. The narrow passageway behind the stage was cluttered with instrument cases, cabinets, tables, and chairs. A *real firetrap*, Officer Caruso thought, as he made his way along the corridor.

At the end of the corridor was the entrance to the stage. He looked out, over the shoulder of a stagehand watching the rehearsal on a monitor, and saw that Barnes was in the middle of another story. The stagehand nodded in Barnes's direction. "For a guy that gets paid to conduct he sure talks a lot," he told Officer Caruso. "If I talked that much on the job, not even the Teamsters could save my ass."

"Yeah, I know what you mean," Officer Caruso said, and he continued on his way to the coffee table. He headed past the stage door and down a stairway. At the bottom of the stairs he came upon the coffee table, and he poured himself a cup of coffee. He was in no hurry to return to the rehearsal. He found himself enjoying the feeling of playing hooky.

Officer Caruso brought his coffee into the musicians' lounge, a large, well-appointed room with comfortable-looking sofas as well as tables and chairs. An enormous television sat on a table in one corner. A few ushers in red jackets and dark pants, older men in their fifties and early sixties, sat reading newspapers. They ignored the patrolman.

"Julie—you know, the tympanist—tells me this guy Barnes is no musician," one usher said to another.

"How'd he get so famous then?" asked the other.

"Who knows? I hear his wife has a lot of pull. Guy's supposed to be some kind of big name in England. I think he was Smith's idea, anyway. Figured he'd be a good draw."

"You kidding?" asked the other usher. "How good a draw do you need when you're doing a Mozart premiere, for crying out loud?"

The first one shrugged and went on reading his newspaper.

The general lack of respect for Barnes surprised Officer Caruso. He stepped into the hallway again. Opposite the musicians' lounge were the private dressing rooms for the conductors and the two soloists. Next to the dressing rooms was a large bulletin board. Officer Caruso paused to read the notices. Most had to do with rehearsal times and information about an upcoming Symphony trip to Japan. Other, smaller notices, posted by the orchestra members themselves, offered season shares in a ski lodge in New Hampshire or instruments or cars for sale. One of the bassoonists was looking for other musicians with whom to share a Caribbean cruise.

"Not a bad life," Officer Caruso said aloud. Then he read an announcement of a vacancy in the New York Symphony's flute section. The starting salary was listed at $51,025 a year. "Jesus," he said. "They make more than *cops*. A *lot* more."

Next to the announcement about the flute vacancy was posted a long profile about Barnes on the bulletin board.

The article came from the Arts & Leisure section of the previous Sunday's *New York Times*. Officer Caruso sipped his coffee and read about the guest conductor. The article noted that Barnes had been hired directly out of music school to direct the then struggling Royal Symphonic Society of London; that the R.S.S. had flourished under his baton; and that he had abandoned the modern repertoire of his predecessor in favor of a steady diet of Beethoven, Mozart, and Brahms.

The article did not contain a word about Barnes's ability as a conductor. It also failed to mention the death threats. Officer Caruso, who, as his name suggested, was a fan of orchestral music and of opera, found it strange that there was no gushing, or even qualified, praise of Barnes anywhere in the profile. No one—not the profile writer, not even Carnegie Hall ushers and stagehands— had a kind word for Barnes.

Officer Caruso heard voices behind him. He turned and saw the orchestra musicians carrying their instruments down the stairs. He checked his watch: it was only ten minutes past twelve. Barnes must have ended the rehearsal early. The players streamed past the patrolman, some stopping for coffee, others heading directly into the lounge. A man and a woman, both carrying violins, stepped past him.

"I can't believe he never noticed. I played the whole Agnus Dei an octave too low," said the man.

"Tin ear," said his companion.

This is pretty strange, Officer Caruso told himself. Everybody's *picking on Barnes*. And then he turned to finish reading the article.

At that same moment, no one in the crowded hallway— not Officer Caruso, not any of the orchestra members, not even a plainclothes detective pouring himself a cup of coffee at the end of the corridor, noticed that someone had just dropped an envelope in front of Barnes's dressing room. The envelope fluttered through the air and landed in the middle of the corridor. The person who dropped the envelope looked both ways, and, as casually as he could manage, slid the letter with his foot halfway under Barnes's door. He glanced around, decided that he had gone undetected, and stepped quickly away.

SIX

Donald Bright usually arranged the seating plans for concerts in alphabetical order, although he made exceptions for tall people and usually placed them in the back row. Two sopranos, Alison Gardiner and Corinne Gates, usually found themselves side by side at rehearsals and performances. They became friends despite, or perhaps because of, the gap in age between them. Alison was twenty-two and a graduate student in voice at the Manhattan Conservatory of Music. Corinne, who had trained in voice at the same school fourteen years earlier, was thirty-six. Corinne did promotional work in the New York office of a German classical music recording label.

"Oh, by the way," said Alison. "You'll never guess what happened to me last night." They had just ordered lunch in a soup-and-salad restaurant around the corner from Carnegie Hall. Symphony people called the restaurant the "Help Wanted" because the management had so much trouble holding on to their staff that they never took the sign out of the window.

"You went to a bar," Corinne said. "You met a fabulous guy, he's nothing like the other ones, and you spent the night at his place."

Alison stopped short. "How did you know? Who told you?"

"Nobody told me," said Corinne. "Just a lucky guess. I know you."

"Want to hear about him?" Alison asked, a bit miffed. Alison, tall and willowy, had boundless, if justifiable, confidence in her ability to attract the attention of men. She was dressed, as she often was during warm weather, in blue jeans and a white cotton blouse. Corinne wore a turquoise dress and no makeup.

"Not really," said Corinne, but she knew she had no choice. People who knew Corinne and Alison wondered what brought the two together as friends. They seemed to have little in common aside from their alphabetically proximate last names. Corinne, in fact, found Alison's busy social life a source of entertainment and vicarious satisfaction. Alison had more than enough social life for both of them. Alison liked men.

Corinne admired Alison's ability not to let her emotions interfere with her libido. Alison's involvements with men followed a pattern that Corinne had long ago charted: a chance encounter; one night to three weeks of intense passion; a gradual loss of interest on Alison's part; his phone messages unreturned; no hard feelings, but no goodbyes.

Corinne's only social life consisted of an on-again, off-again relationship with Kevin Riordan, a classmate from the conservatory who was now the assistant general manager of the Symphony. They had been alternately breaking up and resolving their differences for three and a half years. Otherwise, their relationship was solid, dependable, and compared to Alison's brief attachments, a little boring.

"He's about six-two," Alison said, describing her latest find. "He played lacrosse for Johns Hopkins. He's a liquidity trader on Wall Street, whatever that means. He lives on Washington Square Park, in one of those cute little brick buildings. He knocked down all the walls in the apartment. It's just one giant bedroom."

"Perfect," said Corinne. "You were made for each other."

"That's what *I* was thinking. That's why I figured it would be okay."

"Hey, Alison," Corinne said, always uncomfortable when sounding older and wiser, "I thought we talked about this last month. Aren't you afraid of, you know, getting something? How do you know this guy is clean?"

Alison looked pensive. "Well, we kind of talked about it—*indirectly*."

"Which means what?"

"Well, on the way from the bar to his place—and it happened to be a *very nice bar*, by the way. It had a fireplace. Anyway, he mentioned that a woman he knew had just started going out with a guy who was bisexual, and he said he thought that was just *crazy*, because everybody knows that a woman who sleeps with a bisexual is putting herself at an incredible risk."

People at tables nearby stopped talking, and some of them stopped eating, the better to hear Alison.

"I figured he was trying to signal me that he was concerned about sexually transmitted diseases and that he himself was healthy."

"But you didn't come right out and ask him?" Corinne asked, uncomfortably aware of the attention of the people around them.

"Are you kidding?" Alison asked, appalled. "It would have ruined the mood."

The people at the next tables laughed and returned to their own conversations.

"I see your point," Corinne said diplomatically. "But you just told me a few weeks ago that you were going to change your behavior because you don't want to get infected by some guy you meet in a bar. Life was so much easier when *I* was in college. All you could get was pregnant."

"But I *am* changing my behavior," Alison insisted.

"But you said you went to bed with him."

"I did."

"The same night you met him."

Alison nodded. The people nearby were listening again.

"Then what was so different?" Corinne asked.

Alison made a face. "I was too terrified to enjoy myself."

Corinne had to laugh. "You're too much," she said.

"I actually did bring it up afterward," Alison said, defending her actions. "I told him I was a little nervous, because from the point of view of health, it was like I had gone to bed with every woman he'd ever slept with."

Now even the waiters were paying attention.

"Makes sense," Corinne acknowledged. "What did he say to that?"

Alison's expression was rueful. "He told me I'd *like* them. He said most of his old girlfriends usually got along."

"A fine romance," said Corinne. "Will you see him again?"

"I don't know," said Alison. "He gave me his card. He said I could call whenever I wanted."

"He gave you his *card*?" Corinne repeated, amazed. "Didn't he ask for *your* number?"

Alison shook her head. "He says he always loses numbers."

"Men make me sick," said Corinne. The waiters, trading grins, went back to serving food.

"He had a nice apartment, anyway," said Alison, as their lunch arrived. "Not to change the subject or anything, but what did you think of this morning?" Now her tone was as offhand as she could manage. She flipped through her score and ignored her food.

"Think about what?" Corinne began to eat her salad.

"About the rehearsal."

"Donald seemed pretty down," said Corinne.

"I wasn't talking about Donald," Alison responded.

"Well—we sounded pretty good, I guess. What little we actually *sang*."

"I'm not talking about the *music*. I mean, what did you think about *him*?"

Corinne looked up quickly. "Who, Barnes?"

"Yeah, Barnes," said Alison, hoping she sounded casual.

Corinne took her time answering. "He's a good conductor, I guess—the R.S.S. is very popular in London—and he's really not the chowderhead that Donald makes him out to be—"

"That's *not* what I mean," Alison interrupted.

"What *do* you mean?"

Alison pretended that she was studying a line of music in the score. "I think he's incredibly good-looking," she said.

"He's okay," Corinne allowed.

"Only okay?"

"Yeah, he's okay."

"Well, *I* think he's more than just okay," said Alison.

"Everyone's entitled to their opinion," Corinne responded.

"Is there something wrong?" asked Alison.

"No, not at all."

"No?" asked Alison. "Then why did you react that way?"

"React what way?"

"I just mentioned that I thought Barnes was more than okay and you kind of got annoyed."

"No, I didn't," Corinne said, pretending to study *her* score. "You think *every* guy is more than okay."

"Oh," said Alison, who thought that perhaps Corinne was also interested in getting to know Andrew Barnes. *Not that it matters,* Alison thought. *She's too old for him.*

"Was he at the conservatory when you were there?" Alison asked. "You're about the same age."

"He might have been," said Corinne. "I guess I used to see him around."

"That's too bad," said Alison, not hiding her disappointment. "I was hoping you knew him."

"Why is that?"

"You could have introduced us."

Corinne shrugged. "If you want to meet him, you can just walk up and say hello. I doubt he's got an armed guard surrounding him."

"I don't have that kind of nerve," Alison said, starting to eat. "I'm sure he's got women coming on to him wherever he goes."

"Oh, I get it," said Corinne, nodding. "You were thinking of coming on to him."

"No, not at all," Alison said, a bit too quickly.

"Don't be so defensive about it."

"Who's being defensive?" Alison asked, mildly annoyed. "It's just that part of being a conductor means you probably have—I don't know what to call them. Groupies. Hangers-on. Like rock stars have."

Corinne smiled. "Do you think of Andrew Baker Barnes as a rock star?" she asked.

Alison returned a smile. "No, of course not. It's just

that a conductor has a lot of power. He's always the center of attention. You know, he's the maestro. And there's just something attractive about a man who has that much power.''

"Do you get wet every time you see a traffic cop?" Corinne asked wryly. "They've got a lot of power, too.''

"Cut it out," said Alison, laughing at the thought. "You know what I mean. And I think Barnes is physically very attractive, too. I wouldn't call him a hunk, exactly, but he does seem very tall—he must be at least six-one—''

"It's the podium. He's five-ten.''

"—And he's so young to be such an important conductor. He's only thirty-five.''

"Thirty-eight.''

"Still—hey, if you've got no interest in him, how come you know so much about him?''

"Never mind.''

"Has he ever been married?''

"He *is* married.''

"Oh," said Alison, disappointed. "Happily?''

"So-so.''

Alison brightened. "Then maybe there's hope," she said. She wondered, though, why Corinne was so well informed about Barnes. Corinne had never displayed this much interest in any of the other guest conductors who had worked with the chorus.

"Are you planning to seduce Andrew Baker Barnes?" Corinne asked.

"No, I'm not planning to seduce Andrew Baker Barnes, okay? But it wouldn't be the worst thing for my career if he remembered my name.''

"How'll you make him do that?" Corinne asked. "Will you take out an ad in the program?''

Alison glared at her friend. "Very funny. Does he travel with his wife?''

"Everywhere," said Corinne. "She doesn't let him out of her sight for a minute.''

"Why is that?''

"Too many groupies," Corinne said tartly.

"Thanks a lot," said Alison, making a face. "I just

think Barnes is hot. He has nice eyes. I thought he was looking right at me half the time.''

"Well, he certainly didn't try to hide it," Corinne said.

Alison could not believe it. "You noticed it *too*? Really?"

"Mm-hmm."

"You're not teasing me, are you?" If Corinne had been making fun of Alison, the younger woman would have been crushed. When it came to the pursuit and capture of men, Alison had no sense of humor.

Corinne took her time answering. "I hate to say this. *Your* ego doesn't need any pumping up. But he couldn't take his eyes off you."

Alison felt her heart racing. "You're a pal, Corinne," she said, taking Corinne's hand. *"Really."*

"Or maybe he was staring at the girl next to you," Corinne added. "You know, Mary Harvey."

Mary Harvey, who tipped the scales at just over two hundred pounds and who, in the candid opinion of most of the soprano section, looked more like a Harvey than a Mary, was an unlikely candidate for Barnes's attentions. Both women knew it.

"Oh, shut up," said Alison.

SEVEN

Donald's closest friend at Carnegie Hall was the chorus's piano accompanist, James Carver. Donald and James had been working together for three years. They met by chance at a reception in the Austrian consulate in New York. The reception honored the arrival of the Berlin Philharmonic and its famous silver-haired conductor, Herbert von Karajan. James, a light drinker and rarely one to take full advantage of an open bar, was very excited to be in the same room as von Karajan, his favorite conductor. He therefore downed a few more glasses of champagne than usual. He was talking with a serious-looking young couple he had just met when Donald first noticed him. James, six feet six inches tall, was hard to miss.

The champagne had gone to James's head. He found the couple dull, and he wished he could be standing in the fawning knot of people surrounding von Karajan. When James looked past the couple again for another glance at the conductor, they seized the opportunity to leave.

"We're going to a concert," the woman said, her hair pulled back tight in a bun. James did not know that Donald was listening to their conversation.

"Oh, really?" James asked, curious despite himself. "I'm a musician. What are you going to hear?"

Her husband, or boyfriend, or whatever he was, mentioned a fairly well-known modern composer, a German named Funt. "It's a premiere," he said.

James sighed dramatically. "Oh, *him*," he said. "The chief exponent of the Fuck You School of music," he said, loud enough for most of the party to hear. Even von Karajan heard him. "Fuck you, audience! Fuck you, musicians! Fuck you, National Endowment for the Arts, or whoever's paying his rent!"

The couple glanced uncomfortably at each other. Donald, standing nearby, noticed that half the room was watching James, waiting to hear his next pronouncement. James sensed through his alcoholic haze that he somehow had hurt the couple's feelings. He instantly regretted his remark. He tried to make up for his lapse, but he only made things worse.

"If you're going to a premiere of a *Funt* piece," James said, attempting an in-joke poking fun at the composer, "you must be a *friend* of his."

The woman gave him an icy look. "As a matter of fact," she told him, "we *are*. My husband's also a composer, but I don't think you'd like *his* music, either."

James did not like to offend people unless they had offended him first, and suddenly he felt awful. Donald, though, had to keep from bursting out laughing. Before James could offer an apology, the couple abruptly left the room, and James found himself face to face with Donald, whom he had never met before.

"The *Fuck You School*?" Donald repeated, a little grin on his face. "I like that."

James was thoroughly flustered. Here he was shooting his big mouth off, unaware that Donald Bright, one of the most important people in music in the whole city, had been listening.

"I didn't mean—it's just that—" James began.

Donald smiled. "No, I happen to agree with you. I'd just never heard it put that way before. Did you say you were a musician?"

James nodded quickly. "I play the piano and I compose a little, too," he told Donald, and he felt his throat close. After all, it was *the* Donald Bright. He completely forgot about von Karajan.

"But you're not in the Fuck You School, are you?" Donald asked. James sensed that Donald was trying to put him at his ease.

"N-no," said James. "I'm sort of a modern romantic, you could say," and he felt like an idiot for describing himself that way to Donald Bright, but he would have felt like an idiot no matter what he had said.

"I like that," said Donald. "A modern romantic. What the world needs more of. How can I hear your music? Do you have a cassette?"

"I'm giving a recital at Merkin Hall next Tuesday," James heard himself say.

"And your name is?"

"James Carver."

"I'll try to make it," Donald said, and he wandered away to say hello to someone else.

James watched him go. *That was Donald Bright*, he told himself. *The* Donald Bright.

After the reception, Donald forgot the whole incident until he saw the recital listed in the Entertainment Events box in the following Tuesday's *New York Times*. Donald remembered the tall pianist who did not belong to the Fuck You School, and he had no other plans that evening, so he went to the recital. Donald found himself enjoying

James's compositions and his style of playing. The thought crossed his mind that if he hired James as rehearsal pianist, perhaps their relationship might extend beyond the purely professional.

Donald approached James at the little party afterward in somebody's apartment overlooking the park and invited him to be the rehearsal pianist for the New York Symphony Chorus. The previous rehearsal pianist, whom Donald considered a good musician if a mentally unbalanced one, had just quit the chorus to play the organ for the Church of Scientology. James accepted the offer on the spot. James parried Donald's early advances as Donald once had parried Philip Popham's and their relationship had settled into one that was strictly business. James's loyalty to Donald, based equally in gratitude for favors conferred and in expectation of favors to come, knew no bounds.

Now, half an hour after Barnes had dismissed the orchestra and chorus, James and Donald sat on the edge of the Carnegie Hall stage. James was wondering what he could say or do to improve Donald's mood.

"What did you think of the rehearsal?" James asked. His voice had a breathlessly intense quality.

"I hadn't heard the story about the string quartet and the prostitute," Donald replied. "Aside from that, it was the same old Andy Barnes. Why, what'd you think?"

James thought that the rehearsal had been an absolute disaster, and he had been waiting all morning to inform Donald.

"I thought the chorus was excellent, despite the cues that Barnes forgot to give. But the orchestra didn't pay any attention at all! Maybe he'll say something privately to the section leaders."

"I doubt it," said Donald. "He didn't know anything was wrong."

"And the horns!" James added. "They *completely* ignored the dynamics throughout the rehearsal, and he never said anything about them, either! They blew like it was Judgment Day! I know how hurt you were when they gave the piece to Barnes. But just listening to him rehearse has to be salt in the wound."

Neither James nor Donald noticed that Officer Caruso

was standing in the wings, just offstage, and listening to their conversation. Officer Caruso had not intended to eavesdrop. He simply wanted to stand on the Carnegie Hall stage, so that he could tell his grandfather, a music lover, that he had done so. Officer Caruso did not know who James and Donald were.

Donald did not respond.

"I don't blame you for feeling bad," James said patiently, as though to a small child. "After all, it's almost as much *your* piece as it is Mozart's."

Donald laughed. "That's a bit much," he said.

"Actually," James said, and he looked around to make sure that no one could overhear. He did not notice Officer Caruso. "There's a chance that Andy might have to withdraw."

"What are you talking about?" Donald asked, looking sharply at James. False hope was the last thing Donald needed.

"You know those death threats Andy was getting in London?" James asked.

Officer Caruso edged closer. He was surprised to hear the London threats mentioned. He did not know that they were common knowledge among Symphony people.

"What about them?" asked Donald.

"He's getting them here, too," James said quietly.

"Are you *serious*?" Donald asked, wanting to believe it. "How do you know that?"

"*I just do,*" James said mysteriously. "*Trust me.* And if Andy might get killed, they can't let him conduct. He'll have to withdraw. And if *he* can't conduct, who will?"

"*Me?*" Donald asked, grasping matters. He shook his head. "It'll never happen. Andy'll never pull out."

"I hear the threats are *very* persuasive," said James.

Officer Caruso wondered who these two people were and how they possibly could know so much about the death threats.

"*Really,*" said Donald, looking at the television cameras that would record Barnes's performance. "That would be something, wouldn't it?" he asked, briefly allowing himself the pleasure of believing James. "I step in at the last moment. Save the day. That'd be front-page news. You know, that's how Leonard Bernstein got started."

"I'm glad to see you're feeling a little better," said James, who knew that whenever Donald started comparing himself to Leonard Bernstein, his mood was improving.

Donald's mood *was* improving. This was the best news he had heard in six months. Donald found himself recalling the day in boarding school when Mr. Pirante suggested, ever so gently, that he pick up the violin again. The first notes that Donald played, after several years during which he made no music at all, chilled him. He understood that he was regaining a part of himself. He sensed how deep a rut he had been in and that the faint possibility existed that he might climb out. The news that he might conduct the Mass had the same effect. He marveled at James's ability to be so attuned to backstage gossip. He wondered how James had learned about the threats.

For his part, Officer Caruso was wondering the same thing. *Who are these guys,* he asked himself.

EIGHT

As Kevin Riordan, the assistant general manager of the New York Symphony, passed Andrew Barnes's dressing room, he noticed an envelope slipped halfway under the door. Kevin thought of himself as the only normal person backstage at Carnegie Hall. He did not become hysterical in the face of crisis; he neither contributed nor listened to the steady flow of Symphony gossip; he was not trying to seduce any of the young and presumably impressionable ushers. He was responsible, steady, conscious of detail. Had he not been a musician, he might have been an accountant.

Kevin's duties included supervising security matters with regard to the Barnes visit. Kevin had arranged for the police presence inside the hall and for the metal detectors through which all entrants had to pass. A letter under a dressing room door, he reasoned, could be fan mail, a request for an autograph, a phone number from a female admirer, or another death threat. Kevin bent down, picked up the envelope, and opened it.

The envelope contained a brief letter, typed neatly on ordinary white paper:

We will kill you Friday night, during the concert.

The letter was unsigned.

"Kevin, is that you?" asked Elizabeth Garrett-Jones, who was just now arriving from the hotel. Elizabeth was Andrew Barnes's wife. Elizabeth had also been a classmate of Donald, Andrew, and Kevin's at the conservatory. Although Elizabeth and Kevin had not seen each other in fourteen years, they had spoken on the telephone frequently over the last few months. Elizabeth had negotiated Andrew's guest-conducting contract. There was little need for the usual social amenities that accompany reunions between long-separated classmates. Also, Elizabeth was not one to waste social amenities on people from whom she did not need something at the moment.

"Oh, hi, Lizzie," said Kevin, casually stuffing the letter into a pocket. He knew that she hated to be called Lizzie. Kevin was probably the only person on earth who called her by that name. "Nice to finally see you after all those phone calls."

"You look much older than you used to," she said, unlocking the door to her husband's dressing room. "Older than you sound over the telephone," she added unnecessarily. "Won't you come in? Would you care for a drink?"

Kevin, mildly unnerved by the letter, and, to a lesser degree by Elizabeth's unflattering remarks, stepped in.

"I was just reading that article about Andy—" he lied, indicating the profile tacked to the bulletin board outside.

"Good public relations," Elizabeth said approvingly. "A very nice article. Good PR can be more important than talent, don't you think? My Andrew has been detained onstage. A representative from the musicians' union is explaining some work rules to him. We have trade unions at home, and I assumed that he could handle such a meeting without my assistance. I rather hope I'm right. He'll be along shortly. You may wait in here if you like."

Her English accent had a rough, no-nonsense musicality. She had the air of a woman long used to having her way. Her wide brown eyes missed nothing. She was tall, probably a half-inch taller than her husband. She kept her auburn hair in the same page-boy cut she had favored at the conservatory. "Calculating, fierce, impatient, and forceful" was how a newspaper story on Barnes had described her. Kevin heard that the musicians of the Royal Symphonic Society feared Elizabeth Garrett-Jones more than they feared her husband. It was not hard to see why.

Elizabeth closed the door behind them and motioned him to a seat on the couch. She remained standing. If she was aware of his agitated state, which resulted from the threatening letter, she gave no sign of it.

"I'm utterly exhausted," she continued, but she seemed well rested to Kevin. "We arrived the day before yesterday, and I so hate to fly. I'm *parched*. Would you care for something to drink? There's a little refrigerator in the next room. There's also something you Americans call a toaster-oven. As if you expected your guest conductors to do their own cooking. Or perhaps American conductors are partial to toast. Would ginger ale be all right? There's so much of it. I suppose they think that since we're English we should like ginger ale. I'll only be a minute."

"Ginger ale would be fine," said Kevin as she disappeared into the other room. He could not tell whether she was trying to forestall conversation about serious matters or simply trying to keep him entertained until Andrew arrived. Or perhaps there was no point at all to her soliloquies. He remembered from conservatory days that Elizabeth had always preferred speaking to listening.

Kevin had been a Ph.D. candidate in music history at the Manhattan Conservatory and a classmate of Donald and Andrew's. He was one of Andrew's closest friends at the conservatory, but they had rarely seen one another since. Kevin left the conservatory for his Symphony job after he formally proposed a doctoral thesis comparing Italian Renaissance madrigals with 1960s rock and roll. Albert Nouse, Kevin's advisor at the conservatory, thought he detected a hint of levity in the proposal. He suggested that Kevin rethink his commitment to music history. Kevin did so. He quit the conservatory and joined the management of the Symphony, working his way up from usher-trainee to his current position of assistant general manager. Kevin wanted to rise still further and become general manager. He believed that the incumbent, George Smith, was only one more nervous breakdown away from early retirement. Kevin never would have admitted it, but he lived for that day.

Kevin cringed whenever he had to enter the Carnegie Hall dressing rooms. The furniture—two easy chairs, a sofa, and a desk—was modern in an unattractive sort of way. The walls were bare except for a full-length mirror on the back of the door and a makeup mirror over the desk. The walls were neither painted nor papered. They were padded with an unpleasant white vinyl. Soundproofing, Kevin supposed. There were no windows. The carpeting was decent enough—a thick, white wall-to-wall shag that extended into the other room.

Elizabeth emerged with two glasses of ginger ale. "I thought they renovated Carnegie Hall," she began. "One could never tell from the dressing rooms. Some committeewoman or other of the Friends of the Orchestra must have designed it. The furniture is appalling. Still, there's a private shower and bath in the other room, which we don't have in London. Plumbing at the Royal Albert Hall—that's where Andrew conducts—is utterly *prehistoric*.

"Have you ever been to London? It's ghastly in the winter, and it's not much better in summer, either. I'm always trying to get my Andrew to take the orchestra to

Majorca in February, because all it does in London is rain, but my father says it's too expensive. Here.''

She handed Kevin a ginger ale and a napkin and seated herself on the opposite edge of the couch. Kevin knew what her father had to do with the Royal Symphonic going to Majorca—he was the chairman of the orchestra's board and its chief donor. Important decisions were his to make.

"There isn't any ice," she continued. "Which stuns me. You Americans have such a fetish for ice. When we have guest artists from America at Royal Albert Hall, I declare, they're more concerned about ice than acoustics. And in our hotel! Ice machines in every room, on every floor—they must think we're going to store fish. We could open a cannery with all that ice. I hope you're not bored waiting with me for Andrew. I do tend to rattle on a bit. It is *so* nice to sit with you and catch up. How have you been?''

"Well, I—" Kevin began, but Elizabeth cut him off.

She became serious. "My Andrew's in a lot of trouble this time. I fear greatly for his life. You *will* be able to help him, won't you?''

Kevin thought of the letter. "We're doing the best we can," he said.

Elizabeth nodded. She was not listening. "Good," she said. "My Andrew is—how shall I put it? Andrew is a *simple* man in some ways. He gets himself mixed up in things that he doesn't really understand. Politically he's a bit naïve. Naïveté is not against the law, of course, but it can lead to unexpected consequences.''

Her voice trailed away.

"Sometimes I don't know what Andrew will involve himself with next," she said. "It wasn't always this way. I always used to know what he was doing, and with whom. For the last year or two, I've been just clueless. I could have stopped him from doing those benefits. He just didn't *ask* me. He used to ask me about everything. He's just a bit too—shall we say—too trusting of other people. Other people sense that and take advantage of him. He can be *molded*, Kevin.''

"No kidding, Lizzie," said Kevin, looking her over. "Well, I guess that's *your* job in life, right?''

Kevin remembered a time at the conservatory when Andrew had inadvertently risked his entire scholarship. He presented the faculty with a "manifesto," signed by two-thirds of the student body. The students complained that the faculty ignored twentieth-century music. They called for a revision of the curriculum, the formation of a department of modern music, and other changes. The irony, Elizabeth and Kevin both knew, was that Andrew himself neither liked nor understood modern music.

Andrew favored Beethoven, Mozart, Brahms, and a handful of other composers, and had no use for anything else. He presented the students' demands only because he wanted to be thought of as a good guy. He acted without regard for the repercussions that might have attended what the traditionally minded (some might have said hidebound) faculty viewed as insubordination. The account had a happy ending, though. The faculty agreed to offer courses in recent composers and the whole matter was quickly forgotten.

"My husband is not a very religious man," said Elizabeth, ignoring Kevin's affront. "He certainly hasn't found God since the conservatory. But to have not one but two religious groups—the Jews *and* the Arabs—upset at him is terribly disturbing to him. I can't understand either religion myself. Why they want to make the Middle East a butcher shop is beyond me. Although Israel is a perfectly lovely country. We were guests of the Mayor of Jerusalem, what's-his-name. We loved the Old City."

Just then there was a knock at the door. Kevin, so bored that he had been stirring the bubbles out of his ginger ale with his finger, was grateful for the interruption. He was certain that Elizabeth would have given him a detailed description of their stay in the Holy Land. The door opened and Andrew appeared.

"Kevin!" Andrew exclaimed, entering his dressing room and shaking hands and hugging his old classmate. "How the hell have you been? Look at you. You look great!"

"Look at *you*," said Kevin. "The big conducting star!"

Elizabeth was not interested in the class reunion.

"While you two gentlemen are admiring yourselves,"

she said, "I've got some things to attend to. Goodbye, Kevin. A pleasure to see you again." She left the dressing room without a word to her husband.

"It really *is* great to see you," Andrew told Kevin, as he watched Elizabeth go. "Fix you a drink?"

"No, thanks," Kevin said. "Lizzie just gave me a ginger ale."

"Lizzie," repeated Andrew, smiling. "She'd kill me if I called her Lizzie. If I don't call her Elizabeth, she won't even respond. Sometimes I catch myself calling her Miss Garrett-Jones. Have a seat."

After pouring some bourbon from a bottle on the desk, Andrew dropped himself into an easy chair opposite Kevin, unbuttoned his collar, loosened his tie, and raised his glass. "To Mozart," he said. "Without whom—hell, without whom, no Mass in F."

"To Mozart," Kevin said, laughing and lifting his ginger ale.

Andrew Baker Barnes was still so aggressively affable that Kevin had to smile. To Kevin's eye, Andrew looked just as he had at the conservatory. His thick, dark hair hung down over his forehead and reached his equally thick, dark eyebrows. His eyes were bright blue. He wore gray slacks and a starched blue striped shirt. His unwrinkled complexion was that of a twenty-year-old. Andrew was not tall but he was powerfully built. He exuded energy and youth. He could easily have been mistaken for a high school wrestling coach.

"And how about that chorus?" Andrew added. "God, they're good. That's all Donald's doing. The *sound* he gets out of them! Amazing!"

"Funny you should mention Donald," said Kevin. "He's had a lot to say about *you*."

"Oh, really?" said Andrew. "Actually, I'm not surprised." Andrew knew that Donald resented his success in London. "I still look up to *him*. That's the funny part. He's come to London a few times to prepare choruses for concerts and recordings. He's so good I get nervous whenever I conduct around him. The last two mornings, just knowing he's out there, I've been a wreck onstage."

"In that case, you two are even," said Kevin. "Donald's been a wreck in the audience."

"I believe it," said Andrew. "This morning, I goofed a cue to the chorus. Right in the middle of the Kyrie. My first thought was, 'Donald must think I'm an idiot.' "

"You got that one right," said Kevin, who had been hearing Donald's criticisms of Andrew for months. "He doesn't try to hide his feelings, either."

"Not everybody's going to love you," said Andrew, stretching out his legs. "You know, sometimes I think I should give up conducting and do something a little easier," said Andrew. "Like bullfighting, or being a prison guard. I'm worn out, and we've only had two rehearsals. But there aren't too many careers where you can just wave your arms for a couple of hours and pick up a paycheck. I really shouldn't complain."

Kevin laughed. "Is that all there is to it?" he asked. "Just waving your arms?"

Andrew smiled again. "I'm oversimplifying, I guess. But there *are* tougher jobs out there. It's an odd feeling, though."

"What is?" asked Kevin.

"Well, I don't know how to put it," said Andrew. "Looking out at the orchestra and not recognizing anyone. I've grown accustomed to the faces of the Royal Symphonic, you might say." Barnes's accent was American but at moments the rhythm of his speech betrayed his fourteen years in London. He took another sip of his drink.

"Let's not kid ourselves. I'm not the world's greatest conductor. I don't deserve a lot of the good fortune that's come my way. I don't reject it—I enjoy my orchestra in London. Frankly, I love the job. I feel as though I've built something. I can't imagine being happier with the way of life, the little bonuses that come with being music director. I travel a lot, and I meet all kinds of people. I also run into my share of boring failures. Like you, for example," Andrew added, grinning.

"Gee, thanks," said Kevin, smiling back. "First Lizzie dumps on me, and now you do." He wondered, though, why Andrew's tone sounded defensive and almost confessional in their first conversation in thirteen years. He wondered whether Andrew was trying to signal

Kevin that his self-opinion had not expanded along with his reputation.

"Don't pay any attention to my wife," said Andrew. "*I* don't." He grew serious. "Look. Until I became music director of the R.S.S., no one *ever* made a big deal over me. I've been conducting for thirteen years and I'm *still* not used to all this attention."

"Come on," said Kevin. "I can't believe that."

"No, it's true," said Andrew, running a hand through his hair. "Remember Nice?" he asked.

"Sure, why?" After their first year at the conservatory, Andrew, Kevin, and two other conservatory students went backpacking across Europe. Andrew had never been out of the country before. The four music students went to Nice, in the south of France, because they had heard about the nude beaches. Andrew knew of no nude beaches on the Maryland shore.

They arrived at three o'clock on a Saturday in July with no reservations and little cash. The youth hostels were filled and so were all of the cheap hotels. They could not find a room anywhere, so they tried to sleep on the beach. All four were arrested because sleeping on the beach had been prohibited that summer, and they could not read the signs which were, of course, in French. They spent the night in the police station and were turned out the next morning.

"Last month Elizabeth and I went to Nice for a week," said Andrew. "I was doing a benefit concert for a youth group. I love to do benefits. The atmosphere is relaxed, and you can work with kids, which I just love. Anyway, when we got to Nice, they practically gave us the key to the city. I couldn't pick up a check the whole time. People were fighting over whose villa we'd stay in. We ended up staying in three different villas, each with a different view of the Mediterranean, just to keep everyone happy.

"And the *women*. When you and I were there, they wouldn't give us the time of day. Well, *this* time—it was a little different. I felt like a rock star." Andrew chose not to tell his old friend that women came on to him constantly now—at parties, after concerts, in stores, in the street.

"You know what I did in Nice?" Andrew asked. "I went looking for the jail where they'd kept us that night."

"Did you find it?" Kevin asked, remembering. "Our old jail cell."

Andrew shook his head. "They tore it down to build a hotel. I guess it was one of the few jails anywhere with an oceanfront view. Anyway, somehow, I end up humping this unbelievable Danish girl in one of the rooms. Turns out she saw me conduct on a concert series that's syndicated for European television. Elizabeth's idea. Good for my career. Good for a lot of other things, too."

"It's not fair," said Kevin, shaking his head in mock disapproval. "The rest of us have to work for a living, and you get laid wherever you go."

"It was wild," Andrew agreed.

"Well, maybe it *is* only fair," Kevin said. "You *were* the only one of us that didn't get laid that whole summer."

"Don't remind me," said Andrew, making a face.

Andrew's tale of infidelity made Kevin uncomfortable, but Kevin did not want to say so. He chose to change the subject.

"What made you take our offer?" Kevin asked. "We were lucky to get you."

"Hmm? Also Elizabeth's idea," said Andrew. "She told me I needed to broaden my reputation a bit. She feels I'm a big enough star in London, but nobody in America knows my name. She went after the job, and everything just fell into place. You people wanted a guest conductor for the Mass, and you asked me. Why Donald wasn't asked is beyond me."

"It's beyond him, too," said Kevin. "Your timing— looking for a guest-conducting job—let's just say it couldn't have been better."

"My timing?" Andrew repeated. "You mean Elizabeth's timing. It was her idea, remember?"

"Whatever. I've been dealing with her on the phone for months. I deal with all the guest conductors and soloists and their agents, and let me tell you, she's tougher than all of them put together. She's made us do things for *you* we don't do for *anybody*."

"Like what?" Andrew asked, ready to be embarrassed. He left all the details of his guest-conducting contract to Elizabeth. She tended to handle all of their business affairs, which was fine with Andrew. He was dismayed, though, to think that Elizabeth might have made unorthodox demands on the Symphony.

"You kidding?" Kevin asked. "Well, the TV special, for one thing. Charlie Churchill, the superstar ex-weatherman. The Phil Donahue of weather. Now he does these really hot specials on PBS. He just goes around the country doing shows on interesting people. Elizabeth somehow got him to do a show on you."

"You saying I'm not interesting enough for Charlie Churchill?" asked Andrew, teasing his friend.

"No, not at all," said Kevin. "Well, you're borderline. Anyway, *he's* never done a show on classical music before. He's going to introduce you to a whole new audience. He told me he knows absolutely nothing about classical music."

"At least he's honest," said Andrew.

"I suppose," said Kevin. "He practically wanted to know if Mozart was coming to the premiere."

"What did you tell him?" Andrew asked, laughing.

"I told him we were negotiating with Mozart's people, but they hadn't gotten back to us yet."

"Jesus."

"I wouldn't worry about it," said Kevin. "Anyway, then there's your master class. And the press conference this afternoon. Christ, not even *Bernstein* gives press conferences. Do you know how much she's making us spend on the buffet for the press conference? Twenty-six hundred bucks!"

"Really?" asked Andrew, trying to imagine what twenty-six hundred dollars of groceries looked like. It sounded like a lot.

"We've got ninety people coming," Kevin was saying. "Maybe more. This is unheard of for guest conductors."

"Ninety reporters to see me?" Andrew asked, surprised.

Kevin shook his head. "Ninety reporters to eat crab cakes and drink our champagne. We've even got *sportswriters* coming, for chrissakes. Lizzie put out the angle about you being a former wrestler."

"She doesn't miss a trick, does she?"

"Nope," said Kevin. "She's even got the TV cameras coming to your master class. She's going to make you the Pia Zadora of classical music."

"Who?"

"Never mind," said Kevin. "Anyway, thanks to your loving wife, you're going to have the biggest debut of any conductor in this country in years."

"I don't know if 'loving' is exactly the right word," said Andrew, disturbed by the lengths Elizabeth had gone to strengthen his American reputation. "I'd have been happy to stay home with my own group, but she said my career was stagnating. I figured she might have been right. She usually is, in her own crazy way. But I never dreamed she'd make you do all these things. I didn't realize the TV thing was *her* idea. Or the master class."

"She put a gun to our heads," Kevin explained. "We couldn't say no."

"That's my wife," said Andrew, finishing his drink. He shifted his weight in his chair. "Trigger happy as always. Speaking of people with guns to their heads. I've been getting threats ever since we got to New York. At the hotel. Telephone calls. Foreign accents."

"I know," said Kevin. "I've heard all about it."

Andrew shrugged. "Nothing's ever really happened to me, thank God, except for that one time when they got me with the eggs. I was furious. I've had to rearrange my whole life because of the threats. I have to sleep in different places in London, which *is* convenient for other, let's say social, reasons. If you get my drift."

Kevin did, but he said nothing.

"But it's gotten to be a pain in the butt," said Andrew. "I have to take different routes to the concert hall. We spend a fortune on security. I'm told that both of these groups have American branches. It obviously wasn't hard for them to figure out where I was staying. You know, Kevin, the Brits have it all over us when it comes to security. What with the IRA and everything, security in London is just plain tight. You couldn't wander into Royal Albert Hall the way you can wander into places here. I was watching at the stage door this morning. Anybody could get past that guard. He wasn't even checking IDs.

He was talking about alternate-side-of-the-street parking. What is that, anyway?''

Tommy, Kevin thought. ''Alternate side?'' he repeated. ''It's got to do with street cleaning. If you have a car in the city, you've always got to be moving it. That's a pain in the butt also.''

''I wonder what the doorman finds so interesting about it,'' said Andrew. ''He was talking about it for fifteen minutes.''

''You got away after only fifteen minutes?'' Kevin asked, laughing. ''What's your secret? He could talk about alternate sides for days.''

''It took me ten minutes to figure out he was talking about *parking*. Anyway, there's another thing,'' Andrew continued. ''These death threats have—how can I put this? They've taken their toll on my wife's mental health. She hasn't been all that well to begin with over the last two years. Lately it's gotten a lot worse. Obviously her PR sense hasn't been affected, but I think she might just crack from all the strain. If you could figure out a way to guarantee our safety, it would do a lot for her peace of mind. Not to mention my own.''

Kevin nodded. ''Have you gotten any threats in writing?''

Andrew shook his head. ''Why do you ask—'' he began.

''I've been reading your mail,'' said Kevin, and he took the crumpled envelope from his pocket and handed it to Andrew.

The conductor's expression remained impassive as he studied the letter. He passed it back to Kevin with uplifted eyebrows and without a word.

''We've stepped up security around Carnegie Hall, and around your hotel,'' Kevin said. ''I don't know if you noticed the cops wandering around during the rehearsal this morning.''

''Actually, I did,'' said Andrew. ''They were a little disconcerting.'' He stopped and grinned. ''No pun intended,'' he added.

''Cute,'' said Kevin. ''Look. We might be able to get a few extra cops without explaining too much to the press.

And considering that your pals can deliver letters right to your dressing room, it may not be such a bad idea.''

"That would be great," said Andrew. "Listen. I'm meeting Donald for a drink at eight. The bar at the Meridien Hotel. Around the corner. Elizabeth's idea, once again. Show the world there's no hard feelings between Donald and me. Although I'm sure Donald resents the hell out of my coming here and stealing his Mass. Care to join us?''

"Is she bringing the TV cameras, to record the event for posterity?''

Andrew laughed. "I wouldn't put it past her," he said. "Will you come?''

"I'd love to, but I've already got plans," Kevin said, and now *he* seemed embarrassed.

"What's wrong? Is it a woman? Bring her along. No problem.''

Kevin hesitated before he spoke. "I don't think it's such a great idea.''

"Why not?" Andrew asked. "You don't trust me around your women?''

"Does the name Corinne Gates ring a bell?" Kevin asked. Corinne, Alison's friend in the chorus, had been a classmate of Andrew, Donald, Kevin, and Elizabeth's at the conservatory.

"Corinne Gates?" Andrew repeated, nodding. "I see your point. I guess we'll grab a drink some other time. What do you say?''

"You've got it," said Kevin, standing up. "Hey, we're all really thrilled to have you here. Good luck tomorrow night.''

"Thanks," said Andrew, giving a wry smile. "If I don't get killed first, that is.''

NINE

Donald sat at the upright piano near the right side of the Carnegie Hall stage, playing the piano reduction of the score of the Mass. A "reduction" does not refer to the size of the score; it means that someone has taken all of the notes played by all of the instruments and combined them for one person to play at the piano. Reductions allow musicians—singers and instrumentalists alike—to learn how one's own part fits into the whole of the piece. Donald had written the reduction himself and was playing it now because he thought he had heard an errant note in the viola section during the rehearsal of the Credo section of the Mass.

The stage was quieter, much cooler, and in comfortable half darkness with the television lights turned off. As Donald played, a few stagehands rearranged the chairs and music stands. The Symphony's chain-smoking, gray-haired, slightly stooped longtime librarian, Evelyn Jervis, was replacing the Mass scores on the orchestra members' music stands with the scores of the pieces to be rehearsed that afternoon.

Evelyn's musical tastes had evolved considerably in the years since she joined the Symphony. At first she was fairly open-minded and enjoyed all kinds of music. As time passed and some stiffness in the joints took hold, she came to like only those composers whose scores were shelved high enough so that she would not have to stoop to reach them. Among her favorite composers were Albinoni, Bach, and Corelli. She had mixed feelings about Mozart and no longer cared for Verdi, Vivaldi, and, below all, Wagner.

Donald played softly and expressively. He had gone over the piece so often that he could almost play it by heart. He played it so lovingly that one might have thought he was giving a recital for a capacity crowd and not for the few people onstage.

Suddenly, in the middle of the movement, Donald halted. The stagehands, unaware that they had been listening, looked over to see why the music stopped. Donald stopped because he had found the mistake he had been looking for. He was a hundred and sixty measures into the Credo movement. Now he played repeatedly the three or four chords surrounding the false note. "That's really strange," he said aloud. He stared at the score, got up, and went over to the brass section of the orchestra, where Evelyn was replacing scores.

"Evelyn," he said, "you haven't put away the viola parts yet, have you?"

Each instrument had a separate "part" written for it, containing only the notes that it was to play. Only the conductor's score contained all the notes for each instrument.

"Why?" she asked, without looking up. Donald's tone implied more work for her. "You don't want to see one, do you?"

"Could I?"

"Just a minute." Evelyn sorted through an enormous pile of instrument parts and found one for the violas. "Here."

"Thanks," said Donald, opening the score to the Credo movement and finding the measure in question. He put the score on a music stand and picked up a viola that one of the players had left on a chair. He played the line of music leading up to the trouble spot.

"Look at that," he said, and he played it again. Evelyn said nothing. She stood and watched him. He played it a third time and set the viola down carefully. Then he compared the line of music in the viola part with the line of music in the piano reduction. Donald, as editor of the score, had written out each of the instrument parts as well as the conductor's score and the piano reduction. He looked back and forth from one score to the other.

"How do you like that," said Donald, scratching his

head. "I made a mistake." Neither Donald nor Evelyn noticed that Elizabeth had just joined them on the stage.

"What is it?" Evelyn asked.

"It's right here, just before the coda," said Donald. "This F sharp in the parts—it should be an F natural. I can't believe I wrote it that way. It's so obvious. That's just not how Mozart leads voices. He would never use an interval like that. Listen."

Donald picked up the viola and played the line of music with the correction. Evelyn did not hear the difference. Neither did the stagehands. Elizabeth caught it, and she was impressed. She did not say anything, though.

"Is it serious?" Evelyn asked. To her mind, most musicians had unhealthy obsessions over details. Her own obsession with not letting anyone into the Symphony's music library to handle the music scores did not strike *her* as odd, though.

"Well, it's not a life-and-death thing," said Donald. "But they really ought to play the F natural."

"Do you want me to leave them a note?" Evelyn asked. "I could put it in their scores this afternoon."

"Would you mind very much?" Donald asked.

"Oh yes, I *would* mind," said Evelyn, "but I'll do it anyway." She did not see the point, but she had not survived thirty-four years at Carnegie Hall by arguing with people like Donald.

She took out a notepad. "That's, um, measure one thirty-seven, the F sharp in the violas should be an F natural. If you say so."

"It's not what *I* say," Donald said, smiling for the first time. "It's what *Mozart* would say."

"Have you spoken with him recently?" Elizabeth asked.

Donald turned around quickly at the familiar voice. "When did you get here?" he asked.

"A while ago. How *are* you, Donald?"

"Okay, I guess," he said, ill at ease in her presence. "How are you?"

"Just fine, thank you, as always," Elizabeth replied. "Still turning F sharps into F naturals?" she asked, teasing him.

Donald did not find anything funny about the question.

He looked very uncomfortable. "Please don't make this any harder for me than it has to be," he said.

"Make what hard for you?" Elizabeth asked. "I'm afraid I don't understand. Are you coming to Andrew's master class this afternoon? He'd love it if you were there. The Symphony's sponsoring it as a benefit for the conservatory, you know."

Donald still could not believe that Andrew had been asked to lead a master class. Master classes are lecture-demonstration sessions, usually open to the public, in which six or eight music students perform while the teacher, often a famous soloist, instrumentalist, or conductor, offers criticism and advice. In all of Donald's time at the Symphony, they had never asked *him* to lead one. He did not know that Elizabeth had made the master class a part of Andrew's guest-conducting agreement.

"When is it?" Donald heard himself ask. Under no circumstances would he attend, he told himself.

"It's in Weill Hall at three," she said. The Weill Recital Hall, formerly known as Carnegie Recital Hall and lately nicknamed Vile Hall by some musicians who did not care for its acoustics, seated around three hundred and was part of the Carnegie Hall complex.

"I think I'm busy just then," said Donald. "What a shame."

Elizabeth nodded. "It *is* a pity," she said. "You might have *learned* something."

Donald stared at her in surprise. Elizabeth knew she had made her point. "Perhaps you can rearrange your schedule," she added. "Andrew and I would be pleased if you can attend. You'd be so proud of him. He's made *such* progress."

"I hope so for his sake," said Donald, remembering what a disaster Barnes had been in conducting class at the conservatory. The faculty there still could not believe that Andrew had been handed an orchestra upon his graduation. Stranger things had happened, they told each other, although they could not think of any.

"Andrew says you've done an excellent job with the chorus," Elizabeth said, throwing Donald a crumb.

"How can he tell?" Donald asked blandly.

"Rudeness won't take you far in life," said Elizabeth.

"It's worked okay for you," Donald shot back.

"Three o'clock, at Weill Hall," Elizabeth said stiffly. "I'll leave a ticket for you." She turned and walked quickly off the stage. Donald watched her go. He had actually scored a point off her. He went over to the piano. Still standing, he played himself a little flourish. He thought he had earned it.

TEN

Andrew Barnes poured himself another drink and stretched out on the couch in his dressing room to study the score of the Mass. He opened the score to the middle of the second movement, the Gloria, and examined the choral parts. "What great writing," he said aloud. "All this music out of the mind of one man. And if it weren't for Donald, we might never have heard it."

Andrew turned the pages of the score. He thought about how much Donald must resent him for coming in and conducting the score that Donald had found and edited and most likely *knew* much better than Andrew did. Sitting still and studying music never came easily to Andrew. He shut the score again, sat up, sipped his drink, and drummed his fingers on the side of the couch. He opened the Mass at random and looked at the notes on the page. His mind began to wander again.

First he thought about Elizabeth. He felt more and more disturbed about the lengths she had gone to promote his career here in New York. He wondered why she was going to such trouble for him, especially when he considered the ruinous state of their marriage. It did not make sense to him. Then he found himself thinking about the first oboist of the New York Symphony Orchestra, a

tall, stunning, red-haired woman whose presence had
been distracting Andrew from the moment he stepped out
onstage. He fantasized briefly about meeting her after the
next rehearsal and bringing her back to his dressing room.
He would explain about the recalcitrant oboist in Mozart's orchestra and offer her the chance to make up for
the omissions of her predecessor. *Clever,* Andrew
thought. *Very clever.*

Then he remembered a young woman in the soprano
section of the chorus whom he had observed during the
two rehearsals. He wondered how he could arrange to
meet *either* woman. It would not be easy—Elizabeth had
made plans for almost every minute of their trip. She
might have been trying to keep him occupied for just this
reason, he decided. Standing next to the young soprano,
Andrew knew, was Corinne Gates, a woman with whom
he had been close at the conservatory. He wondered
whether he might run into Corinne over the course of the
next few days, and, if so, what he and Corinne might
have to say to one another. He knew that he could not
just ignore her. He could hardly ask her for an introduc-
tion to the young woman she stood beside at the rehearsal. That wouldn't do. He found it interesting that
Kevin and Corinne were seeing each other. He wondered
how serious they were about each other.

Then Andrew thought about the third-chair violinist of
the Royal Symphonic Society and how much he always
wanted to have an affair with *her*. He always liked to see
what she wore to rehearsals. Her tastes ran to leather and
lace, not exactly traditional garb for British violinists.
Andrew often fantasized about slipping away with her for
a weekend in Majorca. He wondered what she would
wear *there*. He did not need to sleep with her, though.
He would have been content merely to rummage through
her closet.

Nothing had ever happened between Andrew and the
third-chair violinist, although she did not seem averse to
a fling with him. Andrew made it a rule not to sleep with
members of his own orchestra. No fishing off the company pier. No such constraints applied in New York,
though.

An incident involving a famous European conductor

came to Andrew's mind. The orchestra resisted when he sought to install a beautiful young woman, rumored to be his mistress, in the violin section of the orchestra. The other violinists claimed that her playing was far below the orchestra's high standards. The conductor retaliated by hitting them right in the wallet. He canceled all recording and touring contracts and reduced his appearances with the orchestra to the contractual minimum.

I wouldn't even dare *pull a stunt like that,* Andrew thought. *Elizabeth's father would fire me on the spot. Although, who knows? Maybe I've got just enough of a following by now to—oh, the whole thing's ridiculous.*

Just then, there was a knock at the door. Officer Caruso stuck his head into the dressing room. He did not expect to find Andrew inside. When he noticed Andrew, he looked apologetic.

"Excuse me, Maestro," he said. "I just wanted to make sure everything was okay in here. I can come back later."

"Come on in," said Andrew, grateful for any interruption. "Have a seat."

"No, I—" The patrolman put up both hands.

"You can take a break," said Andrew, rising and motioning the patrolman to a chair. "I'll pour you a drink, and you'll tell me what it's like to be a policeman in New York City."

"No way," said Officer Caruso. "I can't drink on duty. Actually, I don't drink at all, really." He paused for a moment. "Except for a little wine with dinner with the family on Sundays."

"Never mind," said Andrew. "Come on in. How do you like working in Carnegie Hall? Is this your normal assignment?"

"Uh-uh," said Officer Caruso, taking off his hat and sitting down. Ever since he first met Andrew, he was surprised that a famous conductor would talk to a cop. "To tell you the truth," he added, "yesterday was the first time I ever saw the inside of this place. It sure beats working the subway. You know, my grandfather—he loves music. Listens to opera all the time. He got me interested in it."

"Your grandfather's a big opera lover?" Andrew asked.

"You kidding? With a name like Caruso? My grandfather came to this country when he was seventeen. Never learned English, you believe that? But every night he comes home and he puts on his opera records. He taught me a thing or two about music."

"Your grandfather never learned English?" Andrew asked. "What does he do for a living? How'd he get along?"

"Him?" Officer Caruso asked. "He's retired now. He was a cop."

"Your grandfather was a cop? How could he get a job as a cop if he didn't speak English?"

Officer Caruso shrugged. "I guess he had connections. He had a cousin who was a sergeant. It's not like in music. In music, you gotta have the talent, right?"

"Um, right," said Andrew, looking away for a moment. "So your grandfather walked a beat, but he never learned to speak English? That's amazing."

Officer Caruso was offended. "My grandfather *never* walked a beat. He worked at headquarters. He had a desk job."

"I guess there's a lot I don't know about the New York Police Department," said Andrew.

"I guess not," said Officer Caruso. "And here's something else you don't know. The second violins are screwing around with you. They all played the Agnus Dei an octave too low. I thought I heard it when I was listening to the rehearsal, and then I heard one of the violinists *admit* it."

Andrew was extremely embarrassed. He had not heard it.

"You better say something at the dress rehearsal tomorrow," said Officer Caruso. "Or you'll get totally screwed over in the concert. You hear what I'm saying?"

Andrew was speechless.

Officer Caruso stood and headed for the door. "Listen, I gotta go. But one more thing," he added. "Tell the horns to watch the dynamics. Tell them it's a Mozart Mass, it isn't the freakin' 'Stars and Stripes Forever.' I'll catch you later." He left the dressing room.

Andrew could not believe what he had just heard. He had been conducting since Officer Caruso was a ten-year-old, but the young patrolman had heard things at the rehearsal that Andrew would never have heard. The thought shook Andrew, who began to wonder if he really deserved his job as chief conductor of an important orchestra. *Of course I do,* he told himself indignantly. Andrew knew that his talent lay not in rehearsals but in performances. Still, the idea of the orchestra making fun of him in this manner bothered him, even if it did not altogether surprise him.

Andrew knew that there was a war on between conductors and orchestras. It made perfect sense, when one thought about it. Musicians must be extraordinarily talented to win a job playing for a top orchestra. Growing up, they were most likely child prodigies, better than their teachers from the time they were ten or twelve years old. They reached adulthood with the certainty that they were among the best of their generation at what they did. This adulation, Andrew knew well, often went to the young performers' heads.

Andrew had seen it happen with every youth orchestra he had conducted and every well-known orchestra he had seen perform. When eighty to a hundred certified geniuses were bound together into an orchestra, Andrew believed, with all power and glory vested in one person who just stands there and waves a stick at them—it stood to reason that resentment and friction would result. Conductors, Andrew understood, were responsible for learning the scores they were to conduct, choosing programs of music, and auditioning musicians to create an ensemble sound. Their most important task, though, was to shape all that fractiousness into a single instrument. Doing so with the New York Symphony, Andrew concluded, would not be easy.

He promised himself to begin the final rehearsal the next morning with Officer Caruso's observations. Now, though, he found himself unable to concentrate on his score. He decided to step out of his dressing room and stretch his legs. "Mozart can wait a few more minutes," he said to himself. "What the hell. He's already waited two hundred years."

Andrew finished his drink, set his score on the couch, and wandered into the empty hallway. He noticed the article about himself tacked to the bulletin board and began to read it. " 'My husband brought the Royal Symphonic back from the dead,' says Miss Garrett-Jones. 'I could not be more pleased with his accomplishments.' "

"Next she'll have me changing water into wine," Andrew muttered, and he stopped reading. He looked into the musicians' lounge and saw a few orchestra members and singers making their way through bag lunches or reading newspapers. He noticed the coffee table. "I wouldn't mind some coffee right now," he told himself, knowing that some sort of external stimulation would be required to get him through the rest of the score. As he approached the table a young woman who had just made herself some tea turned suddenly and bumped into the conductor, spilling hot water on his trouser leg.

"Hey, watch it," she said angrily, unaware that she was speaking to Andrew Barnes.

"My fault," Andrew said quickly. "It was *my* fault. I'm terribly sorry. Please forgive me. Let me get some napkins. It's all right. I'm not burned. Your aim is impeccable. These pants needed to be cleaned anyway—"

Andrew grabbed a handful of napkins and patted his pants. He looked at the young woman's face for the first time. She was the soprano he had noticed during the rehearsal. *Okay,* he thought, *the oboist loses.*

"I was just going to get some coffee and have a seat in the musicians' lounge," he told her. "Would you care to join me? After you get a fresh cup of tea, of course."

"Maestro Barnes," said Alison Gardiner, her expression reflecting a mixture of embarrassment and awe. "I'd *love* to."

ELEVEN

George Smith had attended a conservatory in Evanston, Illinois, and therefore was not a classmate of Andrew, Donald, Kevin, Corinne, and Elizabeth's. When he graduated, eighteen years before, he had been a decent if unspectacular violinist. His options were teaching violin, playing with an orchestra, or going into his father's insurance business. George had gone to the conservatory because he knew he had no business sense whatsoever and could not be expected to sell anything, even insurance to his father's long-established customers.

Teaching violin did not appeal to him, either. Children made him nervous. Loud screeches on the violin, such as children tended to make, also made him nervous. In fact, virtually everything in life made him nervous. George had been voted by his high school graduating class in Winnetka, Illinois, "Most Likely to be Overwhelmed by Reality." Unlike most such awards, this one applied to George throughout his adult life.

Most people who met him liked him, even those who found him timid and shy. Studying music had been a wise choice for George. Music allowed him to escape from the pressures of the real world, a place that held no appeal for George at all. Playing music alone in a practice room soothed him. The idea of *performing* terrified him, though. He managed to get through the conservatory with only two performances. Most conservatory students perform dozens of times before they get their degrees.

Since insurance and teaching were out, and arts management required the sort of business skills he knew he lacked, George was down to one option—applying for positions as an orchestra violinist. Reluctantly, he made a tape of his violin playing and sent copies to the forty-one orchestras advertising openings that year for violinists. His lack of enthusiasm evidenced itself in his playing. Only three of the forty-one orchestras invited George to a second-round, live audition.

Second-round auditions are called the "behind the screen" round because large, opaque screens separate candidates from those conducting the auditions. The anonymity the process offers is intended to shield candidates from discrimination based on race, sex, or cronyism. Auditioning live, not surprisingly, made George nervous. He passed only one of his behind-the-screen auditions and eventually, to his deep regret, won a job deep in the Kansas City Philharmonic's second-violin section.

George never learned that he passed the audition not because of his violin playing but because he shared the same last name as the principal benefactor of the orchestra, an artificial-whipped-cream magnate named Ruppert Smith. One of Ruppert Smith's grandsons was known to be a musician, and the people in charge of auditioning violinists mistakenly believed *George* to be that grandson. The behind-the-screen audition did not exactly serve its purpose.

Ruppert Smith's real grandson had never studied music; he merely performed it. He was nineteen and the lead guitarist for a highly popular heavy-metal band called "Grislydeth" (one word). He lived in the Kenmore Square area of Boston with his three stunning girlfriends, who ranged in age from one to five years older than he was. Ruppert the Third, who went by a stage name of Face (short for Scumface), appeared both onstage and in public wearing a leather truss, stud collars on all four of his limbs, and motor oil liberally applied. The group regularly killed small animals in its stage show—gerbils, rats, bats, and, once, an unfortunate tree squirrel all met their untimely demises in loud, smoky Lansdowne Street clubs.

The group's lyrics were unintelligible in performance and barely coherent on the liner notes to its two bootlegged cassette tapes. Nevertheless, because the songs opposed war, condoms, and the Republican Party, Boston music critics frequently described the group as "relevant," "cutting edge," and "in touch with the times." The *Boston Globe* routinely gave Grislydeth's performances more review attention than it gave the Boston Symphony Orchestra. Ruppert the Third, who had dropped out of high school two years earlier to move to Boston and start Grislydeth, was earning approximately five times the average salary of an orchestra musician.

Ruppert Senior, the artificial-whipped-cream magnate, was so disgusted with his grandson's success that he revoked his trust fund and gave the principal to an environmental group concerned somehow with the ozone layer. Ruppert Senior was so delighted to have a Kansas City Philharmonic violinist bearing his name that he gave the orchestra an extra quarter million on the condition that they never admit that George and Ruppert were not related. They never did.

George Smith the violinist knew that he was not as good as the other members of his section, many of whom had won jobs on merit and not through connections. He felt guilty about dragging down the quality of the orchestra and wanted nothing more than to leave. Early in George's second season, Ugo Barelli, chief conductor of the New York Symphony, made a guest-conducting appearance with the Kansas City orchestra. George met Ugo's granddaughter, Maria Barelli, then twenty-three, after Ugo threw George out of rehearsal for missing a cue. Maria was devoted to Ugo, accompanied him on all his trips, and had a tendency to fall in love with musicians he threw out of rehearsals. George, who had never been on a date before, fell quickly in love with Maria, and the two were married later that year on the stage of Carnegie Hall.

Now that George was part of the family, Ugo had a change of heart about his grandson-in-law's abilities and went around telling everyone that Maria had married the next Umberto Poissoni, a violinist famous in Ugo's distant youth. No one but Ugo had ever heard the name Umberto Poissoni, but if Ugo liked him, everyone assumed he must have been good. Despite George's relative lack of talent, Ugo wanted to make him concertmaster, or first violinist, of the New York Symphony Orchestra. George had had enough of performing, though, so Ugo promptly arranged the firing of the Symphony's general manager and gave the job to George as a wedding present. With proper training and experience, George might have been an effective general manager, but the burdens of his new job quickly overwhelmed him. Six weeks after his arrival, the Symphony entered into its first and only orchestra strike. Everyone blamed the strike on George.

The previous general manager of the Symphony, Daniel Perelman, had a degree in cello and an M.B.A. and worked hard at keeping his orchestra members happy. Perelman knew that an unhappy orchestra could translate quickly into bad concerts, worse reviews, and a fall-off in ticket sales and subscription renewals. Strikes often lead to the demise of orchestras when their town or city realizes that it can get along perfectly well without all those concerts. Such has been the case in an increasing number of American cities. Orchestra members, convinced they are essential to a city's cultural life, often find the public's indifference a rude and numbing awakening. More often than not, no financial white knight comes to the rescue of deficit-ridden orchestras. The unintended result of some orchestra strikes is unemployment. The difficulty of finding another orchestral post (typically, 120 first-rate musicians may apply for every opening) gives musicians ample incentive to reach an agreement.

George, the newly minted administrator, therefore came to the bargaining table in a position of strength. The union representative did not even bother calling for a strike authorization vote because he sensed that the musicians would not risk jeopardizing their hard-won jobs. George's own negotiating experience was limited to the purchase and sales of two cars. He had been taken to the cleaners both times. He prepared for the talks with the Musicians Union by going to the library and taking out a few books with titles like *How to Make the Slob Across the Table Give in Completely*.

These books uniformly advocated a hard-nosed approach. George tried that tactic; it failed utterly. For a while he thought that the union people had read the same books. They hadn't. They were simply amazed to see George wipe out decades of labor peace with his "non-negotiable final offer," which included the first pay cut in the history of the Symphony. The union people balked. George would not give in, and so the orchestra struck.

Outside mediators finally came in and untangled the mess, but not before the three-week strike did permanent damage to George's reputation, and, many feared, to George's presence of mind. "George Smith gives nepotism a bad name," Symphony people told one another. Ugo Barelli, who never stepped off Sardinia during the entire strike, lost no confidence in his grandson-in-law, though. Over time, George improved, and was now considered a credible administrator. He could never live down that first failure, though, and his nervousness about every minor detail only increased. Everyone thought George was slowly driving Kevin Riordan, his assistant, 9out of his mind. In short, George was stuck in one of life's most unfortunate positions: everyone he worked with considered him a boob.

That George and Donald each shared the ignominy of having to live down an unfortunate disaster early in their careers might have brought the two men together. It did not. Each man's failure reminded the other of his own. Donald resented George because George basked in the distant, if total, approval, of Ugo Barelli. Donald, whose parents rarely communicated with him, would have enjoyed basking in the approval of an important older music person.

For his part, George had two reasons for not liking Donald. First, Ugo didn't, and George rarely disagreed with Ugo. Ugo's dislike of Donald was fairly mild, though, given Ugo's range of emotion and the speed with which he tossed musicians out of rehearsals. Ugo might not have been Donald's greatest fan, but he would never have thought of firing him. It simply wasn't worth the trouble to Ugo.

George had a second reason for not liking Donald. He did not approve of what he thought was Donald's practice of expecting the men in the chorus to sleep with him whenever he felt like it. George believed that Donald sometimes dropped from the group good singers who were just too heterosexual for Donald's tastes. This was not true, but George believed it anyway. "He puts his gonads ahead of the interest of the Symphony," George once said. In response, Donald described George to a reporter as "Mr. Maria Barelli." Any chance for reconciliation between the two men was shattered.

George licked his wounds in private until Donald's discovery of the Mass. George was not aware of the depth of Donald's animosity toward Andrew Barnes; he only needed to know that there was *some* bad feeling. George, therefore, hired Andrew (on all of Elizabeth's terms) to conduct the Mass as a slap at Donald. George did not realize that his slap was more like a knock-down blow.

George was coming back from a quick lunch at the Help Wanted across the street from Carnegie Hall when Kevin ran up to him on the sidewalk. "We've got a problem with Andy," he said, catching his breath. He had been looking for George everywhere.

"What is it?" George asked nervously. The premiere was also the opening night of the season, and he could not bear to think that something might go wrong. "Is he feeling all right? He looked okay this morning."

"Oh, he feels just great," said Kevin. "But not everybody feels so great about *him*." He fished the threatening letter out of his pocket and handed it to George. "It was under his dressing room door."

"Oh, shit," said George, reading the letter. "Ugo'll have a fit." George was a walking encyclopedia of political protests involving performances of classical music. He went through life dreading the possibility that some sort of terrorist outburst might occur at a Symphony performance, and that he would get all the blame. A clause in Andrew's contract gave the Symphony the right to replace him in the event of credible threats against his life. Ugo, of course, had forbidden Donald to conduct under any circumstances, but only Donald knew the Mass well enough to substitute on one day's notice.

The thought of contacting Ugo and asking for guidance crossed the minds of both Kevin and George. Both men knew, however, that Ugo long ago had tired of the day-to-day affairs of the Symphony and remained on Sardinia, at his thousand-acre goat-and-chicken farm, where there was no telephone, for as long as he could. Ugo was not scheduled to arrive in New York for three more weeks, which made it necessary to hire a series of guest conductors. The orchestra members were no happier about this system than Kevin and George, but no one dared challenge Ugo. Ugo loved his farm. Not even a Mozart premiere could entice him away from his goats. Some orchestra members claimed Ugo was so old that he had conducted Mozart premieres the first time around. Others joked that his affection for his farm animals extended beyond that normally proffered in small, religious southern Italian towns.

Neither Kevin nor George knew what to say. Terrorists made both George *and* Kevin nervous, but not as nervous as contemplating Ugo's reaction to their letting Donald conduct. Just then, Donald and James emerged from inside the hall. The four men greeted one another. They stood under a large concert poster featuring Andrew Barnes conducting, head thrown back, eyes closed, his baton slashing the air.

"George has something to tell you, Donald," said Kevin. "Tell him, George."

"What's up?" Donald asked, his tone friendly if guarded.

George swallowed hard. "Some people are thinking about killing Andy," he told Donald. "We may have to ask you to fill in. Ugo would kill me, but you're all we've got."

Donald's face lit up. George felt a pain in his stomach. "I have to take a Gelusil," he added. "Excuse me. Come along, Kevin."

Kevin, who wished that George could have left his private life out of the conversation, followed George inside. Beneath the poster of Andrew Barnes, Donald looked wide-eyed at James.

"Did you *hear* that?" Donald asked, beaming. "I might just get the concert!"

"I heard," James said excitedly. "I heard."

"Did you *hear* that?" Donald repeated. "I might just get it!"

"I *heard*," said James, sharing in Donald's excitement. Donald had not looked so happy in months. "I was standing right next to you. I heard the whole thing."

Suddenly Donald's face fell. Memories of his three disasters on the podium returned to mind. "Oh, Christ," he said, shaking his head slowly, "I might just get the concert."

THURSDAY
AFTERNOON

TWELVE

Alison and Andrew lay quietly between the damp sheets of Andrew's bed in his hotel suite. Andrew's hands were folded under his head while Alison snuggled against him. Neither of them had spoken for a few minutes. Neither was thinking about the other, for that matter. Andrew's mind was on the rehearsal he had just concluded and on the concert a day away. Alison was thinking about the first time she had ever heard classical music, and how much her life had changed as a result of that performance. Now she wondered how much her life might change as a result of *this* performance. She reflected on the fact that everyone who talked about sleeping one's way to the top always made it sound like an unpleasant and joyless enterprise. Boy, they were wrong.

The first time she heard serious music, she had been a high school freshman, growing up in Minneapolis, which, like virtually every city in the Midwest, considered itself the world's capital of choral music. She met a boy whose father taught music composition at the University of Minnesota. The boy's name was Mark. He was a high school junior. For their first and, as it happened, their only evening together, they used Mark's father's tickets to see a touring company of the Metropolitan Opera perform Wagner's *Die Meistersinger*. Alison went not because she was interested in opera but because she was interested in Mark.

At the performance, just before the curtain rose, Alison felt a sort of full-body shudder. If she had grown up in a less scientifically inclined family (her father was a chemist with 3M), she might have considered it a premonition. She sensed that something odd was going to happen to her that evening as she watched the opera. Until that moment, she had been scared because the opera was to begin at eight and the program said it would not end until eleven fifty-five. She could not imagine anything that could be interesting enough to watch, or to do, for almost four whole hours. She also wondered how they knew it would end at exactly eleven fifty-five and not eleven fifty-six or even a quarter after twelve.

Mark also had never been to an opera. He expected to enjoy it because his parents did, and so did all of their important friends from the Music Department. Mark knew a good deal about Richard Wagner's career and about the plot and music of *Die Meistersinger*. He impressed Alison no end with his whispered explanations of the characters and the story. As the opera went into its second and third hours, though, Mark was surprised to find himself sinking into utter and irreversible boredom. Studying string quartets and piano sonatas with his father was one thing. Playing violin or piano was fine, too. Sitting through four hours of opera, though, was pure punishment for him.

Alison, unaware of Mark's distress, was having a great time. Her favorite moment came whenever the conductor, with a deft flip of the baton, cued the singers to sing. She wanted the conductor to turn around, face the audience, and cue *her*. She tried to hear the opera on its own terms, which meant not listening to Wagner through a filter of groups like the Beach Boys or the Rolling Stones. She concentrated less on the plot, which Mark knew cold, and more on the *sound*—the interplay of voices, the blending of voice and orchestra. Twenty minutes into the performance, in fact, she had forgotten all about Mark.

Mark thought her enthusiasm for opera was contrived. He suspected that she was just as bored as he, and that she was refusing, out of childish stubbornness, to admit it. *This is what I get for going out with freshmen,* he told himself. He endured three hours of music, and then he asked her, during the third intermission, whether they might skip the last act. He had soccer practice the next day, after school, and he did not want to be out too late. Alison looked horrified. They stayed until the end.

When the curtain fell, Alison looked as awake and enthusiastic about opera as Mark had been four long hours earlier. Mark decided that he did not like Alison at all and he would not even try to kiss her goodnight. *That* would show her. To his surprise, though, when the bus dropped them off a few blocks from her house, which was about two blocks from his, Alison nailed him with the most amazing kiss he had ever gotten in his life. Alison was just as surprised, because after all it was only her first date and she had never kissed a boy, and she was not even sure until that moment of how you did it. She worried that she might be a slow learner.

She was a natural, though, and she just held Mark's shoulders with both hands and stuck her tongue into his mouth as though it belonged there, and he was flabbergasted because she was kissing him after he told himself he would not kiss her. He was even more surprised a moment later when Alison disengaged and said, "Thank you for a lovely evening. I can't go out with you again because I have to start training for my career as an opera star."

Mark never went back to the opera, but Alison was convinced that she would make a career for herself in music. A week later, she embarked upon what would become seven years of voice lessons and music study. She was blessed with a beautiful voice, and she wanted to learn how to sing properly. She took singing lessons one day a week and paid for them with money she earned babysitting. After high school, she went, not to college, like most of her friends, but to the Manhattan Conservatory of Music. She was lucky enough to have a series of vocal coaches who did not ruin her voice through improper training, as happens to many aspiring young singers.

The vocal music world abounds with bad teachers. They find themselves drawn by the high pay and the chance to take out their frustrations over their own unsuccessful careers by destroying, consciously or unconsciously, the voices of the next generation. A voice coach sabotaged the career of a singer Alison knew from Minneapolis, a mezzo-soprano named Laura Bartz. The teacher, herself a failed opera singer, pulled strings at a leading opera company and secured for Laura an extremely demanding role in a Wagner opera only two years after Laura graduated from the conservatory.

This may not sound like something to complain about, but Laura, then twenty-five, was neither musically nor emotionally prepared to take it on. The vocal coach cynically and accurately foresaw that the combination of the wear and tear on the young woman's throat (she had to sing for hours) and the humiliating reviews her performance received would cause her to stop singing altogether. If the singer had not been so ill used, she might have gone on to a career far more successful than that of her voice teacher. Unfortunately for her, the teacher knew this and managed to prevent it from happening.

Alison somehow managed to avoid all the bad teachers out there. She received a bachelor's degree in voice from the Manhattan Conservatory and was studying there now for her master's degree. She entered every important competition and audition in New York and won a few awards and prizes, but her professors at the conservatory all agreed that she was years away from any sort of career-making "big break." As she lay next to Andrew Barnes, running her hand slowly across his chest, she thought that perhaps her professors were about to be proved wrong.

"Did I read somewhere that you were a wrestling star when you were in college?" Alison asked. She had done her homework.

"Not quite a star," Andrew said modestly, touching her hand. "Just a guy willing to perform contortionistic acts in the name of sport."

"I don't know," said Alison. "I always thought wrestling looked kind of sexy."

"Only if you're not taking part," said Andrew. "Trust me."

"Mm," said Alison, taking hold of Andrew's hand. "Can I ask you something?"

"Sure, anything."

"What were you thinking about?"

"Hmm?"

"What were you thinking about?" she repeated. "While we were, you know. Doing it."

"Do you really want to know?" Andrew asked.

Alison nodded.

"George Gershwin," said Andrew.

"What?" Alison pulled her hand away. "You were thinking about a *man*?"

"No—I was thinking about *George Gershwin*. You know, *Rhapsody in Blue.*"

"Are you serious?" she asked. She hated to be made fun of.

"Absolutely," said Andrew.

Alison looked up at him, trying to decide whether he was playing a joke on her. "But why?" she asked. "Why would you be thinking about George Gershwin during sex?"

"I don't know," Andrew admitted. "I've been thinking about *Rhapsody in Blue* ever since rehearsal this morning. The part where it goes bum-bum-bum-BUM! Khhh! *De*-da-*De*-da-*De*-da-bum-bum-bum-BUM! Bum-bum-bum—do you know where I am?"

Alison pretended to be hurt. "Weren't you thinking about *me*?" she asked.

"Sure I was," said Andrew, trying to reassure her. He took her hand and placed it on his chest again. "I was just thinking of Gershwin, too. I don't know why. I've never conducted it. I'd like to, I guess."

"You even think of conducting when you're having sex?" Alison asked.

Andrew nodded. He ran his free hand through her hair. "I think about it all the time." He paused, and laughed. "Except sometimes, when I'm conducting."

"Why?" Alison asked. "What do you think about then?"

"Oh, a lot of things. World peace, the colonization of the planets, the melting of the polar icecaps, whether I'm getting enough roughage, whether Elvis is still alive, whether the BBC will ever show *Leave it to Beaver*, how much I'm getting paid per minute, what the Royal Family looks like naked—just the usual guy stuff. The stuff all guys think about."

"Well, what were you thinking about *today*?" Alison asked, playing along.

"You," said Andrew, and he kissed her. Alison decided that she'd let him get away with that *this* time. "Now, you tell me," he added. "What were *you* thinking about?"

"I'd rather not say," said Alison, turning away.

"Why not?"

"You'll get the wrong idea about me," she said.

"I promise you I won't," said Andrew, wondering what she meant by that.

"Actually," said Alison, and now *she* was toying with *him*, "I was thinking of STDs."

"Hmm?"

"Sexually transmitted diseases," said Alison, looking directly at Andrew.

"What?" he said, sitting up quickly. "But *why*?"

"You asked me," Alison said simply. "That's what I was thinking about. I'm clean, so don't get nervous or anything."

"But why were you thinking about *diseases*?" Andrew asked.

"I don't know," said Alison. "I just *was*. You can't control what you think about. How come you were thinking about Gershwin?"

Andrew admitted to himself that she had a point.

"I mean," Alison said, "just say you caught something from somebody. You'd never trust another woman as long as you lived. And you'd always think about how you got it, and where you got it, and everything that led up to it, and you'd be really depressed."

"Makes sense," said Andrew, thinking it over. "I guess."

"Say you caught something from someone you met on a ski trip," said Alison. "You'd probably never want to go skiing again for the rest of your life. You could wipe out sex *and* skiing in one trip."

"Do you ski?" asked Andrew.

"No, never," said Alison. "I just gave it as an example."

"Oh," said Andrew, thoroughly confused by now. Just then, the telephone rang. Andrew tried to reach across Alison, but she held on to his arm and would not let him near the phone.

"I've got to get the phone," Andrew complained.

"Why?" Alison asked mischievously. "*Why* do you have to get the phone?"

"I just do," said Andrew, straining to reach past her, but she would not loosen her grip.

"No, you don't," she said, her tone playful. The telephone kept ringing.

"You don't understand," Andrew said through gritted teeth, still trying to reach past her but not wanting to hurt her. "I paid off the concierge downstairs to call me in case my wife comes into the hotel. You've got to let—" All of a sudden Andrew put a half nelson on Alison. He thrust an arm under her right arm, placed a hand on the back of her neck, and flipped her gently across the bed. She looked dazed.

"What happened?" she asked, rubbing her forehead. "How'd you do that?"

Andrew picked up the receiver. "Hello? Pierre? Is she coming up? . . . Oh, hi, George. No, you're not interrupting anything."

Alison pouted, pretending to be insulted.

"Really? You'd really do that? . . . Then who'd fill in, Donald? . . . You haven't decided anything, have you? Wait and see? . . . Okay, keep me posted. . . . Do I what? Of course I respect your judgment. . . . You respect mine, too? That makes me very happy. Bye now." He hung up.

"What was that all about?" asked Alison. "Who's Donald going to fill in for?"

"Oh no, you, uh, you misunderstood," Andrew said quickly. "My fan club was complaining. They don't like the location of their seats."

"You have a fan club?" Alison asked admiringly.

Andrew nodded. He looked at the clock on the nightstand. "I think we better get dressed," he said. "Elizabeth could be back any minute."

Alison, disappointed, pulled the sheet up over her body. "What's wrong?" she asked.

"We'll just have to save Round Two for later on," Andrew said. "Around seven, right here? Is that okay for you? My wife's going to some kind of reception."

"Okay, I guess," she said in a small voice.

Andrew climbed out of bed and headed for the bathroom. He ran the water.

"Come on," he called out. "Let's make ourselves presentable."

"Okay, I guess," Alison said. Then her spirits rose: maybe he'd go for Round Two in the shower, she thought, and she followed him into the bathroom.

Word spread quickly throughout the chorus and orchestra that Donald might be stepping in for Andrew at the premiere. James, in his own unsubtle way, spread the rumor as quickly and as widely as he could. Alvin Reischel, the second trombonist and gambling czar, began to offer odds on which conductor would appear. Alvin made book on a full line of sporting events. He also offered specialized bets on questions like with which piece Ugo Barelli might begin a given rehearsal or what color tie he was going to wear. Until Ugo caught on, he would wonder why half the orchestra would cheer and half would boo when he started with, say, the Stravinsky instead of the Copland.

Tens of thousands of dollars changed hands every season. Alvin, who set all odds and arbitrated all disputes, usually came out ahead. He made Andrew the two-to-one favorite, but Donald was an interesting proposition at twelve-to-five. Alvin, mindful of Andrew's reputation as a man with an eye for women, wanted to make book on the possibility of his going to bed with a woman in the chorus or orchestra. Alvin had to abandon the idea because the outcome of a bet like that, though extremely appealing to his customers, would have been very hard to prove.

THIRTEEN

Six nervous conducting students, scores and batons in hand, sat in metal folding chairs on the edge of the Weill Recital Hall stage. They looked as though they had not slept in days. Four were men, two were women, all were in their mid-to-late twenties and all were graduate students of conducting at the Manhattan Conservatory of Music. They carried heavy course loads of conducting technique, music history, composition, orchestration, and liberal arts courses like literature and psychology. For the last few weeks, they had put most of their classwork aside to prepare for the master class with Andrew Baker Barnes. Television lights accentuated the signs of sleeplessness in their faces. None of them were pleased to learn that an international audience would watch their errors.

The conducting students were apprehensive about the master class not only because they wanted to do well in front of their peers, their professors, the public, and the television cameras, but also because the conservatory faculty had little good to say about Barnes. He might have been one of their most prominent graduates and the only member of his class to have his own orchestra, but people said there was something unorthodox about him. "He's not a *real* musician," went the whispering campaign against Barnes among the conservatory faculty. "He got very poor grades when he was here." This sense of Barnes as a poor conductor was just what Elizabeth was seeking to counteract.

Andrew had never given a master class for the simple reason that no one had ever asked him to give one. During Andrew's time at the conservatory he had never auditioned for the master classes in conducting because it was not required of him to do so. Andrew did almost nothing at the conservatory that was not required. He knew, also, that the few seats in master classes invariably went to the best conducting students. He had had no illusions during his conservatory days about his abilities on the podium. His approach to conducting was more intuitive than analytical, and he was almost defensive about his inability to describe how he did what he did. Still, he had allowed Elizabeth to talk him into giving a master class here in New York, and the time had come.

Andrew, dressed now in a conservatively tailored blue suit, appeared onstage. The audience of music students, conservatory professors, and members of the public applauded, but only politely. The cameras rolled. Andrew scanned the crowded hall for some friendly faces, perhaps some conservatory classmates, but he recognized no one. He tried to keep from thinking about the death threats, but he reminded himself that the master class audience had been made to pass through metal detectors and was almost certainly unarmed. Half a dozen police officers, including Officer Caruso, had taken up positions around Weill Hall, adding an ominous tone to the proceedings.

Andrew had conducted almost five hundred concerts and had never felt butterflies—until now. *And I don't even have to conduct anything,* he told himself. *I just have to stand here.* Then he felt panic: maybe he wasn't supposed to stand. Maybe he was supposed to sit. But sit where? He looked across the stage and saw a folding chair facing the podium from a distance of fifteen feet. *I guess that's for me,* he thought, and he went and sat down. The house lights were kept on for the convenience of those many members of the audience who had brought scores of Beethoven's Symphony No. 7, the piece the students would conduct. *Wonderful,* Andrew thought, peering into the packed hall. *These people are going to take notes.*

What was he going to tell them? What could he tell them? Andrew had conducted the Seventh Symphony two dozen times. He could *hum* the piece from memory, but his knowledge of the precise markings of the score was skeletal. It occurred to him now that the students probably knew the piece better than he did. The television cameras were as unnerving to Andrew as they were to the students.

The hall grew silent. Andrew wondered whether he was supposed to say something or just ask the first student conductor to begin. Andrew told himself that he should have prepared, somehow. He feared now that he would make a great fool of himself, and he wondered whether this was what Elizabeth had in mind. He looked at the audience again and recognized Albert Nouse, his old conducting professor at the Manhattan Conservatory. *Hasn't changed at all*, Andrew thought. *Still doesn't look a day over ninety.* Seated next to Nouse was Henry Mishkin, an extremely popular music history professor, a Bach expert, and Andrew's only real friend on the conservatory faculty. Andrew nodded to Henry, who smiled and nodded back.

Andrew decided against opening remarks. He motioned to the conductor seated nearest the podium, a taciturn young man with a neatly trimmed black beard. He wore gray slacks and a blue blazer. Andrew offered him a friendly smile.

"Care to start us off?" Andrew asked.

The conducting student shook his head nervously and started to play with his beard. "We're supposed to go in alphabetical order," he said. "I go fourth."

"Okay," said Andrew, forcing a smile. He wondered how he was supposed to have known that. He also wondered what difference it made. Then he decided that he would not have wanted to go first, either. "Who *is* first?" he asked.

Another student, tall, sandy-haired, thin, wearing a green pullover and blue jeans, stood up. His baton was tucked into a dog-eared conductor's score.

"And your name is—" said Andrew.

"Peter Berk," said the student.

Just then, Donald slipped in by a side door. He took a seat in the back. Andrew did not notice him, but Officer Caruso, watching from the back of the hall, did.

"Whenever you're ready, Mr. Berk," Andrew said,

hoping he sounded casual. *Let's get this over with*, he thought. *How long do these things last? Do you take a break after three students? Or every half hour? What the hell is going on here?*

A flurry of page-turning from the audience greeted Peter Berk as he mounted the podium. "Ready?" Berk asked the orchestra.

He's a cool one, this Berk, Andrew told himself. *Probably an honor student.* Then Peter looked to Barnes for permission to begin, and Barnes nodded. Peter lifted his baton, the string section lifted their bows, and conductor and orchestra launched into the first movement of the Seventh Symphony. Peter conducted with authority and with grace. He took an appropriate tempo for the movement—fast, but not too fast. His beats were easy to follow, although many members of the orchestra, made up of Manhattan Conservatory students, knew the piece so well that they did not always keep their eyes on him.

Andrew watched carefully, hoping to find something to correct. *There must be something*, Andrew told himself. Posture? No, his posture was fine. His back was straight but not stiff. The pattern his baton made in the air? Andrew watched it carefully, but it was clear and even—above reproach. His grip on the baton? Nothing wrong there. He was holding it lightly but firmly, just as the textbooks instructed.

What about the way he indicated the crescendo at measure fourteen? *No problem*, Andrew told himself, and he felt himself growing edgy. Peter Berk's gestures were exactly what the score required. *He's doing everything right*, Andrew told himself. The other students noticed Andrew's deepening frown. Their quick intakes of breath could be heard over the orchestra's quiet moments. Peter's conducting was unassailable, they all thought. *If this guy Barnes doesn't like Peter, he'll hate the rest of us.* At the podium, Peter was wondering when Barnes would stop him and give him the benefit of his experience. *The longer he lets me go on*, Peter thought, *the worse it's going to be for me.* He gave Barnes a nervous glance and continued to conduct.

Andrew was no happier than the students. Two minutes had passed and Barnes had found nothing wrong. *They must think I'm an idiot out there,* he thought. Everyone else probably found lots of things to criticize. Andrew asked himself how he had ever allowed himself to be dragged into this mess. Then a passage in the woodwinds brought Andrew back to the first time he heard the piece. A girlfriend of his at the University of Maryland had played the flute in the university orchestra. She first kindled Andrew's interest in classical music and started him on the road to the conservatory. She made him listen to the Seventh over and over again because she was going to perform it in a concert. Although she never said so, familiarity with the Seventh was a prerequisite for the continued success of the relationship.

He played the record a dozen times. It was a scratchy, ancient Toscanini recording with the NBC Symphony. She had bought the record for fifty cents on their first date. The seller was an aging hippie with hair down to his waist who sold records from the back of a Microbus. Andrew played the album, not out of interest, but out of that stubborn chivalrous sense that sometimes comes over men when they want to keep a woman happy.

To Andrew's surprise, though, he enjoyed the concert—not the whole concert, just Beethoven's Seventh. Andrew, at that point, was still planning on a career as a high school wrestling coach and needed to find an academic subject to teach to go along with the wrestling. English, social studies, and math all seemed too dull, and he was never much of a success in science classes. Why not music, he asked himself during that concert. How hard could it be? And it had to be more interesting than sine, cosine, and tangent, or the French and Indian War.

And then Andrew found that he *liked* music, that he had some aptitude for the cello, that he met a lot of interesting girls in the music library, and that a few years in a conservatory might not be the worst thing. And there he met Corinne, and then Elizabeth, and his life changed so quickly when he married Elizabeth and went to London to lead the R.S.S. And now here he was sitting on the stage of the Weill Recital Hall in New York, giving a master class in conducting, and suddenly Andrew made the sickening discovery that two more minutes had gone

by and he had not been paying the slightest attention. In
the audience, Donald, to his own great surprise, found
himself feeling bad for Andrew.

Meanwhile, at the podium, Peter Berk was amazed that
the maestro had allowed him to conduct this long without
stopping. *Maybe I'm not doing such a bad job,* he allowed himself to think. Then he heard Barnes say "Thank
you, that's enough," and he braced himself for the in-
evitable dressing-down. People in the front rows of the
audience thought they saw the muscles in his back and
shoulders tense, as if he were preparing to receive a blow.

To Peter's great surprise, Andrew merely asked,
"Who's next?"

Peter gave Barnes a long look. What did the maestro
mean by that, he wondered. Had he done a good job or
a poor job? Barnes's expression—affable but confused—
offered little comfort. Peter returned to his seat, but not
before the audience gave him a spirited ovation in which
Barnes, smiling now, joined wholeheartedly. Peter ex-
haled deeply and turned to the student next to him.
"Guy's hard to read," Peter whispered, and the other
student nodded quickly.

The second conducting student, an intense, auburn-
haired young woman wearing a dark blue dress, stood at
the platform.

"And your name is?" Barnes asked.

"Suzanne Harris," she said. "May I begin?"

"Please," said Andrew.

Suzanne started the movement, and the same thing
happened again. Andrew could find no fault with her
conducting, and after thirty or forty seconds of intense
concentration his mind started to wander. He began to
think about Alison. *This won't do,* Barnes told himself.
I've just got to pay attention.

In the audience, a concerned Professor Mishkin leaned
toward Professor Nouse.

"He isn't listening," said Professor Mishkin.

"He's listening," Professor Nouse responded. "He's
just not *hearing.*"

Suzanne Harris, in fact, had made a few errors obvious
to most of the conducting students in the hall. Donald

noticed every mistake. Had Andrew been listening, he would have heard them, too.

At last Andrew himself heard a mistake. *Oh, thank heavens,* he told himself. And then, another moment of panic: *What if I'm wrong?* He stood up. "Right there," he said, hoping he sounded authoritative. "Just for a moment."

The student conductor brought the orchestra to a quick halt. All eyes—orchestra, students onstage, and the audience—were on Barnes.

"After the two full rests," Barnes said. "YAH-ta-ta YAH-ta-ta in the violins, do you know where I am?"

Suzanne Harris's eyes scanned the score. "One eighty-one?" she asked quickly, rubbing her chin.

"Fine," said Andrew, taking command. "I'm at measure one eighty-one, the violin entrance. And then the second violins come in two bars later down a third? Right? Does everyone have the place?"

A blizzard of page-turning ensued as the orchestra and the audience looked for measure 181 in their scores.

"It's marked *pianissimo*, right?" Barnes asked Suzanne, who checked her score and nodded.

"And what came just before was double *forte*, right?" Barnes asked. *How on earth do I remember all this,* he asked himself.

Suzanne checked her score and nodded again. She was watching Barnes, unconsciously rubbing together the palms of her hands.

"Okay," said Andrew. "Double *forte* to *pianissimo* is a long way, right? Beethoven is asking for an *enormous* change of volume here. If I'm not mistaken, this is the biggest sudden change in volume in the whole symphony. You just had the whole orchestra playing very loud. You've got all the woodwinds—the flutes, everybody— playing at the top of their ranges. Am I right? It's shrill, it's loud, it's a very big sound. Right?"

Suzanne Harris swallowed hard and nodded. People in the audience started to sit up in their seats. Even Donald was impressed.

"And you go from all those instruments booming away," Andrew was saying, "to what? To the first violins, all alone, exposed, sweet, and *soft*. Above all, soft.

Could I please have everyone playing your last pitch at, what is it, measure one seventy-eight? Just give me your pitch, sustained at double *forte*.''

The orchestra obliged and a long, loud chord ensued.

''*Good*,'' Barnes shouted over the orchestral din, ''first violins on the G natural, *pianissimo—now!*'' The soft, quiet strings replaced the loud music of the earlier chord.

''*That's* the kind of contrast Beethoven is asking for,'' Barnes concluded, speaking softly over the gentle sound of the violins. ''And who are we to turn him down? And then make those dotted eighth and sixteenth notes *dance*. Make them beautiful. Don't be afraid. It's not Morse code, it's music. YA-ta-ta, YA-ta-ta. You've got to *feel* it. Take it again, please, from—what's a good spot to get into it?''

The violins halted themselves. Suzanne Harris examined her score again. ''How about one sixty-eight?'' she asked.

''How *about* measure one sixty-eight?'' Andrew repeated. The orchestra members checked their parts, decided it was a good place to come in, and took up their instruments. Suzanne lifted her baton, the orchestra began, and this time she demanded—and received, to the satisfaction of the audience and Andrew Barnes—the great change in volume that Beethoven had requested. Suzanne glanced at Barnes, as if to ask whether she should keep going, and Barnes nodded.

Andrew resumed his seat. *Where the hell did* that *come from,* he asked himself. *How did I remember that it goes from double* forte *to* pianissimo *right there?* He watched the camera crew depart, satisfied with their footage of Andrew in action. They wanted to set up their equipment in time for the beginning of the press conference. They also wanted to hit the buffet table, about which they had heard rumors.

And then Andrew remembered. His first year final examination in conducting at the Manhattan Conservatory consisted of conducting the school's orchestra—an earlier version of the group playing for Suzanne Harris. The piece Andrew conducted was the first movement of the same Beethoven's Seventh Symphony. The performance, which went badly for Andrew, also had been videotaped.

Barnes then had to suffer the ignominy of watching the tape played back to his classmates.

Professor Nouse—now seated beside Henry Mishkin in the audience—had stopped the tape almost every twenty seconds to point out something else that Barnes had done wrong. Barnes got a D for the year. After class, Nouse took him aside and suggested, ever so politely, that he think about a different line of work. Arts management, maybe, or even music therapy. At that point in his career, Andrew had not expected to become a conductor, but still, the experience had not been much fun.

Andrew had managed to suppress the memory of that final exam—until now. To his surprise, he remembered every wrong move that he had made, every incorrect motion to the orchestra, every wrong tempo, every wasted gesture. All he had to do now was wait for the student conductors to make the same mistakes. As good as the students were, Andrew realized that they were making some of the same errors that he had made a dozen years earlier.

By five o'clock, all six students had conducted large chunks of the first movement of the Seventh, and all were grateful to Andrew for his insightful comments. (Donald only stayed for forty minutes, though, forced to make the grudging admission to himself that Andrew came off well.) All six students left the stage certain that they were better conductors for their brief tutelage with Maestro Barnes, and all would append the experience to their résumés. Andrew felt a bit like a fraud, although he was relieved not to have made a fool of himself onstage. He acknowledged the audience's applause at the end of the class without a trace of a smile, until he saw that Mishkin was looking approvingly at him. Then Andrew's own expression lightened.

On his way out, Albert Nouse turned to Mishkin. "I was pleasantly surprised," Nouse admitted. "Andy's ear has gotten a lot better since when *we* had him."

"I don't think we really appreciated him in those days," Mishkin said, smiling. "A fine young man."

'Of course,'' murmured Elizabeth as he delighted ''. And then the deep

FOURTEEN

Elizabeth Garrett-Jones paused at the bulletin board
across from her husband's dressing room. She reread with
satisfaction the profile on Andrew. She was the one who
had posted it.

Elizabeth had not attended the master class. She had
not seen Andrew conduct in over a year. Now she
watched the orchestra members filing past. The afternoon rehearsal had just ended, and they were coming
offstage. Down the corridor, pouring coffee for herself,
was a woman who, to Elizabeth's eye, closely resembled
Corinne Gates, a classmate of hers at the Manhattan
Conservatory.

While Elizabeth felt little remorse over Donald's un-
happiness, she retained a shred of guilt for those rare
occasions when Corinne Gates came to mind. After fourteen years, Elizabeth did not recall all the details, but
she remembered that Corinne and Andrew had been involved before she and Andrew started to spend time together. Elizabeth was certain, though, that the woman
down the corridor who looked like Corinne Gates in fact
was Corinne Gates.

"Why, Corinne, what are you doing here?" she asked.

"Elizabeth Garrett-Jones," Corinne replied, non-
plussed. "After all these years."

Orchestra members and ushers stepped quickly past
them, unaware of the chance encounter that Corinne had
hoped to avoid.

"How about a cup of coffee?" asked Corinne, breaking the silence, motioning to the coffee machine behind
them. "For old times' sake."

"Of course," murmured Elizabeth. "I'd be delighted." And then she repeated: "Why, Corinne, what *are* you doing here?"

"I'm here to fix the pipe organ," Corinne said tartly.

Corinne and Elizabeth had met in the Manhattan Conservatory Chorus, and they had not seen one another since then.

"I don't think I want any coffee after all," said Elizabeth, looking Corinne up and down. Corinne led her to a table in the musicians' lounge. "Aren't you as surprised to see me as I am to see you?" Elizabeth asked.

"Not really," said Corinne, opening a container of cream and pouring some into her coffee. "It's not exactly classified information that you married Andy."

"You still haven't told me why *you're* here." She became suspicious. "You haven't come to see my Andrew, have you?"

"No, I haven't come to see *your Andrew*. I happen to sing with the New York Symphony Chorus. See my score?" In fact, though, Corinne was backstage because she wanted to bump into Andrew, quite by accident, of course.

"Oh," said Elizabeth, visibly relieved. "Dear Corinne, still singing in the chorus."

"Spare me."

"How long has it been since we last saw one another?" asked Elizabeth.

"Fourteen years," Corinne replied matter-of-factly. "Not since graduation from conservatory. I've followed your career, of course."

"I beg your pardon? *My* career?"

Corinne stirred her coffee. "As Andy's nanny," she said, without looking up.

Elizabeth's eyes flashed. "*You* might spare *me*," she said.

"Forgive me. Your career as Andy's wife. Let's try to be civil."

"*Do* let's try," said Elizabeth. "I so hate scenes."

"That makes two of us," said Corinne.

"You must have been expecting this. Our bumping into one another. You seem so calm."

Corinne smiled, trying to hide the turbulence *she* felt.

"You're right," she said. "I thought we might meet. But why should I be anything but calm?"

"Well," said Elizabeth. "If I knew that at any moment I should encounter the woman who stole off with my fiancé I should feel a bit ill at ease, don't you think?"

"Fiancé? We were never engaged."

"I always thought you were."

"First I ever heard of it."

"Oh, I see," said Elizabeth. "I could be mistaken."

"How generous of you."

"I thought we were trying to keep things civil."

"So we were," said Corinne. "How's London?"

"It's all gotten so terribly boring, frankly. I rather enjoyed the first few years of it—the social whirl, the parties, my Andrew's first few seasons. But lately a kind of sameness has crept in. The same parties year after year. The same faces. Wherever one goes one finds great mobs of people who want to meet us and talk to us. It's gotten dreadful, frankly."

"It doesn't sound that bad to me," said Corinne, sipping her coffee. "Parties? Mobs of people? It sounds a lot better than what I've been doing."

"Which is?"

"PR work, singing in churches here and there, putting my life back in order after a short marriage. Getting by."

"Oh, you pitiful thing," said Elizabeth, putting her hand atop Corinne's. Corinne gently moved her hand away.

"It's not that bad. I'm not exactly a pitiful thing. Actually, I've been going out with Kevin Riordan. He was a classmate of ours. I don't know if you remember him."

"Of course I remember him," said Elizabeth. "But the thought of divorce is so *frightful*, don't you think?"

"You're right," said Corinne. "I wouldn't even wish it on you."

"I see," said Elizabeth, as if Corinne's words confirmed a longstanding suspicion. "You're still angry with me."

Corinne looked up. "With you?"

"Yes, with me," said Elizabeth. "Over Andrew."

Corinne sighed. "Not really." She paused. "I'll bet you never lost much sleep over it."

"Well, no, of course not—what's *that* supposed to mean?"

"Never mind."

"No, I want to talk about it," said Elizabeth. "What do you mean, you bet I didn't lose any sleep over it?"

"Everybody can hear you," said Corinne. Others, including the two ushers seemingly welded to their seats near the entrance to the lounge, were beginning to pay attention to the two women.

"Are you suggesting that I lacked a conscience?" Elizabeth whispered angrily. "Is that it?"

"You didn't seem too bothered at the time."

Elizabeth paused. "You're right," she said. "I wasn't. But you forgive me now, don't you?"

"What difference does it make?"

"It makes a *great* difference," Elizabeth insisted.

"Please, keep it down," said Corinne, embarrassed. Everyone else in the musicians' lounge had stopped talking, and Corinne and Elizabeth were center stage. *Am I the only one in the world who doesn't like to hash things out in public?* Corinne asked herself. "I don't think this is anybody's business but our own," she said aloud.

Elizabeth, oblivious to the attention of the others in the room, was still waiting for an answer.

"If forgiving you will keep you quiet," said Corinne, "then I forgive you." *This I didn't expect,* Corinne told herself.

Elizabeth closed her eyes and moved her head back slightly. "Darling Corinne, you can't know how much this means to me."

"You're right. I can't."

"Please. Don't spoil things. We were just getting along so well. We *were* awfully good friends in conservatory, weren't we? We did those wonderful string quartets, you and I and Donald and my Andrew."

"Those *were* good times," said Corinne, wishing that Elizabeth would stop referring to Andrew as "her" Andrew. Corinne wondered whether Elizabeth did it just to upset her. Remembering Elizabeth as she did, it was entirely possible. "I have a lot of happy memories," Corinne added. "I just don't think about them much."

"*I* do," Elizabeth said earnestly. "Those might have

been the happiest days of my life. Even before my Andrew—forgive me. Even before Andrew and I—became close.''

This made no sense to Corinne. ''Your husband conducts the most popular orchestra in London! You just told me that you go to balls and parties every night! How can you possibly say that conservatory was a better time for you?''

Elizabeth lowered her eyes. ''It's not all I thought it would be,'' she said in a small voice.

''What's not all you thought it would be? Being in high society—although I suppose you were born to that—or being married to Andy?''

''Both.''

''What's wrong?''

''Andrew has *changed* over the years since we married,'' Elizabeth said bitterly. ''He's just not the same man.''

Corinne was guarded in her response. ''How so?'' she asked.

''It's hard to say, exactly. When we met he was just a boy. He was unsure of himself. He lacked the courage to go after the biggest, most prestigious posts. He didn't have the courage even to apply for fellowships or awards. He avoided competition like the plague.''

''Andy always knew his limits,'' said Corinne.

''Quite the opposite,'' Elizabeth said firmly. ''He never knew his *potential*.''

''And that's where you came in?''

''In a manner of speaking, yes. I tried to nurture him.''

''If only I'd thought of that,'' said Corinne. If Elizabeth caught the sarcastic nature of the comment, she did not show it.

''I remember when I first saw him,'' said Elizabeth, looking at the far wall of the lounge. ''It was during a conservatory chorus rehearsal. He seemed so vulnerable. He seemed so alone.''

''He was going out with *me* at the time.''

''Quite. No offense intended.''

''Forget it,'' said Corinne, looking away. ''Keep going.''

''As I said, he seemed so vulnerable.''

"Not vulnerable," said Corinne. "Manipulable."

"Are you saying that I manipulated my Andrew?" Elizabeth asked, surprised.

"Of course not," said Corinne, sipping her coffee.

"Well, then," Elizabeth continued, "I sought him out. I *befriended* him. Why, there he was, in his last year at the conservatory. He had made not a single application to an orchestra. He had applied for not a single fellowship. Do you know what he wanted to *do*?"

"Mm-hmm," said Corinne. "I only went out with him for two and a half years."

"So you remember," said Elizabeth, a bit miffed because Corinne's remembering undercut the flow of her monologue. "How *extraordinary*, I thought. What a waste of talent and charm and education. Was this all that he could accomplish, given his superlative record at conservatory?"

"Superlative record at conservatory?" repeated Corinne. "Are we talking about the same Andrew Barnes? The Andy *I* remember barely squeaked through. His grades were awful! He failed his second-year music-theory exam! He had to make up an entire semester! His cello teacher nearly had him thrown out of the student orchestra. He never practiced, of course, but he was no Pablo Casals to begin with."

"He did well in the advanced conducting seminar," Elizabeth said stiffly.

"No he didn't. It was pass-fail. *And* he was the *only* student in the class who wasn't given his own concert with the student orchestra."

"It must have been a scheduling problem."

"No. It was a talent problem."

"I'm not sure I remember that," said Elizabeth.

"Of course not. It interferes with your idea of Andrew, the consummate musician. He didn't even want to *take* that seminar until you talked him into it. He knew he'd be out of his league. He wanted to be a high school music teacher. And a wrestling coach, after school. In Maryland. Where he grew up. Not a conductor."

"Of course Andrew wanted to be a conductor! How dare you suggest that I talked him into it?"

"Of course you talked him into it!" Corinne exclaimed. "That's not what he wanted."

Everyone in the musicians' lounge turned to listen.

"He didn't want balls and parties! He wanted a normal, simple life!" She paused, and then she lost her self-control: *"And so did I!"*

"Please, Corinne—" said Elizabeth, but Corinne would not stop.

"He'd tell me about his hometown, and about how much he loved growing up there. And he used to say that his only ambition in life was to go back there and teach music, and coach sports, and try to pay the town back for everything it gave him. I can still hear him saying that!

"And he would have been a great music teacher, that's for sure. The kids would have loved him because he was such a great guy and a good athlete"—Corinne was near tears—"and I can't believe I'm saying these things. And Andy used to talk about *taking me with him.* And maybe if you'd never come along he *would've* taken me with him. And we would have gotten married, and we'd be living in his hometown, and none of the awful things that happened to me would have happened—"

Corinne began to cry.

"Oh, my dear Corinne—" Elizabeth began.

"I can do without your sympathy, okay?" Corinne found a handkerchief in her purse and dabbed at her eyes. "Look at me. I promised myself this wouldn't happen. But there it is. And it's *all your fault.*"

Elizabeth noticed that the eyes of the room were upon them.

"Please, Corinne—" she said softly.

"Don't 'please Corinne' me, okay? I've always wanted to get this off my chest. You stole Andy away from me not because you loved him. That would have been one thing. I mean, that's life, I guess. You stole him away because you knew you could manipulate him and make a conductor out of him—and he had as much business conducting as—as you do! You latched on to Andy because you thought you could *control* him! You figured that since he had so little talent he'd be completely beholden to you, and that way you could run the whole show!''

''Corinne—please—not here—couldn't we step into Andrew's dressing room—''

Corinne cut her off.

''No, we *can't* step into Andrew's dressing room. And now you're sad because Andy came into his own socially. Oh, I'm sure it was rough on him at first. A varsity wrestling captain from the Maryland shore suddenly leading a symphony orchestra in a foreign country. And I'm sure he felt totally out of place in the beginning. But Andy's nobody's fool. He could see after a while that all your fancy friends were just people, and that there was no reason to be afraid of them. And once they got to see what a good guy he was, it was no wonder he was out every night. You lost control of him, that's all. And it's just destroying you, isn't it?''

''How *dare* you say such things?'' asked Elizabeth, her voice up an octave and a half. ''And how do you know so much about my Andrew?''

''Your Andrew's life is hardly a state secret. Everyone in the music world knows what a playboy he is. It's common knowledge. Or don't they tell *you*?''

''That's quite enough!'' Elizabeth said. She stood. ''I think that we've said more than enough already. Good day, Miss Gates, or whatever your name is.''

''It's still Gates. And I've got some more news for you, Miss Garrett-Jones. If I were you I'd keep a close eye on your Andrew while he's in New York because I know of at least one woman in the chorus who fully intends to give him what you don't!''

Speechless, Elizabeth glared at Corinne and stomped out of the lounge. The others present pretended that they had not been listening. Corinne tried to regain her composure.

''Are you all right, miss?''

It was one of the ushers.

''Just fine, thank you.'' Corinne forced a smile. ''It's always emotional when you meet an old friend, don't you think?''

FIFTEEN

Andrew, accompanied as always by Officer Caruso, went directly from the master class to the press conference in the Carnegie Hall Patrons' Room. The session would give the American music press its first look at the guest conductor. Andrew took stock of all that had happened since breakfast: Alison was a pleasant and welcome surprise. The master class with Mishkin and that old bastard Nouse in the audience could not have been more of a triumph. If he ignored the fact that the Symphony musicians had made a fool of him in rehearsal, and that the terrorists were threatening to kill him if he did not withdraw from the concert, he was enjoying a perfect day.

"You did a good job in that master class," said Officer Caruso, as he and Andrew approached the Patrons' Room. "I might have handled that third kid a little differently. His legatos could have been a little smoother, don't you think?"

Andrew stopped and turned to look at Officer Caruso. "No, I don't think," he said. He did not want the young patrolman to dispel his sense that he had handled the master class well.

"On second thought," Officer Caruso said diplomatically, "I think you handled him perfectly."

"Thanks," said Andrew. He checked the knot in his tie, cleared his throat, prepared a winning smile, and strode inside. Officer Caruso followed him in.

The ninety-five reporters present, representing news and music publications, as well as most of the local television and radio stations, barely responded when Andrew entered. They sat low in their chairs with the look of people who had eaten and drunk too much too quickly. Elizabeth had provided enough food for a hundred and fifty, but almost nothing remained. The theme was Maryland cuisine, symbolic of Andrew's home state and his American upbringing. Elizabeth believed that the "American homecoming" angle was the best way to guarantee sympathetic coverage for her husband.

The press had consumed twenty-six hundred dollars' worth of Maryland crab cakes, Maryland oysters, Maryland clams, terrapin, wild duck, fried chicken à la Maryland, green peas, coleslaw, cantaloupes, peaches, Maryland beaten biscuits, and for dessert, Maryland apple pie. They washed it down with four cases of Maryland rye whiskey and two cases of California champagne. (The caterer had offered to provide a Maryland champagne, but Elizabeth turned it down. She told him that when it came to authenticity, you had to draw the line somewhere.)

Elizabeth hoped that the journalists would get a little bit tipsy, look upon Andrew with a warm glow, and write nice stories. Instead, the representatives of the media ate and drank themselves into a collective stupor. It was no one's fault, really. The room was hot, the hour was late, and Andrew had been detained for twenty minutes signing autographs and shaking hands at the Weill. Meanwhile, three wire-service reporters had fallen asleep in the back row. Even the film crew shooting the Barnes special had overindulged. The sound man was sound asleep. The camera operator had spent the last ten minutes focusing on the left breast of a woman reporter leaning against the buffet table. Elizabeth's public relations campaign had hit its first snag.

Donald watched Andrew enter the room. "Here comes the bar-mitzvah boy," he muttered under his breath.

The television lights went on and blinded Andrew for a moment but he recovered and went to join Donald Bright at a table covered with microphones. Andrew had not known that Donald would be present. The reporters gave them both glassy-eyed looks.

"What's going on?" Andrew whispered to Donald, smiling all the while for the still photographers, who were as wobbly as the reporters.

"They're all shit-faced," Donald whispered back.

Gretchen Hemenway, a youngish, blond, unrelievedly serious administrative assistant to the chorus and orchestra, stood near Donald and Andrew, who shook hands and smiled for the cameras. Gretchen did not drink and did not approve of those who did. She also did not approve of Alvin Reischel's gambling pool, and she once tried to rat on him to George and Ugo. Unfortunately for Gretchen, George and Ugo were two of Alvin's biggest customers. George bet and lost small sums on horses who had names connected somehow to music—names like "G String," or "William Tell." Ugo bet large amounts on Italian club soccer. Ugo, in fact, bet on anything Italian. Alvin, nobody's fool, always let him win.

"Ladies and gentlemen," Gretchen began, "we apologize for being unable to grant you individual interviews with either conductor, but there were just too many requests."

This was not true. There had been only two requests. Elizabeth had told Gretchen that there had been dozens. Gretchen, who had never met Elizabeth before, had no reason to doubt her.

"As you all know," Gretchen continued, "Maestro Barnes is the music director of the Royal Symphonic Society of London and this is his debut as guest conductor of the New York Symphony. First question?"

Donald had given countless interviews and press conferences, in Europe and New York, relating to his discovery and editing of the Mozart manuscript. Never before, though, had he shared the Mass spotlight with someone else. It pained him to do so now. The fixed half-smile on his lips was a slight clue to the disappointment he felt. To make matters worse, the reporters were not even looking at him. They had never seen Andrew before. Donald was no longer at the center of the story about the Mass.

Andrew, for his part, thought that Elizabeth had deliberately gotten the reporters smashed so as to embarrass him. He promised to tell her off when they were alone next. He often promised himself to tell her off for one thing or another. This time, though, he meant it.

A long and embarrassing silence ensued. No one asked

anything of either Donald or Andrew. Everyone present only wanted to go home and sleep.

"Doesn't anyone have a question for our two maestros?" Gretchen asked nervously. If the press conference were to be a disaster, a strong possibility at the moment, she would have to answer to George.

"Maestro Barnes," asked a reporter, to Gretchen's enormous relief, "how does it feel to conduct a Mozart premiere?" The reporter was a recovering alcoholic who happened to be on a diet and thus had avoided the overindulgences of her colleagues.

What a dumb question, Donald thought, glaring at the reporter. *I should never have taken part in this thing.* In truth, though, Donald would have loved to answer a question like that.

"It's a wonderful feeling," Andrew said. He tried to look modest. "I'm delighted that the Symphony invited me to do the Mass." As Andrew spoke, Donald rolled his eyes and asked himself how much more of this he could stand. "—But the man who really ought to be conducting the premiere," Andrew continued, "is the man to my left, who *found* the Mass in the first place."

Donald raised his eyebrows in surprise. *Of course it's easy for him to be generous,* Donald thought. *He's got the concert and I don't.*

In the back row of reporters, Gretchen Hemenway had taken a seat next to James Carver. "That was nice," Gretchen whispered to James. "Do you think anybody's listening?"

"He's not a bad guy," James whispered back. "Just a bad conductor."

"—So if you want to know about the Mass, you might as well ask Donald. He knows the piece better than I ever will."

"Maestro Barnes," asked another reporter, reading slowly and carefully from notes, "you were twenty-four when you were named head of the Royal Symphonic. How did a man that young get such an important post?"

"By 'young' you really mean 'inexperienced,' don't you?" Andrew replied. "I used to lie awake nights wondering the same thing, actually. And I'm sure half my orchestra felt the same way. But you must remember that when I took the job, the R.S.S. was under water. They probably couldn't get a qualified conductor, so they were forced to turn to me.''

Another reporter raised her hand. The press had begun to remember that their role in life was to ask questions. ''The Royal Symphonic has a reputation for playing it safe,'' she began. ''Is it true that you have an aversion to modern and experimental music?''

''I haven't had a virgin in weeks,'' Andrew quipped, to no laughter. He gave a quick shrug. ''If this were London, you'd all be on the floor. The question is, am I averse to experimental music? Not at all. I just refuse to play most of it in concert. You must remember that most experiments—musical, scientific, whatever—*fail*. I try not to subject our audience to things I'd never play on the stereo for guests at home.''

The same reporter persisted. ''But if every orchestra felt the same way you did, wouldn't it be discouraging for composers?''

Barnes grinned. ''Most modern composers *should* be discouraged. Unfortunately for you New Yorkers, your Maestro Barelli is very committed to new music. My sympathies.''

He acknowledged the reporters' laughter with a grin and then launched into a set piece criticizing modern music that he had delivered many times before.

''Beauty went out of music,'' Andrew told his audience, ''when audiences—wealthy individuals, the Church—stopped hiring composers. Archbishops and archdukes may not have known a G clef from a grand piano, but they knew what they liked. Today, though, government arts councils are the primary sources of money for composers. Government officials, luckily for them, don't have to sit through the pieces they've commissioned.'' Andrew paused for a moment. ''Although if we went back to the old system,'' he added with a grin, ''we might end up with pieces called, I don't know, 'Concerto for Donald Trump.' ''

Andrew looked pleased as more reporters joined in the laughter. Then he asked, ''Couldn't we move away from this line of questioning? Isn't there something you'd like to know about the Mass?''

"I completely agree with his criticism of new music," James whispered to Gretchen. "Except for the kind of music *I* write."

"How do you prepare for a concert, Maestro Barnes?" asked a reporter.

"Hmm," said Andrew, rubbing his chin. He noticed that Donald was not having much fun and he decided to cheer him up.

"Normally I listen to records of a piece," he said. "I take a look at the score, and I just try to get the *feel* of what the composer was after. Now, *Donald* here would do a lot more than that—he probably wouldn't listen to recordings at all. He wouldn't want to be influenced by other conductors' interpretations. He'd study various editions of the score, compare them for discrepancies, learn every line of every instrument in the piece. He'd know it cold, whereas I just have a sense for what goes where. I conduct with my heart while Donald conducts with his heart and his head. You really might have a few questions for him."

"Why doesn't he just bend over and kiss Donald's ass for the six o'clock news?" James asked Gretchen.

Another reporter raised a pencil into the air. "We understand," she began, "that there have been some threats on your life. Would you care to comment, and what are the chances that you might be forced to step down and not conduct tomorrow night's concert?"

Andrew, surprised that the press had learned of the death threats, gave the reporter a bland look. "My, aren't we well informed?" he asked. He was not happy to discuss the matter. "There have been some, let's say, threatening remarks in my direction, but the security people here at Carnegie Hall seem to have matters firmly in hand. I think it's a bit early to say whether I might step down—"

The reporter interrupted him. "In other words, you're saying there *is* a chance that you might not conduct tomorrow night?"

The room was still as Andrew decided how best to answer. James though Donald was holding his breath.

"I don't think security matters are a fit topic for press conferences," Andrew said, a bit heatedly, and then he seemed surprised at himself for the amount of emotion he had allowed himself to display. "Let's just wait and see," he added, his tone conciliatory. "These things invariably sort themselves out. You'll see."

"Maestro Barnes," asked another reporter, "is there any connection between the fact that you were asked to give a master class as a benefit for the Manhattan Conservatory and that your father-in-law, the chairman of the board of your orchestra, is giving the conservatory a donation of a hundred and fifty thousand dollars?"

Aha! Donald thought triumphantly. *That explains everything.*

Andrew did not try to hide how stunned and outraged he felt. He had no idea that Elizabeth and her father had arranged any sort of donation. He thought that the conservatory had invited him to lead the master class strictly because he was a decent conductor.

"I've got a photocopy of the check, if you want to see it," the reporter added, trying to sound helpful.

Andrew did not want to see the check, but many of the other reporters did. They crowded around the reporter who had asked the question and stared at the check. They sensed the possibility of scandal, although they were not sure what the whole thing was about. Only the reporters from music magazines knew what master classes were, but the other reporters sensed that revelation of a payoff plus an outraged celebrity usually added up to a front-page story.

Just then, both Andrew and Donald noticed that Elizabeth was entering the Patrons' Room from a door in the rear. She surveyed the near-total alcoholic devastation in the room and thought for a moment that perhaps she *had* overdone things. Andrew gave her a searching look and then he smiled to the reporters. When Donald saw her, he quickly looked away.

"I'm suddenly reminded of a story," Andrew said, glaring at Elizabeth again.

"What a surprise," James told Gretchen, who gave him a blank look. Gretchen did not really approve of James, either.

"An orchestra conductor," Andrew began, "was having an affair with a young woman in the chorus. They were having a *great* old time of it, but after three weeks the conductor's *wife* caught on.'' Andrew paused for dramatic effect and looked around the room. His gaze settled on Elizabeth, who knew the story well. He told it whenever he was mad at her.

"Tearfully," he continued, "the poor wife confronted her husband's agent at teatime in a certain hotel lobby where he was known to be found. She asked him what to do.

"He wanted to be helpful, but he didn't quite know what to say. 'But, my dear,' the agent said, sipping his tea''—Andrew gave a comic impression of the man daintily holding a teacup, his right pinky extended—" '*whatever* are you worried about? He's conducting *better than ever!*' "

The reporters laughed. Elizabeth glared at Andrew, who looked at her long enough to see that he had gotten his feelings across. Then Andrew smiled. "I've been hogging the microphones long enough. Any questions for Donald, or anything specific about tomorrow night's performance? Anyone for more champagne?"

"Please, no more champagne," said a reporter rubbing his forehead.

A reporter in the next-to-last row began to snore.

"If there aren't any more questions—" Andrew said. "Thank you all very much for coming. I hope you all enjoy the concert."

He and Donald stood up and shook hands and smiled for the cameras. "I wonder what kind of story we'll get out of that," Andrew told Donald.

"Story?" Donald repeated. "These people don't even know what building they're in."

Andrew nodded. He glanced at Elizabeth, who had buttonholed a woman reporter from a local news program. Elizabeth was trying to convince her to do a live preconcert interview with Andrew during Friday's six o'clock news. Andrew shook his head and sighed. *She just won't quit,* he told himself.

Andrew was hungry. The sight of the picked-over buffet table sharpened his appetite. He had to sneak a quick dinner—after all, he would meet Alison in his hotel suite in about an hour, while Elizabeth attended a reception somewhere else. He began to feel better.

SIXTEEN

My grandfather says that in fifty years there won't be any more symphony orchestras,'' said Officer Caruso.

"Really?" asked Andrew, licking chicken grease off his fingers. He and Officer Caruso were sitting and eating dinner in the last row of the highest balcony in Carnegie Hall. The press conference had ended twenty minutes earlier. Officer Caruso had kindly saved some food for Andrew, who had not eaten since breakfast. Elizabeth, furious with Andrew for telling the story about the conductor, was changing her clothes in Andrew's dressing room. A Musicians Union meeting had taken over the musicians' lounge, forcing the two men to find somewhere else to eat within the confines of Carnegie Hall. At the suggestion of Andrew, they had taken their food to the balcony.

Officer Caruso nodded. "He says they're getting out of touch with the public. He says that since composers aren't writing orchestral music that people want to hear, orchestras will soon be like dinosaurs.''

"Too big to survive?" asked Andrew, nibbling on a fried chicken wing. "With brains the size of peas? This is really good.''

"Oh, he doesn't mean anything insulting. He just says good music is like good food for an orchestra. He says if composers don't write good music, orchestras will starve and die.''

"Your grandfather doesn't like modern music?''

Officer Caruso made a face. "He said they have no right to even *call* it music."

"Your grandfather sounds like a very smart man," said Andrew.

"He said he wants to meet you," said Officer Caruso. "But he says he never heard of you."

"If he never heard of me, why does he want to meet me?"

"He thinks maybe you can get him Barelli's autograph. He figures all you conductors are friends. You're all in the same profession. Like cops."

"If that's what he thinks, then there's a lot *he* doesn't know about conductors. How come he likes Ugo so much, anyway?"

"My grandfather?" asked Officer Caruso. "He likes Ugo because Ugo conducts a lot of operas, and because Ugo's Italian. My grandfather says you have to be Italian to understand music."

"You have to be Italian?" asked Andrew. "That leaves me out."

"Yeah, or at least from Europe," said Officer Caruso, looking in the bag of food for something else to eat. He and Andrew had gone through everything, though. "He says Americans don't understand music."

"A lot of people feel that way," said Andrew, thinking back to his early days, and lack of acceptance, in London. Most American orchestra managements seem to agree—few have ever hired American-born chief conductors. "So in fifty years I'll be out of a job?" Andrew asked. "Is that what your grandfather thinks?"

Officer Caruso nodded. "If you live that long."

"I'd settle for getting through this weekend," said Andrew.

"No kidding," said Officer Caruso. "If something happened to you, do you know what would happen to my record at the Department?"

"You'd get in trouble?" asked Andrew, finishing his chicken.

"I'd be in a lot of trouble. That's why I'm guarding you so carefully."

"Thanks," said Andrew, making a face.

"Don't mention it," said Officer Caruso. "How come you wanted to sit up here, anyway?"

"I don't know," said Andrew. "I guess I like the view. I sat up here once for a concert. Leonard Bernstein conducted."

"Is that right?" said Officer Caruso, who did not want to hear about the concert. He had something he wanted to discuss with Andrew. "Hey. How come a guy like you's got so many enemies? You're almost like a regular guy."

Andrew laughed. "Almost, huh? Well, how do you know I'm not in love with myself?"

"I don't know," admitted Officer Caruso. "Maybe you are. But you've still got all these people angry at you."

"You mean those religious groups?" said Andrew.

"No, I'm not talking about them. I'm talking about right here in Carnegie Hall. *Everybody's* on your case."

"Like who?" asked Andrew, concerned.

"Like every time I turn around," said Officer Caruso. "The stagehands. The ushers. The violinists. Everybody's always knocking you."

Andrew thought it over. "Maybe I'm not stuck-up enough for *them*."

"Yeah, maybe," said Officer Caruso. "They probably aren't used to a conductor who's a good guy. My grandfather says most conductors are assholes."

"People here are probably very loyal to Donald," Andrew reasoned. "You know, the choral conductor. I just didn't realize how deep that loyalty went. Even the stagehands and the ushers? Jesus."

"*Donald,*" repeated Officer Caruso, putting things together. "That's the guy. He was sitting next to you at the press conference, right?"

Andrew nodded.

"He was at your master class, too. He came in late. I don't know if you saw him."

"Really?" Andrew asked, feeling self-conscious. He was certain that Donald must have seen through his performance. "*He* was there?"

"He conducts if something happens to you, right?" asked Officer Caruso. "He's like your understudy?"

"I guess so," said Andrew. "You could say that."

"And he conducts the concert even if they only *think* something's going to happen to you?"

Andrew nodded.

"This morning," said Officer Caruso, "after the rehearsal? I went out onstage, you know, just to tell my grandfather I did it, right? So there's Donald and he's sitting and talking to this really tall, thin guy—you know who I mean?"

Andrew thought for a moment. "That must be his rehearsal pianist. I've seen him."

"Well, the tall guy knew you were getting death threats here in New York. Nobody knew that, except top management of the orchestra. So how did *he* know?"

"I have no idea," said Andrew.

"You didn't tell him, did you?"

"Of course not," said Andrew.

"I'm going to keep an eye on him," said Officer Caruso. "You want some more chicken?"

"Huh? Oh no, thanks," said Andrew, checking his watch. "Look, we've got to get back to the hotel. I've got, um, an appointment at seven. You coming?"

"Sure," said Officer Caruso, wrapping up the remains of his dinner. "I'm supposed to follow you everywhere. Remember?"

"I remember," said Andrew, a bit grumpily. His appointment, after all, was with Alison. He hoped Officer Caruso had a sense of humor—and a Continental blind eye.

THURSDAY
EVENING

SEVENTEEN

While Andrew was attending to his "appointment" in his hotel suite eight floors above, Donald Bright sat at a low table in the bar of the Meridien Hotel and wondered why he had allowed himself to be roped into yet another event on Elizabeth's calendar. He sipped his glass of white wine, ate salted peanuts from the little bowl on the table, and waited for Andrew and Elizabeth to appear.

Donald passed the time making a list of all the reasons why Andrew was not nearly as good a conductor as he was. Had *Andrew* found the Mass in that Vienna library basement, Donald told himself, he would never have recognized it. Donald found the manuscript in a leather pouch containing letters of Franz Schubert. He immediately recognized Mozart's handwriting and could tell in seconds that this piece was unknown to twentieth-century ears. *Any* musicologist might have done that, Donald told himself modestly. Well, any *musicologist*—but not *Andrew*.

Even if Andrew *had* recognized the handwriting as Mozart's, Donald told himself, he could never have produced from the manuscript a modern score, as Donald had. Musical notation has changed since Mozart's day and an editor is required to put a score in terms that today's musicians can readily understand. Donald extended his sabbatical from the Symphony chorus by three months and worked fourteen hours a day preparing the score for performance. If he had left New York shamed by his failure on the podium, he returned in triumph with the score of the Mass. *Andrew* editing a score? Donald asked himself. *Andrew* wouldn't have known where to start.

The catalog of Andrew's sins multiplied. *Donald* was an expert in virtually every period of music history, from Gregorian chant through music composed and performed on computers. Donald believed that conductors were supposed to be educators. They must be alive to the tension between giving audiences what they want to hear and retrieving neglected works from the past. Conductors, Donald believed, were obliged to expand the horizons of their listeners. *Andrew* knew only one small segment of musical history, the century and a half between Haydn and Brahms. Andrew, Donald believed, expanded no listener's horizons.

Donald could tell when orchestra members deliberately made mistakes, just to test his ear. Andrew had no idea, as the second violins proved conclusively this morning. Donald asserted control from the downbeat of rehearsals. If the past two mornings were any indication, Andrew did not know how to get an orchestra *silent*, let alone how to make it play well. Donald communicated ideas about music through his baton and his hands. Andrew only told jokes. Donald began to feel better. He ordered a second glass of wine.

Donald believed that an orchestra conductor must be capable of auditioning musicians and selecting those players who will blend in musically and personally. Sometimes when new conductors are appointed, they fire all the musicians considered too loyal to the previous conductor. Donald knew that such wholesale purges often eliminated excellent musicians and were to be avoided. Another problem conductors face is how to ease out those musicians past their prime. They certainly cannot be marched behind the hall and shot; their removal is one of the most delicate operations a conductor faces.

Donald considered himself an expert at creating a sense of ensemble, as he did with the chorus. He was sure that he could do the same thing with an orchestra, given the chance. *Andrew*, on the other hand, was known to leave all personnel decisions to others—primarily to Elizabeth. Thinking about Andrew's shortcomings made Donald feel better. Donald's superiority, he decided, even stretched back to childhood. Donald, after all, had been a child prodigy. Andrew only took up cello in college.

Conducting concerts was another matter, Donald glumly acknowledged, as the waiter brought his second glass of wine and a fresh bowl of peanuts. In theory, Donald believed, he was any conductor's equal. He knew, though, that theory and real life were two different things. Ugo Barelli had been conducting for forty years and, to the best of Donald's knowledge, had never blown a concert. Donald thought Andrew had never done an especially *good* job, for that matter. However brilliant Ugo might have been in his youth, Donald considered his conducting technically unsound. Of course, Donald considered the conducting of all but two or three conductors (himself included) technically unsound. And then there was Andrew. Andrew had been leading the Royal Symphonic for thirteen years and his reviews had steadily improved. But what did reviewers know about conducting, Donald asked, to console himself. Donald had conducted just three times in Carnegie Hall, and each concert had been an utter disaster.

"It's not fair," Donald said aloud.

Just then, Andrew arrived, accompanied by Alison Gardiner. Both looked freshly showered and seemed a bit tipsy—they had shared a bottle of champagne in Andrew's Jacuzzi. Andrew and Alison, in fact, had taken full advantage of Elizabeth's absence from their hotel suite. Death threats seemed far from Andrew's mind.

"Hello, Donald," Andrew said cheerfully. "Sorry I'm late. You know Alison. She sings for you."

"You're not late. Hello, Alison." Donald spoke without warmth. It seemed wrong to Donald that Andrew would bring a member of his chorus to their meeting. "I see that you've made the acquaintance of Maestro Barnes," he told her.

"We met this afternoon," said Andrew, taking a seat and motioning to Alison to do likewise.

"Hi, Donald," said Alison, sensing Donald's discomfort. *I hope he doesn't throw me out of the chorus for this,* she thought.

Donald cast a disrespectful glance at Alison's wet hair. *Andrew moves fast, all right,* he thought.

"What did you think of the rehearsal this morning?" Andrew asked, posing the question out of respect for Donald's musicianship.

Donald paused before he answered, evidently searching for the right words. "Andy," he said, the disdain in his voice unmistakable, "I don't think you could have done a better job."

Andrew heard only praise. "Why, thank you," he said. He was beaming. He turned to Alison and arched his eyebrows, as if to ask whether she had heard Donald's kind words. "Coming from you, Donald, well, I'm honored. Say, what does a guy have to do to get a drink around here?" He grinned, and he asked, in a self-mocking way: "Don't they know who I am?"

"The waiter was here a minute ago," said Donald.

"I think we held the press off pretty nicely, eh, Donald?" Andrew asked. "Those drunken sods."

"We were unforgettable," Donald replied. He could not take his eyes off Alison's wet hair. "I hate to spoil the party," he added, rising, "but I've got some work to do before tomorrow morning's rehearsal."

"Oh, stick around," said Andrew. "Elizabeth's dying to see you again. She'll be here any minute. She says you two had a nice chat onstage today."

At the sound of Elizabeth's name, Donald obediently sat down again. He wondered whether Andrew intended Elizabeth and Alison to meet. Or maybe they already knew about each other. What a strange world it was.

"This is crazy," said Andrew, craning his neck around. "Don't they have any waiters in this place? I'm dying of thirst. I'm going to the bar and ordering something. What can I get you, Alison? We just met this afternoon."

"Um, white wine," Alison said, wishing that Andrew had not repeated that fact.

"Be right back," said Andrew, and he went off to the bar.

Neither Alison nor Donald could think of anything to say. They did not wallow in uncomfortable silence for long, though. Just then Elizabeth wandered over to the table.

"I say, Donald! How nice to find you here. Is this your

fiancée? Have you seen my Andrew about? I've just returned from a *dreadful* reception. Contributors are the
most boring people wherever one goes. They all want to
impress me with their knowledge of music. Frightful.
Oh, *there* he is, over by the bar. I should have guessed.''

''I—I better be going,'' said Alison, looking panicked.

''But we haven't been introduced! I'm Elizabeth
Garrett-Jones. My husband is Andrew Barnes.''

Okay, they haven't met, thought Donald.

''I'm—I'm Alison Gardiner. I'm in the chorus. Nice to
meet you.''

The two women shook hands.

''Donald,'' said Elizabeth, chiding him, ''you didn't
tell me your fiancée sang in the chorus.''

''Must have slipped my mind,'' Donald growled, looking at the floor. *Fiancée?* he thought. *Where'd she come
up with that?*

''What part do you sing, dear?'' Elizabeth asked Alison. ''Why, your hair is wet! You shouldn't be going
about with wet hair! You have an important concert tomorrow! You could catch cold! And no one's said anything to you! Am I the only person around here with the
slightest bit of common sense?''

''Excuse me,'' Alison said, remaining calm. *Wait
till Corinne hears about this,* she thought. ''It's been
nice meeting you, Mrs. um, Barnes. I've got to go—
someplace. Goodbye, everybody.''

Alison practically bolted from the table. Donald was
speechless. At length Andrew returned, saw the change
in cast, and quickly adjusted.

''Hello, darling,'' he said, brushing Elizabeth's cheek
with a kiss. ''Care for some white wine? I thought you'd
be along just now.''

''Why, thank you,'' she said, accepting the drink and
taking full note of Andrew's wet hair. ''Pity that your
fiancée couldn't stay,'' Elizabeth told Donald. ''She
seemed charming.''

Andrew and Donald exchanged glances.

''How was the reception, dear?'' Andrew asked, hoping to change the subject.

''Perfectly awful. As expected. I knew I'd find you in
the bar. Andrew, I'll just have a taste of this, and go up

to bed. I'm still worn out from the trip. And this has been the longest day.''

"Darling, that's fine," said Andrew. "Donald and I have some catching up to do."

Elizabeth sipped her drink and stood up. "Do excuse me, then," she said. And to Donald, she added: "I am *so* glad you're working for Andrew again. We enjoy it so much. Good night."

And she was gone.

Neither man spoke for a long time.

"Thanks for covering for me," Andrew told Donald. "I owe you one."

"Forget it," said Donald, who felt a stirring of pity for Elizabeth. Donald might not have liked the way she treated him, but he did not want to see her humiliated in public. "How could she not have understood what was going on?" he asked.

"Oh, she knew exactly what was going on," said Andrew, shaking his head. "This isn't the first time."

"Forgive me for asking a personal question," said Donald, "but doesn't it make you uncomfortable to do this kind of thing in front of your wife? She seemed to know you'd be down here in the bar."

Andrew took a long pull on his drink before he answered. "To be honest, our marriage has deteriorated to the point where—I don't know. It just doesn't seem to matter anymore. You could say this is the way we communicate."

"How could she have thought that Alison was my *fiancée*?" Donald asked. "Who could she have been fooling?"

"She wasn't fooling anybody," said Andrew. "Except herself, maybe. It's a combination of resignation and self-deception on her part. I'm sorry I put you through this. I suppose it's put a damper on our evening. My fault. I should never have brought Alison here."

"Unless you *wanted* Elizabeth to know about her," said Donald.

"The delicious thrill of almost getting caught," said Andrew. "I never thought of that."

EIGHTEEN

As she walked to James Carver's apartment, a fourth-floor walk-up studio on Fifty-fifth Street west of Tenth Avenue, Janet Ikovic, the soprano soloist in the Mass, caught a glimpse of herself in a store window. Despite the way she felt, she had to laugh. She was the only woman on Tenth Avenue on this warm September evening wearing a wool scarf and a ski hat. *I look like a cross between a bank robber and a street person,* she thought. *If only I'd been wearing this stuff yesterday and the day before.*

Janet and James had met four years ago when Janet was singing at a music festival. James occasionally accompanied Janet at her recitals and had helped her get the solo part in the Mozart Mass, her first important role. Janet's involvement in the Mass seemed doubtful just now. She had developed a sore throat and a case of swollen glands. She could barely talk. She could certainly not sing.

Two things that Janet's first vocal coach had told her fell into the category of things heard once and never forgotten. This coach taught at the Eastman School of Music in Janet's hometown of Rochester, New York, where Janet's father worked as a research chemist for Kodak. One was a story about two nineteenth-century Italian tenors, one of whom has lost his singing voice by his fortieth birthday while the other sang professionally into his late fifties. "It is because you sang with the principal of your voice," the latter chided his unfortunate colleague, "but *I* have sung only with the interest."

The story came to mind whenever Janet heard a singer

her age failing to conserve her talents. Janet would never throw her voice away, singing too loud or too often, or by taking on roles that she was too young to handle well. She would sing only with the interest, never with the principal.

The other thing Janet frequently recalled was her teacher's "Theory of the Three Dumb Things." The theory worked this way: do two dumb things within forty-eight hours—get drenched in a rainstorm, sleep in the direct path of an air conditioner—and nothing will happen to your health. Do *three* such dumb things, though, and a cold is *guaranteed*. Every time Janet came down with a cold or a sore throat, she would run through the previous forty-eight hours of her life and the three dumb things would announce themselves with annoying clarity.

This time was no exception. *I went out with my hair wet Tuesday morning, when it was only sixty degrees out,* she told herself as she reached James's building. *I slept only three hours Wednesday night because I had to finish learning my part in the Mass. And number three—I just plain oversang.*

She knocked on James's door and he answered. Her outfit alarmed him. A soprano wearing a scarf the day before a concert was never a good sign. "How's your throat?" he asked, by way of greeting. Janet entered his apartment, which was barely large enough for his grand piano and an extra-long futon mattress on the floor. She headed for the futon.

"If I'm so smart," she said, stretching out on her back and speaking in a low, hoarse voice, "then why am I so sick?"

"Tea with lemon," James announced, heading for the kitchenette. "The water's on. Tea with lemon *and* honey."

"Ugh, not both," said Janet. "That sounds disgusting."

"Rest your voice," James called. "I'll do all the talking. How bad to you feel?"

"Very," said Janet, taking off her hat but not her scarf and stretching out on the futon. "My throat's sore. I had chills all afternoon. My whole body feels like I just stepped out of the swimming pool, and both of my cats are avoiding me.''

"Maybe you're allergic,'' James said. ''I hate cats.''

"Well,'' said Janet, ''I hate people who hate cats.''

"You're pretty snippy today,'' said James. ''Did you go to the doctor?''

"Don't have one,'' said Janet.

"You *don't* have a doctor?'' James asked, amazed. ''I have *five*.''

"What do you need five doctors for?'' Janet asked, amused.

"One for each important part of my body,'' said James, making tea. ''Want to hear what they are? In order?''

"Actually, no,'' said Janet. ''I have a gynecologist, but I doubt he wants to see my swollen glands.''

"You sounded okay at the rehearsal this morning,'' James said. ''Your duet with the tenor went really well.''

"Thanks,'' said Janet. ''He's been hitting on me, that tenor. He asked me out for drinks.''

"What did you say?'' asked James.

"I said yes, but then I asked if we could make it tomorrow night instead. After the concert. My throat hurt too much. The idea of sitting and making small talk was just too painful.''

"Did it hurt during the rehearsal?'' James asked.

Janet shook her head. ''I only started to really feel it afterward,'' she said. ''I could feel my throat tightening up after the Christe Eleison and I knew I was in for it. I tried to sing this afternoon but I was so flat and scratchy I sounded awful.''

"Maybe that's why your cats were avoiding you,'' James said. He set a tray down before Janet. On the tray were a mug of tea, honey, lemon slices, and milk.

"Thanks,'' she said. ''What's going to happen if I can't sing tomorrow? This was supposed to be the beginning of my career, not the end of it.''

"You've got twenty-four hours to get better,'' he said. ''You'll be fine.''

Janet rolled over on the futon and looked up at him. ''How can you be so sure? What if I'm *not* fine? Either I'll have to withdraw or I'll go up there and I'll sound awful. And I'll never get another booking as long as I live.''

James sighed. The hardest part of accompanying sopranos was helping them over colds, bad reviews, and ex-boyfriends, he once decided. And in that order.

"Hey, is it true that Donald may conduct tomorrow night?'' Janet asked, changing the subject since James was a little slow in getting his sympathy going.

"We can always hope,'' James said.

"Is Andrew really getting death threats?''

"That's what people are saying,'' James said, his tone guarded. "What have you taken for your cold?'' he asked, changing the subject for reasons of his own. James had intended to spend the day working on his new piano sonata. Instead, he could think only of the threats he had made against Andrew's life—first, the ones over the telephone, and then, this morning, the letter he had dropped at Andrew's door.

When he first conceived the idea to scare Andrew off the platform, he thought that Donald would be delighted. Everyone would think that the threats came from one of the religious groups that had been harassing Andrew in London. No one would suspect a choral pianist. Now, though, after seeing how nervous Donald became at the prospect of conducting again, and after seeing all those policemen wandering around Carnegie Hall, James wished he had never gotten involved. He was no longer certain that Donald would be happy about what he had done.

"What have I taken?'' Janet repeated, noticing how distant James had become. "Nothing, really. Aspirin. A Contac. That's it.''

James snapped out of his reverie. "What's the point of getting sick if you're not going to take *real* drugs?'' he replied.

"I gargled with salt water all afternoon,'' said Janet, trying to sound helpful.

"I've never been much for natural healing,'' said James.

"I've also been chain-sucking Sucrets.'' Janet scooped some honey into her tea. "That's everything I can think of. That and sleeping.''

"There's always cortisone," James said, trying to come up with a better idea.

"Now what are you talking about?" Janet asked, sipping her tea and staring out the window, her mind blank. James's ideas were odd sometimes, but his presence was soothing.

"Well, it's not exactly the greatest thing to do for your throat," James said. He regretted even having brought it up. "An hour before the concert you get a cortisone injection from a doctor. You'll sing just fine but you'll pay for it for a week. Maybe longer."

"What do you mean, I'll *pay* for it?" Janet asked.

"You probably won't be able to talk for a week," James said.

"If I can't sing this concert, I won't *want* to talk," Janet said. "Do you think this is, you know, psychosomatic? Maybe I just wasn't *meant* to do this concert."

"I think you should think less and just drink your tea," said James.

"You should have heard me this afternoon. After you left my dressing room. It was awful. No head voice, no overtones. This isn't supposed to happen the day before the concert."

By "no head voice" and "no overtones" Janet meant that her sinuses were so blocked that the sound of her singing could not resonate through her head. Ordinarily, when she sang, her entire breathing apparatus, from her diaphragm through her mouth and nose, became a single column of air. She thought of it as vibrating like a violin string, creating sound waves. To lose her "head voice" was to become unable to create a full, rich sound. A stuffed head distorted her ability to tell whether she was singing on key. Usually her voice would go flat.

"Just drink your tea," said James. "If you want, I'll get you an appointment with one of my doctors so you can get the shot. It's a good thing they don't give singers drug tests after concerts because tomorrow night you'd fail for sure."

"Hey, wait a minute!" Janet said, sitting up. "If I can't talk for a week, how am I going to sing the other two concerts? I'm getting paid to do three concerts, not just one."

James shrugged. "You'll just have to call them Saturday morning and tell them you can't go on. Medical reasons. They'll go out and find someone else. But you've got to do the Friday night concert, because that's the one that'll get reviewed."

Janet looked puzzled. "I call Saturday morning? Why don't I just call them now so they'll have more time to get a replacement?"

"If you call them now," he explained patiently, as if to a small child, "they'll just get someone else for all *three* concerts. You can't call them until after you've got Friday night under your belt."

"But—" Janet frowned. "Is that . . . legit? Shouldn't they just get someone else for all three concerts?"

James gave her another dirty look. "It's only your career," he said. "And besides, everybody does it."

Janet held her mug in both hands. She had never faced an ethical dilemma before with regard to singing. A long time passed before she spoke. "Well, I *guess* it's okay," she said reluctantly. "It just doesn't seem a hundred percent right to me."

Now she tried to convince herself that her behavior was ethical. "As long as there's a *chance* I can sing on Saturday, I guess I'm not lying to them by not calling now. Okay. I'll do it."

"Good," said James. "You look like you're feeling better already."

"I'm not," said Janet. "By the way, which of your five doctors would give illegal drugs and cortisone shots to sopranos with sore throats and big concerts?"

James laughed. "Any one of them," he said.

NINETEEN

Corinne Gates turned out her bathroom light and joined Kevin, who was already under the covers. She lay on her side with her back to Kevin, who began to trace patterns on her back with a finger.

"Uh-uh," she said quietly. Kevin stopped for a moment. Then he started again, this time with his whole hand.

"No," said Corinne, slightly more emphatically, twisting away and lying on her stomach. Kevin and Corinne had reached the point in life where privacy becomes as important as having another person beside you in bed. They did not see one another every night but they saw each other often enough to know that their relationship was on solid ground. Neither could tell whether they were scared of commitment in general or merely commitment to each other.

"What's wrong?" Kevin asked.

"Nothing's wrong," she said without looking up.

"Talk to me," said Kevin, sitting up.

"There's nothing to talk about."

Kevin did not say anything. He knew that Corinne would speak her mind without prompting, given enough time. So he waited.

"It's Andy," said Corinne.

Kevin yawned. "I figured," he said.

"Then if you figured," said Corinne, "why'd you have to ask?"

"Okay, I didn't figure," Kevin admitted. "But I should've. Right?"

"I ran into Elizabeth today," said Corinne. "Backstage."

"Did you knock her over?"

"Huh?"

"You said you ran into Elizabeth, so I asked if you knocked her over. It's just a joke."

Corinne gave a half laugh. "I should've," she said. "I told her a few choice things, though. That woman can really bring things out in a person."

"No kidding," said Kevin, remembering how difficult she had been during the negotiations on Andrew's contract.

"But now I feel terrible," Corinne added. "I almost want to call her and apologize."

"Why? What'd you say?"

Corinne turned over and sat up. She looked at Kevin. "Nothing much," she said. "Just that one of my friends from the chorus was planning on sleeping with Andy."

"You told her *what*?"

"Why not?" asked Corinne. "It's the truth."

"Where'd you hear something like that?" Kevin asked.

"From the horse's mouth."

"Who's that, Alison? The one that gets around?"

Corinne nodded. "She said going to bed with Andrew might be good for her career. If she *really* wanted to help her career, she should try sleeping with *Elizabeth*. Andy's got no more authority at that orchestra than you have here."

"No wonder Alison never comes on to *me*," said Kevin, laughing. "I thought it was my dandruff, or my bad breath. That explains everything."

"Yeah, that explains everything. But it was strange to hear Alison just coming and saying she wanted to go to bed with Andy. Like he was just some star or something."

"But he *is* a star," Kevin pointed out. "As hard as that may be for us to believe, since we knew him when he was failing conducting class. But to everyone else, he's a famous conductor. A genius."

"Yeah, but still."

"She didn't know about you and Andy, did she?" he asked.

"No, I doubt it. That would have just been cruel. She's not cruel. She's just young."

"And we're old?"

"*You're* old," said Corinne, poking him in the ribs. "You're an old fart."

"An old fart?" Kevin repeated, smiling. "Last week you called me an old prune. I don't think I'm making progress." He was glad to see that she was feeling better. She had not been herself all evening. Kevin suspected that the cause was seeing Andrew, but he did not want to ask. "Feeling any better?" he asked.

"A little," said Corinne, giving a look that told Kevin how happy she was to have him in her life. "Thanks."

"It's strange," said Kevin. "Seeing Andy again. He barely asked anything about *me*, about how I'm doing. He just talked about himself."

Corinne nodded. "That *is* strange," she said. "You two were such good friends."

"I remember when he started going out with Elizabeth," said Kevin.

"Yeah, so do I," said Corinne, her expression deadpan.

"I'm sure you do," said Kevin. "I never thought it would last."

"Maybe it won't," said Corinne.

Kevin looked at her. "You know what I mean. I didn't think it would last long back then. I thought neither of them were taking it very seriously."

"Boy, were you wrong."

Kevin nodded. "It's funny. After he started going out with her, I never saw him. He just disappeared—he was out with her all the time. It's like Elizabeth took him away from both of us."

Corinne didn't say anything.

Kevin paused before he spoke again. "Well, enough about them," he said. "Let's talk about us for a minute." He reached across and ran a finger through her hair. Talking was the last thing on his mind.

Corinne slipped under the covers. "I'm kind of tired," said Corinne. "You understand, don't you?"

Not really, Kevin thought. "Of course," he said gallantly, as she reached out and turned off the light.

TWENTY

Andrew did not return to his hotel suite until well after midnight. He had gone out with Officer Caruso for a few beers at a bar near his station house and ended up meeting six or seven of the young patrolman's colleagues. To his surprise, Elizabeth was sitting up, waiting for him.

"You're angry with me," said Elizabeth. She was wearing a bathrobe and sitting on the couch, reading a magazine. "I can tell."

Andrew did not say anything.

"I don't know where you've been tonight and I don't care with whom and I don't want to know. Is that all right?"

Andrew nodded.

"You must have been angry with me," said Elizabeth. "You told that awful story about the conductor. You know I hate that story."

Andrew waited.

"You must think I got those reporters drunk on purpose. Maybe that's why you're cross. Well, it's not true."

Andrew did not respond.

"And this is hardly the first time my father spent a lot of money on your career. I don't understand why you should suddenly find that offensive."

She did not wait for Andrew to say anything. "Maybe it's the television program that you don't like," she added. "I hired a very popular American as the announcer. He knows nothing about music—he's perfect. He's done everything I've told him to do. Or maybe you're unhappy with me because I found you this Mass in the first place. Your name is going to be linked with that of

136

Mozart. If I had known that that would offend you, I would never have arranged for it."

Andrew went to the refrigerator/bar unit and poured himself a drink. He raised an eyebrow to Elizabeth to ask if she wanted one. She nodded. He made both drinks and placed hers on the desk.

"I wish things weren't this way," Elizabeth said, as she went to get her drink. "I wish things were like when we first got married. But no, you'll say. You'd hate that, wouldn't you? To be under my thumb. That would be dreadful, wouldn't it?"

Andrew continued to remain silent, although he marveled, as always, at her capacity to understand with precision his feelings.

"You don't *have* to say it," said Elizabeth, sipping her drink. "We understand each other without words. That's the beauty of our marriage."

"That's enough," said Andrew.

"Not quite," said Elizabeth. "No matter how angry you are with me, please don't bring girls back to our room. To *my* bedroom. This is a large hotel with plenty of other rooms, and if there's no room here, then go to another hotel. Or to *her* place."

"Darling, what makes you think I brought a girl back to our room?"

"Please don't try to lie to me," said Elizabeth. "Pierre told me. The concierge."

"Pierre?" Andrew repeated. *But I paid him off,* he thought.

"Don't blame *him*," said Elizabeth. "Every time I enter the hotel, *he* jumps to his telephone. I assumed you were paying him off to warn you if I was coming up to the room. I told him that I would have him fired if he didn't tell me what was going on."

"What do you want?" Andrew asked wearily. "What is it this time?"

Elizabeth finished her drink. "I'd like you to remain celibate between now and the concert, as hard as that may be for you."

Andrew did not say anything.

"I hope you won't mind terribly. You *are* conducting a Mass tomorrow, not some horrible Gershwin piece."

"Please don't criticize Gershwin in front of me," said Andrew.

"But out of respect for my wishes, and out of respect for the Mass itself, I'd be pleased if you didn't get laid between now and eight o'clock tomorrow night."

"What does my getting laid have to do with the Mass?" Andrew asked. "I'm not an archbishop. I'm just a conductor."

Elizabeth sipped her drink. "Didn't you tell me you never had sex the night before a big wrestling match? Back when you were in university?"

Andrew nodded. It surprised him that Elizabeth actually remembered something he had told her about the past. "So what?" he asked.

"You said sex before a match was bad for your legs," said Elizabeth. "Perhaps you should look at concerts the same way."

"I don't conduct with my legs," said Andrew.

"Maybe you should," Elizabeth said archly. "It might be an improvement."

"You're in a great mood, aren't you?" asked Andrew. "Hey, I conduct a hundred and fifty nights a year. Do you expect me to go that many nights without sex? Is that what you're saying?"

Elizabeth stirred her drink. "Art often requires sacrifice, don't you think?"

"Don't be ridiculous," said Andrew.

"Well," said Elizabeth, "if that's how you feel about it, I suppose I have no choice. I've actually taken some action to restrict your mobility tomorrow."

"You *what*?" Andrew asked. "What did you do?"

"You'll find out tomorrow," Elizabeth said, delighted with the consternation she knew she had provoked in him. "In light of the threats against your life, you might just end up thanking me." She put down her drink and headed for the bedroom. "Good night, Andrew."

She left the living room of the suite and Andrew heard her lock the bedroom door behind her. Andrew looked first at the bedroom door and then he looked at the couch, where he would spend the night. This was hardly the first time that Elizabeth had banished him from the bedroom.

"Restrict my mobility?" he said aloud. He did not like

the sound of those words. Elizabeth had set traps for him in the past, and he had always managed to elude them. As soon as he could determine what she had done this time, he could begin to find his way around it. He liked the idea of trying to surpass Elizabeth's ingenuity. Perhaps that was what kept them together. He looked at the couch again.

Donald, oblivious to the domestic dramas playing themselves out in bedrooms and hotel suites across the city, sat at the piano in his office at Carnegie Hall, playing the piano reduction of the Credo movement of the Mass. Going home was always the worst part of Donald's day. Nothing was waiting for him there; moreover, he was an occasional insomniac. He often stayed in his office until one in the morning, working. This time, as he played the chords of the Mass, he thought back to the gathering earlier that evening in the Meridien bar. Donald never would have imagined taking Elizabeth's side in a dispute, although just that had happened. There remained in Donald's heart a place for all those who had stayed with him until he no longer fit into their plans: his parents; Mr. Pirante; Elizabeth. He felt a stirring of pity for Andrew. Living with Elizabeth could not be the easiest thing in the world, Donald imagined. And then he thought: Why am *I* pitying *him*? *He's* got *my* Mass!

He played for a few more minutes, turned off the light, and went home.

FRIDAY
MORNING

TWENTY-ONE

Corinne Gates approached the stage door at the Fifty-sixth Street entrance to Carnegie Hall fifteen minutes before the final rehearsal was scheduled to begin. Once again Andrew Barnes would lead the orchestra, chorus, and soloists in a run-through of the Mass. This rehearsal would represent Andrew's last chance to assert some authority over the orchestra. Corinne waved to Tommy, the security guard, as she stepped past his booth.

"Just a minute," he said. "I need some ID."

"Since when?" Corinne asked, surprised. She had never been stopped before.

"Since that Officer Caruso said so this morning," Tommy growled, none too pleased with his new responsibility.

"Tommy, are you gonna tell me you even have to check *my* ID?"

"Officer Caruso told me to check 'em all," Tommy said, with the weariness of someone to whom a younger man assigned a pointless task.

Corinne flipped through her purse and found her chorus membership card.

"I didn't even know I still had it. Okay?"

"Thanks. Sorry to bother you."

"No problem," said Corinne.

"Hey, you know who you just missed meeting? Leonard Bernstein."

"Really?" Corinne asked. "What's *he* doing here?"

"You kidding?" Tommy asked. "He's the guy conducting the Mass tonight."

Corinne shook her head. *Oh, Tommy,* she thought. "That's not Bernstein. That's Barnes."

"Same thing," said Tommy. "Listen, I wanted to tell you. My wife's got that friend of hers back in the hospital with the lukomania."

"Lukomania?" Corinne repeated.

"Yeah, lukomania. It's pretty serious."

"I'm gonna be late for the rehearsal," Corinne said. "I'll see you later, Tommy."

"Okay," he said reluctantly. Corinne was one of his best conversation partners and he always hated to see her leave. "Have a nice day, now."

"You too, Tommy," said Corinne, and she put her purse away and went inside. At the stage door, Tommy stopped a short, elderly man struggling under the weight of a tuba.

"Could I see some ID, please?"

The tuba player looked bewildered.

"Aw, nuts," said Tommy. "Forget it. Just go on in."

Officer Caruso emerged from Carnegie Hall just as the tuba player entered. Out of sheer nervousness, he had arrived at the hall at six in the morning to supervise security matters including the installation of the metal detectors. He was not aware that Carnegie Hall did not open until 8 A.M. He therefore spent two hours in the Carnegie Deli, which somehow seemed appropriate, drinking coffee and reading the *Daily News.*

"Hey, Tommy," he said, "how come you let that guy go through?"

Tommy, annoyed, looked at Officer Caruso. "Because he's the tuba player, that's why."

"How do you know he had a tuba in that instrument case?" Officer Caruso asked.

"Because he always has a tuba," said Tommy. "He's a tuba player. Look, you do your job and I'll do mine, okay?"

"Okay," said Officer Caruso, hurt. "Don't get so testy. I'm just trying to help."

"Some help," said Tommy.

Officer Caruso and Tommy glared at each other, and

Officer Caruso went back into the hall. For once, Tommy did not tell him to have a nice day.

Donald Bright had just gathered up his conductor's score and a yellow pad when a familiar-looking person stuck his head through his office door.

"Got a minute?" he asked, giving Donald the jolliest grin Donald had ever seen in Carnegie Hall. The man was six feet three inches tall and weighed at least two hundred and fifty pounds. Donald tried to remember where he had last seen him.

'Hey, aren't you, um, Charlie Churchill, the weather guy on Channel Nine?" Donald asked.

"*Former* weather guy," said Charlie Churchill, giving Donald another grin. He was always delighted to be recognized.

"What can I do for you?" Donald asked.

"I'm covering the Mass for PBS."

"Are you putting me on?" Donald asked. He knew that there would be a special, but he did not know that Charlie Churchill would be the host.

"Scout's honor, Mr. Bright. You *are* Donald Bright, aren't you? Choral conductor? Guy who found the Mass?"

Donald nodded.

"Well, I'm supposed to interview you. Get ninety seconds for the special."

"They sent a *weatherman* to cover a mass?" Donald asked.

"Meteorologist," Charlie corrected gently. "I moved out of weather because I want to broaden my horizons. It was actually my wife's idea. She thought my career was stagnating. May I come in?"

"Um, sure," said Donald, and he watched Charlie Churchill's camera crew set up their equipment. "But I've only got a few minutes. I'm supposed to be at the dress rehearsal."

"No problem," said Charlie. "Ninety seconds is all I need, as long as it's a *visual* ninety seconds. You're the first conductor I've ever interviewed. I thought I'd practice on you before I did Barnes."

"Good thinking," said Donald, his pride wounded.

He did not say so, though. He wanted to be on the special, even for a mere ninety seconds. "Where do you want me to stand?" he asked.

Charlie looked around the room. "Why don't you just sit at your desk? That always seems to work."

Donald obediently went and sat behind his desk.

"Ready, guys?" Charlie asked. The crew looked at their equipment and nodded. "Okay. I'm talking to Donald Bright, who's the choral conductor here at Carnegie Hall. Now, Donald, who's the greatest conductor you've ever seen?"

Donald answered without hesitation. He looked seriously, thoughtfully, into the camera. "Leonard Bernstein. His brilliant compositions to one side, he's a master of what's called the 'grammar of conducting.' He gets so deeply into a score—he knows what's going on in every measure, every chord—I try to model myself after—" He noticed that Charlie Churchill was frowning and shaking his head. "What's wrong?" Donald asked.

"It's not exactly what we're looking for," Charlie said delicately. "I mean, I don't want to put words in your mouth, but you get into, what was it? Chords? Measures? That's pretty complicated stuff, know what I mean? Look, I got into trouble with my producers whenever I went beyond cloud formations on the radar! You can't go over the heads of the audience, you know what I mean?"

Donald looked confused. "I thought this was for PBS," he said.

"Yeah, but they're running it against the Cosby show," said Charlie. "You give 'em that measure-and-chord shit and they'll be punching the remote control. Can't you make it a little more, you know, *visual*? And let's move away from Bernstein. Everybody knows about him already, know what I mean?"

"Okay," said Donald, unsure about what Charlie wanted. He only wanted to answer the question honestly. He revered Bernstein. He thought for a moment, and an idea came to him. "Oh, I've got something," he said.

"Great," said Charlie, giving Donald another big grin. Donald gave the camera an uncertain look. "We still rolling?" Charlie asked. "Donald Bright's the choral conductor here at the New York Symphony. Donald, who's the most *exciting* conductor you've ever worked with?''

Donald gave a relaxed smile. "Robert Shaw," he said, as Charlie Churchill's face fell. "Shaw conducted the Atlanta Symphony. He used to wear a blue nylon turtleneck shirt to conduct, no matter how hot it was. He'd sweat like a bastard in that thing. He'd always have a towel slung over his shoulder, but he'd never wipe the sweat off his face."

Donald did not notice that Charlie and his crew were exchanging looks of utter boredom.

"An hour into rehearsal, you felt like he might just keel over and die at any moment, because he was working so hard and sweating so much. But as a result, you'd work like crazy for him. You'd march to hell and back for him. And he pulled things out of people that they never knew were inside of them.

"And today," Donald continued, unaware that Charlie's technician had stopped the tape, "there's a whole generation of choral conductors who wear blue nylon turtlenecks to rehearsal and carry towels over their shoulders and sweat like bastards and never wipe their faces. Quite a legacy. But it works, so you can't argue with it—what's wrong?''

Charlie Churchill was shaking his head. "I guess you don't understand what we're going after," he said.

"I guess I don't," said Donald, annoyed by now. The story about Shaw was one of his favorites and it usually went over very well.

"You see," Charlie explained, "this is a special about *Andrew Barnes*. So I ask you who's the greatest conductor, and you're supposed to say *Barnes*. And then you tell me why, *visually*, for ninety seconds. Instead, you start talking about all these *other* people. Jesus!''

Donald seethed. He stared at Charlie Churchill.

"Look," Charlie continued, trying to reason with Donald, "I was in weather seven years and one thing I learned is that *everything in life is just like weather*. People don't care about next year and they don't care about last week. They don't care what they ate yesterday, they don't care if they got laid yesterday. They only want to know about *the next five days*. You follow me?''

Donald closed his eyes and sighed. *Why me?* he was thinking.

"And Barnes is happening *now*," said Charlie. "He's the *five-day forecast*. These other guys—Bernstein, that other guy with the shirt—they're yesterday's weather! They're outta here! People want to hear about Barnes, okay? *Barnes*. You want to take it again?"

Donald stood behind his desk. "Get out," he said quietly.

"But—" said Charlie, not understanding.

"Get out of my office. Now!"

"But, Donald—"

"NOW!"

"Okay, okay," said Charlie, glaring at Donald. "Come on, guys, let's get out of here. What a sorehead. Jesus. To think I nearly gave him a Charlie Churchill autographed umbrella. Unbelievable. Hey, Mrs. Barnes said you'd be easy to talk to. She said you'd say anything to get on TV. Boy, was *she* wrong!"

Charlie and his crew left Donald's office and slammed the door behind them. Donald closed his eyes and thought of Elizabeth.

"She never quits," he said.

TWENTY-TWO

Donald Bright and James Carver took their seats in the twelfth row of Carnegie Hall and watched the chorus members file onstage.

"You're not going to believe what just happened," Donald said to James. He had not yet recovered from his interview with Charlie Churchill.

"Why? What happened?" James asked nervously. He

thought it might have something to do with the threats.
James was exceptionally ill at ease this morning because
he thought that one of the policemen, a young one, was
watching him.

"Never mind," said Donald, opening his score, leaving James to ponder what Donald would not tell him.

The orchestra members took their seats, tuned up, fell
silent, and waited for Andrew Barnes to appear. Andrew,
looking more relaxed than at the two previous rehearsals,
stepped with authority onto the podium. He turned to
address the second violins.

"Ladies and gentlemen," he began, "could I please
ask you to watch yourselves in the Agnus Dei? Yesterday,
a few of you didn't know which *octave* you were in. All
right?"

Eyebrows shot up across the orchestra. *So he really
did hear it,* the musicians thought. They quickly revised
their impressions of Andrew. In the twelfth row, Donald
and James were speechless.

"And I might ask the brass section," Andrew continued, "to be a bit more aware of the dynamics. You rode
roughshod over some very delicate places yesterday
morning." He paused for effect. "This isn't a Sousa
march, you know."

The brass section looked at Andrew with great surprise. They sat up in their chairs and resolved to play
more carefully. The first oboist looked especially approvingly at Andrew. He still had not approached her, to
her disappointment. She also knew the story about Mozart's unwilling oboist and would have welcomed the opportunity to rewrite one small piece of music history.
Affairs of the heart notwithstanding, in the ongoing war
between conductors and orchestras, Andrew knew that
he had just pulled off a successful sneak attack.

The entire orchestra responded to his comments and
played in a professional if not overwhelmingly inspiring
manner. The chorus and soloists tried not to overtax their
voices on the morning before the concert. Janet Ikovic
barely sang at all. Paul Martland, the tenor, passed the
time in between his solos thinking about where he would
take Janet after the concert. He knew where he wanted
to take her, but back to his hotel room would be a bit

too forward, he decided. The hotel bar would be just right. Andrew, for once thinking about nothing but Mozart, guided the performers through the entire first half of the Mass without a pause. Then he announced a fifteen-minute break. Most of the musicians remained onstage, chatting among themselves about Andrew's surprising resurgence. Someone must have told him to say those things about the Agnus Dei and the brass section, the orchestra members concluded—he could never have figured those things out for himself.

During the break, George came up to Kevin backstage. "Guess what," George whispered.

"Surprise me," said Kevin.

"Elizabeth. She called the police and had them put a cop right in front of the door to their hotel room. Right after the rehearsal, they're marching Andy back to the hotel, and he'll stay in the room all afternoon until the concert. That way the terrorists can't get at him."

"That way Andy can't get at the sopranos," said Kevin, laughing. "She doesn't care about terrorists. She just wants to keep him from getting lucky." He grinned. "What are wives for?"

"Terrorists could be trying to kill our conductor right this minute and all you can do is make jokes," sniffed George.

"A sense of humor wouldn't kill *you*," Kevin said, walking away. He had been in a foul mood himself, a function of Corinne's rejection of his attentions the night before. "Everybody's so tense around here. Jesus."

Onstage, the break ended. Andrew raised his baton and quickly began the second half of the Mass, hoping to complete it before the large rehearsal clock on the back wall of the Carnegie Hall stage struck noon. During performances, some decorative woodwork hides the clock from the audience. The rehearsal clock exists because union rules guarantee the orchestra members time and a half for each hour or fraction thereof beyond the contractually arranged rehearsal time. Andrew was able to complete all but the last thirty measures, a series of choral Amens, when time elapsed.

The abrupt ending, with the music stopping seconds before the witching hour, left all concerned with an uncomfortable feeling of incompletion. Under the current salary scale, however, the last thirty measures would have cost the management of the New York Symphony Orchestra four thousand eight hundred dollars.

Andrew smiled good-naturedly. He clasped his hands and shook them to indicate pleasure with the musicians' efforts. The chorus responded with polite applause. The orchestra ignored him. They packed up their instruments, made jokes about the lost overtime, and wondered aloud who would be conducting the Mass. Meanwhile, Alvin Reischel's odds had dropped to eight to five in favor of Donald and increased to three to one on Andrew. He was still finding plenty of takers.

Whenever guest conductors appear with a leading symphony orchestra, the management distributes opinion surveys to all the players. The questionnaire asks such things as "Do you enjoy working with this guest conductor?" "Would you like to see him/her invited back?" "How would you rate his/her musicianship, conducting ability, and ability to run a rehearsal?" Thus management can protect its players from incompetent or overly unpleasant conductors. The survey is placed on the chair of each musician prior to the last rehearsal; the results are never made public.

Andrew knew of the questionnaires because the Royal Symphonic players answered similar ones when guests came to conduct in London. Half of the New York Symphony musicians, however, did not even bother to answer the questions, itself a sort of negative response to Barnes's performance. Andrew noticed that thirty or forty forms were left untouched on the floor of the stage. His comments about the Agnus Dei and the volume of the brass section were not enough to win the respect of the entire orchestra. Most of the players continued to feel the usual sort of antipathy for a guest conductor whom they considered not quite on their level. Andrew tried not to appear overly chagrined. He decided that a bunch of unanswered questionnaires would be far less embarrassing than a flood of negative ones.

After the orchestra departed, the chorus members made

their way offstage. Andrew remained perched on his conductor's stool, watching Alison Gardiner. Officer Caruso stood at the edge of the stage, waiting to escort Andrew back to the hotel. Andrew was effectively isolated from Alison, and from every other young woman in the borough of Manhattan.

Alison, who did not know about Andrew's quarantine, gave him a look that asked, "Are you busy later?" Andrew responded with an expression combining enthusiasm and regret. "I'd love to, but I can't," was the message he tried to convey. Alison responded with a glance that said "Oh, well," but she thought that Andrew was no longer interested in her. She tried to hide her disappointment.

"Chorus interruptus," Corinne joked to Alison. Corinne was unaware of the byplay between Alison and Andrew. "Story of my life," she added.

The women were waiting for the line of chorus members to move so that they could leave the stage. The exit offstage was blocked with other singers.

"Hmm?" said Alison, still watching Andrew.

"You couldn't take your eyes off Andy during the whole rehearsal," Corinne told Alison.

They approached the exit door. "And what's so unusual about watching the conductor?" Alison replied. "Doesn't everybody?"

"Not the way *you* were watching Andrew."

"How was I watching him?"

"You couldn't take your eyes off him. Not even to look at your score."

"I happen to have studied the score," said Alison, growing annoyed. "What's gotten into you today?"

"Nothing's gotten into me," said Corinne. "I just think you spent yesterday making yourself memorable to Andrew Barnes."

Alison crossed her arms. "And what if I did?" she asked. "Really, Corinne, what's with you? Why should you care if I slept with Andy Barnes or not? I thought you'd be happy for me. You usually are when I have someone new to tell you about. And besides, if you didn't want to hear about him, *you didn't have to ask*, did you?"

Corinne stiffened. "I'm sorry if I don't seem happy enough for you," she said.

"What's gotten *into* you?" Alison asked, upset with Corinne. "Are you jealous because he's a famous conductor? Did you see him first? Is that it?"

Corinne put a hand over her eyes. "I'm sorry. I just got carried away. Forgive me."

Alison looked dismayed.

Corinne gave an embarrassed half-smile. "I don't know. I just got carried away—I'm sorry."

"Well, in that case," said Alison, "do you want to hear about yesterday afternoon? Or last night?"

"Absolutely not," Corinne said abruptly. "I'll see you later, okay? I just have to get out of here. I'm sorry."

Corinne stepped away without another word.

"What got into *her*?" Alison asked herself, shaking her head. Then she turned around and walked toward Andrew Barnes's dressing room. She had something she wanted to leave for him, a small gift that might help Andrew remember her after the Mass concerts were over. She would leave it by his dressing room door. It never occurred to Alison that someone else might find the gift before Andrew did.

"What did you think?" James asked Donald, as Donald finally closed his score.

"It's getting better," Donald admitted grudgingly. "Except for the fugue in the Credo. *That's* still a hash."

The part of the Mass to which Donald referred was an extremely complicated two minutes of music. Mozart divided the chorus there into eight parts—high and low basses, high and low tenors, and so on. A conductor who failed to keep up with his chorus in the fugue would soon find the piece crashing down in a confusion of voices. This was exactly what had happened to Andrew each time he had rehearsed it.

"Are you going to say something to him?" James asked. "Help him out?"

Donald thought back to his conversation with Andrew the night before. He shook his head. "I don't think so," he said.

TWENTY-THREE

A few minutes after the rehearsal ended, an aggrieved Charlie Churchill buttonholed Elizabeth backstage.

"Boy, what a sorehead that guy Donald is," he told her. "Jeez."

"What's wrong?" asked Elizabeth, alarmed. An unhappy Charlie Churchill could mean a bad show about Andrew. Elizabeth might not like the way Andrew treated her, sleeping with sopranos in their own hotel room, but she was not about to slow down her public relations campaign on his behalf.

"He wouldn't talk about Andrew," said Charlie. "He talked about all these guys I never heard of."

I'm going to kill Donald, Elizabeth thought. "Can't you use any of what he said?"

Charlie made a face. "Are you kidding? Not a word. What a waste of tape! He doesn't understand TV! He kept talking about—" He tried to remember. "Chords. Can you imagine?"

"He gets that way," Elizabeth said, expression deadpan. "Is there anything *I* can do?"

"You bet there is," said Charlie. "I've got a minute-and-a-half hole in the show. How am I supposed to fill that? The whole thing's already scripted. I've said everything *I* know about music, which is practically nothing. And my producer's going to kill me when he finds out I blew the interview. I got a problem, lady."

"Yes, you do," Elizabeth agreed. "What if I gave you something to say about music? Something that would make your producer think you were highly intelligent."

"Could you do that for *me*?" Charlie asked, playing

along. Charlie did not like her condescending tone, but he sensed that she might come through for him.

"If anyone can," said Elizabeth. "Why don't you tell your viewers that the key to my husband's success is his ability to convince an orchestra that the concert they are performing is the most important one in their careers?"

"Hold it! Hold it!" Charlie said. "This could be good! Let me get my notebook!"

Elizabeth waited patiently as Charlie dug a notebook and pen out of his jacket pocket. If the BBC did a special on Mozart, she told herself, the narrator would likely possess an advanced degree in musicology. America was a very strange place.

"I haven't taken notes since junior college," Charlie was saying, pen and notebook poised. "Okay, I'm ready. Fire away."

"Ninety-nine percent of musicians' lives," Elizabeth began, speaking slowly, as if she were giving dictation, "ninety-nine percent of musicians' lives are spent in solitary confinement, practicing alone in a room for six to eight hours a day. Or they are in rehearsals, repeating the same line of music over and over again."

"Over and over again," Charlie echoed, as he wrote.

Elizabeth glanced at his notes to make sure that he was getting it all down. To her surprise, he was.

"My husband's intensity on the podium," she continued, "makes clear to musicians that they aren't in a rehearsal studio or off by themselves in a practice room. They are performing for people who have given their time and money to hear good music played expertly and enthusiastically. Does that help?"

"—Expertly and enthusi—how do you spell . . . oh, never mind. Hey," said Charlie, his trademark grin in place again, "this is great material! Thanks!"

Elizabeth gave Charlie a little smile. She wanted to tell him she thought he was a boob, but she refrained.

"See you later," Charlie said. "I want to get this on tape while it's still fresh in my mind."

"Good luck," said Elizabeth, and she walked away.

"Ask anybody on my staff for a free Charlie Churchill umbrella," he called out to her. "You've earned it."

Elizabeth did not respond. Charlie did not care.

"Come on," he told his crew, who had been sitting around, bored, throughout the rehearsal. They were looking forward to taping the next Charlie Churchill special, an exposé on teenage runaways in Times Square. "Set up right here," he said. Then he looked around the backstage area and shook his head. "No, I've got another idea. Let's go up to those boxes. It'll be really visual. Quick, before I forget this stuff. Gee, she talks fast."

Ten minutes later, Charlie Churchill was leaning against the edge of a first-tier box and looking earnestly into the camera. Over his vast shoulder was the empty Carnegie Hall stage. "You know," he told the camera, "being here at Carnegie Hall reminds me of something most people don't really take into account when they go to concerts. Did you know that ninety-nine percent of musicians' lives are spent in solitary confinement, practicing alone for six to eight hours a day. . . ."

TWENTY-FOUR

I'm really sorry to have to do this," said Officer Caruso, as he deposited Andrew in his hotel suite. "You can't come out of there until seven o'clock, when you go back for the concert."

"It's not your fault," Andrew said glumly. He sat down on the couch and kicked off his shoes. "You're just doing your job, right?"

"You got it," said Officer Caruso. "I should have gotten ten some lunch while you were still conducting. I don't get any relief until five."

Andrew thought it over. "Look, there's no law that says I can't buy you lunch, is there?"

"You mean leaving the hotel?" asked Officer Caruso. He shook his head. "I can't let you do that."

"I meant room service," Andrew explained. "Why don't you give them a call and order us both some lunch? I owe you a favor for your brilliant comments yesterday. It was like a different orchestra this morning."

"Gee, do you think it's okay?" asked Officer Caruso. He tried to remember whether there was anything in the manual about eating lunch with somebody you were supposed to be guarding.

"I don't see why not," said Andrew. "Look, I'm going to change. Tell them to bring up a couple of hamburgers and fries, okay?"

"I've never called room service," said Officer Caruso, looking doubtfully at the telephone.

"Nothing to it," said Andrew, as he went into the bedroom. "It's just like the drive-through window at McDonald's. Dial four."

Officer Caruso studied the instructions on the telephone and dialed four. "They have McDonald's in England?" he called to Andrew as the concierge answered.

"Hello, this is, uh, the room of Mr. Andrew Barnes. You know, the conductor. Could you bring us two hamburgers, two large fries, two vanilla shakes, um, and two boxes of cookies for dessert? . . . You don't have cookies? How about ice cream sundaes? That's great. . . . Twenty minutes? Can't you make it any quicker? . . . Okay. Room 814. Thanks."

He hung up. "All set," he called out to Andrew, who was still changing. Officer Caruso noticed Andrew's baton resting on his Mozart score. He glanced at the closed bedroom door and picked up the baton. He studied its cork grip and ivory shaft. "This is great," he said aloud. "My grandfather would love one of these."

He made a few conducting motions with the baton. He thought briefly about pocketing it—maybe sticking it down his trouser leg. Then he remembered first that Andrew would notice it was missing and second that he was a policeman and it wasn't right for policemen to steal. He set the baton down on the table. Then he sat on the couch and picked up Andrew's conductor's score of the Mass. He turned the pages slowly. Andrew emerged from the dressing room, dressed more comfortably in blue jeans, a white button-down shirt, and a pair of high-top basketball sneakers, a gift from a youth orchestra in the south of England.

"Ever seen a conductor's score?" Andrew asked, rolling up his sleeves.

Officer Caruso shook his head. "No, never."

"Then how do you know so much about music?"

"I told you," said Officer Caruso, flipping through the score. "I listen to my grandfather. This is really neat. Look at that. Each instrument has its own line of music. Oboe, clarinet, trumpet, trombone, first violin, second violin—hey, you fixed *their* wagons today. You were great."

"Thanks," said Andrew.

"It's interesting," said Officer Caruso. "You notice there isn't any flute in this piece?"

Andrew had not noticed. "Really?" he asked, looking at the score. Officer Caruso was right—there was no line of music for flutes.

"Mozart thought flutes didn't belong in sacred music," said Officer Caruso. "He thought they didn't sound serious enough."

"I didn't know that," said Andrew, impressed by Officer Caruso's knowledge of music. If anyone had asked him, he would have sworn that there were flutes in the Mass in F.

"Yeah, it's true," said Officer Caruso, studying the score. "Oh, I get it. These are the lines for the chorus, and these are the soloists. When I was a kid, I used to think the composer wrote the melody and then all the instruments just kind of improvised, just like a jazz band. I was twelve years old before I knew that composers did their own orchestrations."

"I was twenty-one before I learned that," said Andrew. "Actually, it's an interesting thing. A lot of melodies in this Mass are actually borrowed from Mozart's earlier compositions." He was anxious to show the young patrolman that he knew something about music, too. "Donald Bright says that he recognizes seven different melodies that Mozart recycled in the Mass."

"Really?" said Officer Caruso. "I recognized nine."

Andrew did not know what to say.

Just then, they heard a key turn in the lock. Officer Caruso panicked. "Oh, no," he said. "I should have been outside the door. This could be the PLO. Get in the bedroom, quick."

"But it's probably just Eliz—" Andrew began.

"Quick!" shouted Officer Caruso, pulling out his service revolver and dropping to a shooting stance. He had both hands on his gun, which was pointed at the door. The door opened.

"Police! Freeze!" yelled Officer Caruso.

It was Elizabeth. "I beg your pardon?" she said, looking curiously at Officer Caruso. She ignored Andrew. "I thought you were supposed to be *outside* the door, guarding my husband, not inside, playing cops and robbers."

"Hello, darling," said Andrew. "Frankly, I don't think I could feel safer." Andrew patted the young patrolman on the shoulder. "Why should I worry about international terrorists when I've got Officer Caruso?"

An embarrassed Officer Caruso replaced his gun in its holster. Andrew sensed that Elizabeth was upset over something. "What's wrong?" he asked.

Elizabeth did not respond. Instead, she took a cassette tape from her pocketbook and held it up for Andrew and Officer Caruso to see.

"Darling, if they've made a taped message, we *simply* must get it to the police immediately," Andrew said. "Where did you find it?"

"At first I thought it was some sort of bomb," she said. "It was leaning against our dressing room door. So I asked that elderly doorman to come and pick it up for me. When it didn't explode I opened it, and this is what I found."

She handed the cassette box over to Andrew. Officer Caruso watched with great interest. Inside, Andrew found a cassette and a note, which read, "Andy—I thought you might like a souvenir of our time together. Love, Alison." The note also provided her telephone number and address.

"Enjoy the rest of your afternoon," said Elizabeth. "Officer Caruso, should any young sopranos come up to this suite this afternoon, I trust you will tell them that Maestro Barnes is not accepting any visitors.''

"Yes, ma'am," Officer Caruso said meekly.

Elizabeth left the suite. She nearly walked into the room service trolley that a busboy was pushing. She glared at the busboy and walked to the elevator.

Neither Officer Caruso nor Andrew knew what to say as the busboy wheeled in their lunch. Andrew tipped the busboy, patted Officer Caruso on the back, and said, "Come on, let's eat."

TWENTY-FIVE

While at the conservatory, Donald had begun the practice of clipping from newspapers and magazines articles on conductors and conducting. He thought the articles would be helpful as his career progressed. He saved them in manila file folders and had a desk drawer full by now. If he were to prepare a chorus for a certain well-known guest conductor, he had only to rummage through the articles to learn about the visiting maestro's strengths and weaknesses, his likes and dislikes.

Donald had never intended the file to be a collection of stories about Andrew Baker Barnes, but as time passed, it turned out that way. Articles on other conductors might or might not find their way into the folders. Pieces on Andrew invariably did. Every so often, if Donald was in a bad mood and wanted to depress himself further, he would take out his Andrew file and read.

Now, at two o'clock, only six hours before the concert, Donald still did not know whether he would be a spectator or the central figure tonight. He found it hard to concentrate on his work. Before the news from George,

Donald had planned to use the afternoon to work on the next piece the chorus would sing, a concert version of a Verdi opera. Mail had been piling up for days in his office. He looked through the stack of concert announcements and press releases. He glanced at a letter from a London orchestra, most likely announcing an American tour. It had been made to resemble a personal letter. *Good PR,* Donald thought, tossing it back on the pile.

Donald opened a desk drawer and removed his Andrew file. He went back to the first year's folder and flipped through the clippings. He came to an article entitled "Can Barnes Save the Royal Symphonic? Sir Anthony Garrett-Jones Wagers £10 Million On Unknown American." The piece appeared in a fourteen-year-old issue of a magazine called *Music in Britain* and was the first profile ever to appear on Barnes. Donald smoothed the clipping on his desk and read it for perhaps the hundredth time.

" 'When I talk to kids about Beethoven,' " the article quoted Andrew, " 'I talk about him in terms of the Beatles. Most people think about Beethoven as some sort of musical god who dropped from the heavens and left behind nine symphonies, five piano concertos, thirty-two piano sonatas, one opera, and whatever else, all in one big package, all at the same time. When I go to schools, and I go often, I try to get kids to think about Beethoven as a human being.

" 'Look at it this way. The Beatles had a number of different periods in their career. The early rock 'n' roll stuff, like "I Wanna Hold Your Hand" and "She Loves You." Rough edged. Raucous. Great fun, of course. Then their middle period, when they were a little smoother, a little more cynical. *A Hard Day's Night. Rubber Soul. Revolver.* And finally comes the more sophisticated, complex music. *Sergeant Pepper. The White Album.* And my favorite, *Abbey Road.*

" 'Kids can relate to the idea that the Beatles who recorded "A Day in the Life" had travelled a long way from their "She Loves You" days. And a kid who can grasp *that* is on his way to understanding that the young, optimistic Beethoven who wrote the Opus 18 string quartets was in many ways a different man from the complicated old man who wrote the *Ode to Joy.*' ''

Donald knew there was something unhealthy in his careful maintenance of a file on Andrew's career. He justified the practice with the thought that these articles would have been written about *him*—had Elizabeth not left him for Andrew. Donald sat at his desk now and read about Andrew, his orchestra, his acclimation to life in London, his stormy marriage, his domineering father-in-law (who bankrolled the orchestra and ran it along with Elizabeth), and his firm tenure in the gossip columns of Fleet Street. If Andrew Barnes was not a musician's conductor, he was certainly a success as a ladies' man.

The picture of Andrew Barnes that emerged from Donald's collection was that of a man at first timid and unsure in his job and surroundings, but one who rapidly grew accustomed to success. Andrew had given the *Music in Britain* interview at a time when he had little confidence in his ability to discuss, let alone conduct, classical music. Andrew seemed painfully aware of his limitations as a musician. He was quick to point them out to reporters and to members of his orchestra. An example: ''When Beethoven conducted the premiere of his Seventh Symphony in 1813,'' he told *The Economist*, shortly after his arrival in London, ''he was stone-deaf. The orchestra completely ignored him and played the piece by themselves. How much worse a job could *I* do?''

As time passed, though, profiles of the conductor contained fewer and fewer references to his shortcomings and more stories about the soloists and conductors with whom he now mingled and performed. The reviews of his concerts—cut out of the *Times* of London, to which Donald subscribed solely for this purpose—suggested that his conducting improved steadily after his first few years. Andrew never performed music that he did not like. To others he left the complex and bizarre. To his own audience he offered the comfortable and the pleasant. London did not lack for orchestras committed to new music. Barnes's diet of Beethoven, Mozart, Haydn, and Brahms packed the vast Royal Albert Hall night after night, season after season.

As his stardom grew, Andrew retained his common

touch. He was Andy, never "Maestro," to his musicians and his public. He invariably admitted all the autograph seekers to his dressing room after concerts, to the deep displeasure of his wife. Once, Donald found a suggestion in *Private Eye*, a London magazine, that Andrew admitted them *because* it displeased her. And he was tireless in his visits to schools and universities, a boyishly handsome cheerleader for the classics, captivating students with his Beatles-to-Beethoven comparisons, displaying the same ease and grace that attracted women somewhat closer to his own age. Donald could not help but feel jealous. This was the life that *he* was supposed to have led. And if he had gotten a chance to lead that life, he was certain, he would have done it even better.

James Carver tapped gently on Donald's office door and quietly let himself in. Donald looked up at his visitor.

"Coming to keep me company?" Donald asked.

"I thought you could use someone to talk to," James said, and he closed the door behind him and folded himself into a chair opposite Donald's desk. In truth, *James* needed someone to talk to. He was so nervous about his plan for installing Donald as conductor for the Mass that he could not stand to be alone. If anything, he was more nervous now that his plan seemed to be working.

Donald nodded. "This is turning into the longest day of my life."

"Mine, too," said James, with good reason. It had just occurred to him that calling in death threats might be some sort of criminal offense. "I hear they're not letting Andy out of his hotel room," he told Donald. "Security reasons."

"Who's idea was that, George's?"

James shook his head. "Elizabeth's," he said.

Donald laughed. "That's great. Good for her. Keep him away from my sopranos."

"Elizabeth said that next she wants to keep you away from your tenors," said James.

Donald stopped laughing. "That's not funny," he said crossly.

"Sorry," said James.

"It'll take more than an armed guard to keep Andy

away from young women," said Donald. "Elizabeth hasn't got a prayer of stopping him."

The mention of Elizabeth's name triggered something in James. "How did you and Elizabeth get started, anyway?" he asked.

"Do you really want to know?" Donald asked.

"Do you mind talking about it?" asked James. This was just the sort of social history that James adored. "Only if you're comfortable talking about it."

"I don't see why not," said Donald. He shifted his weight in his chair. "She and I started going out just after I won the prize for best student in the first year conducting seminar. There wasn't much competition that year, but I was awesome. She was a violin student. Not half bad, either. She used to audit the conducting classes. She said conducting fascinated her and that it was the one thing she wanted to do more than anything else."

"Why didn't *she* try it?" asked James.

Donald made a face. "She couldn't beat time. At *all*. She was even worse than *Andy* was, and that's saying something. She actually tried to conduct a Rossini overture in a conservatory orchestra concert. The *William Tell*. Hardly a challenge for a conductor. Kid stuff, really. She got twenty bars into the piece and she lost her nerve. Just stopped conducting and stood there frozen. By the time she recovered, half the orchestra slowed down and half sped up. It sounded awful. It sounded like a composition by Pierre Boulez."

"She must have felt terrible," said James.

Donald nodded. He paused for a moment. "I never dreamed the same thing would happen to me," he added.

"You shouldn't dwell on that one concert," said James. "Anyone can have *one* bad concert. And you told me it wasn't your fault—it was the lighting—or the air conditioning—or *something*—"

"It wasn't anything like that," said Donald. "It was my fault. I blew it. I just screwed up, that's all. I screwed up all *three* times. It was *three* times, not just one. And the same thing could happen to me tonight."

James wanted to keep Donald from thinking about stage fright. "Tell me more about Elizabeth," he said. "How did she react?"

"After *her* screw-up?" Donald asked. "She never went near the baton again. Maybe she had more sense than I do. But she kept coming to conducting class just the same. The odd thing was that she never watched the teacher. She wouldn't even look at him. Or even pretend to be paying attention."

"What was she looking at?"

"At us. The students. She would watch our faces as we were watching him. I noticed it for the first time a few weeks after her conducting disaster. Other people in the class picked up on it, too, and commented on it. There was something very odd about it. She would even come into the practice rooms, where we would conduct a score to a phonograph record, and watch, and never say a word. She just had an effect on people. No one would ever ask her to leave."

"And *you* were engaged to her?" James asked, getting to the part that most interested him.

Donald nodded. "Don't sound so surprised," he said.

"I'm sorry," said James, shaking his head slowly. "It's just hard to imagine."

"It *is* pretty hard to believe," Donald said. "The conducting students all used to go out together in the evenings. She'd buy. She was practically the only one who could *afford* to. Elizabeth never noticed *me* until I won that prize. By then she was putting less time into her violin and more time into hanging around with conducting students."

"Were you attracted to her?"

"Not especially. I don't think I was attracted to anyone back then. I was a real grind. All I did was study scores."

"Wow," said James, who had been more a free spirit than that when *he* was at the conservatory.

"She invited me to her apartment—she was the only one with an apartment then. Some apartment. On Central Park South. Balcony, and everything. I'd never seen anything like it. The rest of us lived in the dorms. She served me dinner, and then, well, one thing led to another.

"And word got out at the conservatory that she and I were a pair. *I* certainly didn't tell anyone. I was afraid she'd deny it. The other fellows in the conducting class came around and congratulated me on my good luck, and they all asked what my secret was. Frankly, I was wondering the same thing.''

James's expression registered disbelief.

"I was sure she'd get bored with me after a while and move on to some other guy. I mean, what could *I* offer *her*?''

"You make it sound so—economic,'' said James.

"I guess I felt that way at the time,'' Donald admitted. "Anyway, she stayed with me for two years. I won the third-year conducting prize, and just after that, she proposed.''

"*She* proposed?'' James asked.

"She didn't exactly *propose*, but that was the upshot. She told me that her father was going to give an enormous gift—millions, really—to the Royal Symphonic Society. The conductor then was that guy Biederman, who was so involved with twentieth-century music. Elizabeth told me that the orchestra was very badly managed. Her father was going to give the money, but there were a few strings attached.''

"Like what?''

"Well, first, he had to become the chairman of the board of the orchestra. Second, *he* would get to pick the new conductor. Her father hated twentieth-century music. No offense to you, of course, James. Anyway, the new conductor had to have free rein to hire and fire in the orchestra. Totally remake it. Turn the whole thing around.''

"He wanted to buy himself an orchestra?'' James asked.

Donald nodded. "An orchestra, or an airline, or a Greek island. He wanted some visible place to park some of his money. Most wealthy people are content to just buy themselves a seat on an orchestra board, but he wanted the whole thing. I met him a few times. A domineering kind of guy. You know, the kind that has to be in control of the situation? He bought the R.S.S. because it combined his philanthropic urge with his love of music. And he made his offer, and they accepted, on his terms.

"And he asked Elizabeth to go out and bring him back a conductor. He would have given the orchestra to *her*, but she just couldn't cut it. It was big news at the time, when her father took over, because in England people don't go out and buy orchestras. It's not like here.''

James looked thoughtful as he tried to absorb all this new information. ''And that's why she was studying you in conducting class?'' he asked.

''I didn't understand it at the time, of course. No one did. Well, somehow she settled on me. I suppose I was the most promising student, since I'd won those prizes. And I was something of Nouse's pet. Elizabeth told me she wanted to marry me and take me to London and get me the position of principal conductor of the Royal Symphonic.''

''And what did you say?'' James asked.

''I said yes.''

''But she married Andy,'' said James. ''What happened?''

Donald sighed. ''As you can imagine, I was pretty excited. I was in my early twenties and I was going to have my own orchestra. I threw myself into planning changes for the R.S.S. All kinds of changes. Programming. Personnel. Even marketing. And Elizabeth and I would go out to dinner—I ate so well that year—and I'd tell her about all of my plans.

''And it bothered me—it really *hurt* me that she didn't get excited when I talked about what I wanted to do. Actually, she would look more and more frightened. At first I tried to ignore it. And then after a few months, whenever I brought up the orchestra, she'd change the subject.

''I didn't know *what* to think. I was hardly in love with her when the whole thing started. But I guess I got used to the idea that we'd be, you know, spending our lives together. Like business partners, I guess.''

''And?'' James prompted, on the edge of his chair.

''And then one fine day she and Andy were walking hand in hand through the conservatory cafeteria, and she left me a note in my mailbox a day or two later that said to come get my stuff. She put it all in boxes and left it with her doorman.''

''She didn't even tell you to your face?''

Donald did not respond.

"I never knew any of this," James said, fascinated. "Weren't you just *devastated*?"

Donald nodded. "My whole career, my marriage—well, not that I cared about marriage, or anything. But my plans for the orchestra—it all just vanished."

"Why'd she leave you?" James asked. "Especially for him! Was there a fight?"

Donald laughed. "We never fought. The problem was that we had different ideas about running the orchestra. The *real* problem was that I had ideas in the first place."

"I thought she picked you because you had talent—you won all those prizes."

"That might have been true at first. But she dumped me because if I had been principal conductor, *I* would have *run* that orchestra."

"Which is what *she* wanted to do."

"Exactly."

"And that's why she left you for Andrew, because she thought she could control him," said James. "And through him, control the orchestra."

"You're catching on quickly."

"And you *really* never fought?" James asked. He could not believe that Donald kept silent after receiving such abusive treatment.

"There was nothing to fight about," said Donald. "As I said, we were never really in love. But when it ended, I guess I felt—I don't know. Insulted. Used, maybe."

"And?" James asked. Hearing this sort of intimate detail was what James lived for.

"Well," Donald admitted, "you could say we had words. After it was all over."

"Like what?"

Donald shrugged. "I guess I told her she was a manipulative bitch and a repulsive woman. That she had no heart. That kind of thing."

"*Really?*" James asked. He tried to imagine Donald telling Elizabeth off. "You said all that?"

"All that and more. I told her that if it weren't for her father, the closest she'd ever come to a symphony orchestra is if she bought a ticket. I figured that as long as we were breaking up, it ought to *sound* like a breakup." Donald laughed. "I guess I approached it like a music score. I wanted to get the dynamics right. Make it sound right for the audience.''

"You never let go of your work," James said admiringly. "Was there an audience?"

Donald nodded. "It happened in the conservatory cafeteria. I think everybody in the whole school heard about it, even the deans.''

"Wow," said James, shaking his head slowly. "What did *she* say?"

Donald laughed again. "She said, if I could conduct with my dick, I could satisfy all of my life's ambitions at the same time."

James was stunned.

"It's true, of course," said Donald, still laughing.

James let out a low whistle. "No wonder she's still so mean to you."

Donald nodded. "You noticed. And then she got her father to give *Andy* the R.S.S. job. And the rest is history."

Donald paused for a moment. "The whole thing just shook me," he said. "I was going along so well, and then, boom. I think I never got all of my confidence back. Maybe it's why I screwed up those concerts. Maybe it's why part of me doesn't want to conduct tonight."

"But why not?" James asked. "The Mass in F is your piece!"

"It isn't *my* piece. It's Mozart's. It's really Andy's. *He's* the one they picked, not me."

"It's *your* piece. It's been just eating you alive that Andrew is conducting it."

"Could you tell?" Donald asked blandly.

"You hardly kept it a secret," said James, on the verge of telling Donald about his threats. "I felt awful for you. I just kept thinking that there had to be something I could do, maybe say a few words to management—"

Donald laughed. "If Ugo and George don't listen to me, what makes you think they'd listen to you? There was *nothing* you could have done to help me get this concert. Short of making the death threats yourself."

James looked away. Donald did not notice.

"Boy," said Donald. "I'd hate to be the guy who's been making those threats." He stretched back in his desk chair and folded his hands behind his head. "When the cops track him down, they'll beat the crap out of him. You know, rubber hoses, Chinese water torture—the whole nine yards."

James gasped. "What makes you say that?" he asked nervously.

"Oh, come on, it's obvious," said Donald. "He could give them all kinds of information about terrorists. He could tell them about what's planned, and how they get their training, and where their money comes from—once they find that guy, they'll never let go of him."

"But—but—don't they have to let people out on bail?" James asked. He saw himself being led away in handcuffs, his head bowed so that the photographers could not take his picture.

"That guy?" said Donald. "They'll set his bail at a million dollars. Ten million. It's funny. I think *I* have problems. I'd hate to be in *his* shoes."

"I know what you mean," said James, looking at his own shoes.

TWENTY-SIX

Remote control in hand, eyes on the television screen, sipping a drink, and aimlessly changing the channel, Andrew was sprawled on the couch in his hotel suite, bored out of his mind. Waiting for word from Kevin or George about whether he would conduct or not had gone from agonizing to merely tedious. He felt cut out of the decision-making process. The prospect of terrorists did not especially scare him. The worst thing that could happen was that he might be cut down in a blaze of glory, baton in hand, laying down his life on the Carnegie Hall stage. It was, he figured, his only ticket to conducting immortality.

Andrew was not in the mood to read one of the novels he brought with him from London. He certainly had no interest in studying the score. He did not know where Elizabeth was. He knew that she was out there somewhere in Manhattan, enjoying the fact that she had turned her husband into a prisoner for a long afternoon. Officer Caruso stood guard outside his door.

Andrew wanted to invite Alison back to the hotel room, despite her concerns about sexually transmitted diseases. "It wasn't very nice of me to tell her I was thinking about Gershwin," Andrew said to himself. "Maybe if I'd put it differently—'When we make love, I hear music.' No, she'd think I was making fun of her. Maybe I was, just the same. I almost feel as though I ought to apologize." Then he decided that she probably could not get past Officer Caruso, so there was no use in thinking about it.

Then Andrew heard a knock at the door. *Alison?* he asked himself. *Or maybe that unbelievable oboist. Wouldn't that be something.* Both options were unlikely, but Andrew was an optimist. He clicked off the television. Then he ran into the bathroom, and poured his drink down the sink. He hurriedly straightened up the living room, ran a hand through his hair, tucked in his shirt, and opened the door.

It was Officer Caruso.

"Oh," said Andrew highly disappointed. "What's up?"

Officer Caruso looked sheepish. "You mind if I—"

"If you what?" asked Andrew, not understanding.

"I know I'm not supposed to leave the door, but I really need to, uh—"

"Oh, of course," said Andrew, catching on. "Right through that door."

Andrew watched him walk to the bathroom. *What a rotten job,* he said to himself. *He's got to be as bored as I am. At least I can watch TV and drink.*

Then it dawned on Andrew that he could escape the prison of his hotel suite, but only if he hurried. He felt his back pocket for his wallet, looked out into the hallway to make sure no other policemen were standing nearby, and bolted. He ran to the emergency exit on the hallway, down six flights of stairs, out the service exit, and into the daylight of West Fifty-sixth Street.

In Andrew's hotel suite, Officer Caruso was emerging from the bathroom. "I meant to tell you," he said. "That soprano soloist isn't going to make it—" He stopped talking when he noticed that Andrew was not there. He looked into the bedroom. No Barnes. He ran to the open hallway door, panicked, said "Oh shit," and grabbed his walkie-talkie.

"They got him," he yelled. "The PLO—they got the conductor!"

The PLO did *not* have the conductor. Andrew was perfectly safe, walking up Broadway amid the afternoon crowd. He stopped at a hot dog vendor and bought himself a can of soda. He continued to make his way up Broadway, enjoying the sunshine, his anonymity (he could never have gone unrecognized in London), and above all, his sudden freedom. He was extremely pleased with himself for having escaped his hotel room. Then it occurred to him how absurd it was for a grown man to have to escape his own hotel room. Once again the theme of *Rhapsody in Blue* came into his head, and he hummed as he walked and drank his soda: "Dum-dum-dum-DUM! Khhh! DEE-da-DEE-da-DEE-da DUM-dum-dum-DUM, DEE-DA-DUM—"

Andrew stopped in front of an electronics store at Broadway and Fifty-eighth. The sign read "Liquidation Sale—Going Out of Business." Andrew was pleased—he thought he might score himself a bargain. He finished his soda while looking at the portable radios, tape recorders, cameras, and other gear in the store window. "Time to buy myself a present," he said, and he went into the store. He emerged ten minutes later with a pocket compact disc player and a lightweight pair of headphones. Next he went into a record store and bought himself a CD of Leonard Bernstein conducting *Rhapsody in Blue*.

From the record store he walked two blocks to Central Park. He planned to spend the rest of the afternoon sitting on a park bench, watching the people go by, and listening to Gershwin.

* * *

"He's *WHAT*?" George yelled into the telephone. "The *PLO*? From his hotel room? Well, find him, for chrissakes!"

George hung up and ran into Kevin's office down the hall.

Kevin had been looking over a newly arrived orchestral score composed by one of the chief contributors to the Symphony, Harrison Hardy. Hardy's family had made an enormous fortune in tin. Harrison gave the Symphony half a million dollars a year with the expectation that the orchestra would perform all of his compositions. The most charitable things Kevin could say about Harrison Hardy's compositions were that they were infrequent and that they were nicely copied out. Harrison paid a lot of money to a highly skilled music copier to write out his ideas. His ideas, unfortunately, were terrible.

Two years ago, the orchestra held its nose and performed his *Symphony for Elvis*. Last year's work, *Rio Blanco*, a tribute to peasants killed in the Hardy family tin mines, was scored for tenor saxophone and orchestra because Harrison believed, somehow, that Ecuadoran villagers liked modern jazz. Few Ecuadoran villagers in fact had any exposure to modern jazz. In Kevin's hands now was Harrison Hardy's latest accomplishment, a light opera based on Hitchcock's film *The Birds*.

Beads of sweat formed on George's forehead. When Kevin saw how pale George looked, he felt a pain in his own stomach. Although Kevin knew a lot about classical music, nothing in his background had prepared him for coping with kidnappings of conductors. George stood there, afraid to speak.

"What's going on?" Kevin asked nervously. He did not like the way George looked. George's eyes were extremely wide, giving him a vulnerable, puppy-dog look.

"The PLO grabbed Barnes," said George. "From his hotel room!"

"No, come on," said Kevin. "Why would they do that?"

"Maybe they've seen him conduct," said George, who looked so sad that Kevin wanted to hug him, or tell him everything was going to be all right, even though, quite clearly, the reverse was true. "Ugo's going to kill me. Everyone's going to blame *me* for this."

"Why?" asked Kevin, not understanding.

"Because whenever anything goes wrong around here, I get the blame," said George, sitting down. "It isn't fair. I should never have left Kansas City."

Kevin had to know whether this business about Andrew and the PLO was true or whether the strain on George had simply become too great and he had hallucinated it. He settled on a delicate approach.

"Now tell me what happened to Andrew," Kevin said. "Did somebody call?"

George nodded.

"Was it the PLO?"

George shook his head.

"Was it the police?" Kevin asked.

George nodded.

Oh my God, thought Kevin. *Something* has *happened to Andrew. And they really will blame George.*

"What did the police say?" Kevin asked.

"They said—they said—"George was sniffling—"they said that the policeman on duty went inside—into the hotel room to make sure everything was all right—and some men from the PLO came up and—"

George was trying very hard not to cry.

"You're being brave, George," said Kevin. "I admire that. Now, what happened next?"

George looked gratefully at Kevin. "You're a very nice man. Did I ever tell you that?"

"No," said Kevin, embarrassed. "You never did. Thank you."

"So then these men held out their guns and said 'We're with the PLO and we're taking Barnes,' and they locked the cop in the bathroom and they took Barnes away."

Kevin suddenly needed to sit down.

George nodded. "It's too bad, isn't it?" he asked. "Andrew seemed like such a nice man. Now they'll take him to Lebanon, and we won't see him for two years."

Lebanon? thought Kevin. "Um, George," he said, "maybe you ought to take it easy this afternoon. You know, take the afternoon off. How's that sound?"

"I couldn't do that," said George, shaking his head.

"I'm supposed to be in charge here. Ugo would be furious."

Kevin sighed. "Ugo probably would be," he said. "But Ugo isn't here. You should rest. Okay?"

"I guess I'd like to go home and go to bed," said George, looking sadder and sadder. "I'll ask Maria to make chicken Tetrazzini. She always makes chicken Tetrazzini when I don't feel well."

"Really?" Kevin asked, interested. "She makes a good chicken Tetrazzini? I love chicken Tetrazzini." Kevin thought of himself as something of a gourmet chef and was always on the lookout for new recipes.

"We should have you over for dinner sometime," said George, momentarily forgetting about his crisis. In fact, Kevin had been working directly under George for more than five years and had never been invited to dinner. George always meant to have Kevin over, but somehow he never got around to it. "Maybe after this whole thing blows over," George added.

"That would be very nice," Kevin said patiently. The time had come to focus George on the matter at hand. "But tell me, should we have the concert, even though Andrew is missing, or should we cancel it? What do you think we should do?"

George thought it over. He blew his nose again. "If we have it," he said, "then Donald'll *have* to conduct. Ugo'll be pissed. He hates Donald."

"He doesn't hate Donald," said Kevin. "*You* hate Donald."

"I don't hate him," said George. "I just wish he didn't have to call me Mr. Maria Barelli. I don't go around calling him Mr. Fudgepacker, do I?"

"George—"

"Wouldn't it be a much nicer world if people could actually come right out and tell each other how much they liked and respected each other?" asked George.

"That would be wonderful," Kevin agreed. "Can't we just concentrate on tonight?"

George nodded. He tried hard to concentrate. "If we don't have the concert, it'll cost, um, about fifty-six thousand dollars in receipts at the gate, plus another ten thousand or so in concessions, plus the cost of returning the money to the ticket buyers, plus the fee we're getting from PBS for the special. Plus we've got all those souvenir programs at three bucks a pop. And the Philadelphia Orchestra's doing the Mass next month, and the L.A. Philharmonic's doing it in November. So we'll lose the premiere, and all the money, if we don't go ahead. We've got to do it.''

"Okay," said Kevin. *Thank you, Jesus,* he thought, *for restoring George's brain.* "Do you want to tell Donald, or should I?"

"Would *you* mind doing it?" George asked. He felt worn out from his efforts of concentration. He sensed that he was losing his grip again. "I really don't think he respects me."

"Of course he respects you," said Kevin. "And I'll be happy to do it. Maybe you should just go to your office and rest, okay?"

George thought it over.

"Okay," he said.

"And don't tell *anybody* what's happened, okay?" said Kevin.

"Okay," said George.

"Promise?"

"Promise."

"There's a good fellow," said Kevin, patting George on the back. "Now you go to your office and I'll have them send you something to eat. Okay?"

"Even the caterers don't respect me," said George.

"Yes, they do," Kevin said soothingly. "They just told me yesterday what a good job you do."

"They *did*?" George asked, rising. "See? Isn't it nice when people can tell each other how much they like each other? Wouldn't it be nice if the whole world were like that?"

"Now, remember," said Kevin. "Straight to your office and don't tell anyone a thing."

"Okay," said George. "Kevin, you're a very nice man."

"Thank you, George," said Kevin. "And so are you."

"Yes," said George, thinking it over. "And so am I." He walked out of Kevin's office. In the hallway, he ran into a reporter from a local news radio station doing a background piece on tonight's premiere.

"What's new?" asked the reporter.

"The PLO kidnapped Barnes from his hotel room," said George. "They took him away. Donald is going to conduct tonight."

"Are you *serious*?" asked the stunned reporter.

"Yes," said George, nodding his head. "I'm serious." He walked away.

"Mr. Smith—Mr. Smith—" the reporter yelled. George ignored him. He wanted to go sit down in his big, comfortable desk chair, the one Ugo gave him last year as a birthday present.

The reporter ran to a pay telephone and called his newsroom.

"The PLO's got Barnes, the guy who's conducting the Symphony tonight at Carnegie Hall. . . . No, I'm not kidding. I just heard it from the GM of the Symphony. . . ."

Within ten minutes, every radio station in the city had broadcast the Barnes story. News of his kidnapping crossed on the Associated Press wire service at 3:55 P.M. and on the United Press International at 3:58. Police, FBI agents, reporters, and camera crews flooded into the Meridien Hotel and Carnegie Hall, taking statements from everyone they could find. Members of the hotel staff, caught up in all the excitement, were unable to agree on how many kidnappers there were and whether they wore white robes, business suits, or T-shirts and jeans.

So many musicians, stagehands, and technicians tried to get bets on Donald that Alvin Reischel had to lay off some of the action with a guy in the lighting booth named Leo who was thought to have ties to the Mob. The odds on Donald dropped to one to three. Andrew suddenly became a twenty-to-one longshot. If Andrew ended up conducting the concert, Alvin Reischel would be out at least eighteen thousand dollars. Alvin, for the first time in his life, began to root for the PLO.

* * *

In the crowded sub-basement of the Midtown South station house, a detective was asking a very nervous Officer Caruso the same questions he had already been asked a dozen times in the last twenty minutes:

"Are you sure he was kidnapped? Are you sure it was the PLO?"

Officer Caruso decided it was too late to change his story now. He gripped the sides of his chair and stared straight ahead. The room was packed with detectives from Officer Caruso's precinct house as well as representatives of the police commissioner and the mayor's office.

"Yes," he said resolutely, his voice cracking from the strain. "They said they were from the PLO. There were two of them."

"Did they say where they were taking him?" asked the detective.

"Yes," said Officer Caruso, feeling very sorry for himself and wishing that he had not needed to go to the bathroom. It was only his first year on the force. His family would be so embarrassed.

"And where was that?" asked the detective.

"Northern New Jersey." This is where Officer Caruso lived.

"Where in northern New Jersey?" asked the detective, exchanging meaningful glances with an assistant chief of police.

Officer Caruso did not want to say Tenafly, which was his own hometown. "Saddle River," he said. It was the first name that popped into his head.

The detective looked confused. "Saddle River?" he repeated. "Is that technically northern New Jersey?"

"You think these PLO guys are experts in geography or something?" asked Officer Caruso, seizing the offensive.

"Yeah, I suppose you're right," said the detective. "Okay, everybody, let's go."

By four-thirty, hundreds of New Jersey state policemen had surrounded the exclusive suburb of Saddle River, New Jersey, and began to conduct a house-to-house search for the missing conductor while dozens more hovered in helicopters overhead.

* * *

In their hotel suite, Elizabeth watched the policemen dust the furniture for fingerprints. She hoped that they would be successful in their search for Andrew. She did not want anyone to kill him. She wanted to do it herself.

The object of all this attention was sitting on a large rock in the middle of Central Park. He was wearing his headphones and a pair of sunglasses he had bought from a street vendor. He felt bad about sneaking out on Officer Caruso, but he was sure that the young patrolman would not mind. Andrew was enjoying the sunshine, listening to his Gershwin, making little conducting motions and humming quietly to himself, "Dum-dum-dum-DUM! Khhh! DEE-da-DEE-da-DEE-da   DUM-dum-dum-DUM, DEE-da DEE da-da DEE-dee-dee."

TWENTY-SEVEN

"I've always had this fantasy," said Alison Gardiner. She and Corinne were having coffee at the Help Wanted, an uneasy truce in place between them. They knew nothing of Barnes's disappearance.

"Is that so?" Corinne said, pretending not to be interested. She looked out the window. "Look at all those cops."

"It happens right here, in Carnegie Hall," Alison said, oblivious to Corinne's lack of interest. "I'm with a guy and he buys tickets to an entire box of seats in the first tier." Alison was referring to the lower of two levels of boxes that circle the hall. Ticket holders reach their box by passing through a small anteroom. Each anteroom has its own door.

"You know those little rooms," Alison continued,

"between the hallway and the box? Where you hang your coat? Now, if you buy all the tickets in a box for a concert, no one can come in. And no one could *see* in. It would be amazing. Wouldn't it be great to make love with a guy on the floor of an anteroom *during a concert*? They even have mirrors!"

Corinne stifled a yawn. "Is that your fantasy?" she asked, sounding unimpressed. She admitted to herself, though, that it might be fun.

Alison nodded. *"Look what I have,"* she said. She took an envelope from her purse and emptied its contents, eight tickets, on the table. "A high school orchestra's doing a free concert tomorrow afternoon. I got a whole box! When I told the guy in the box office I wanted a whole box, he thought I was crazy. So I told him I had a nephew in the orchestra. Pretty smart, huh?"

"Yeah, pretty smart," said Corinne. *Some people have all the fun,* she thought. Then she wondered when fun stopped being a priority in her own life.

"The only problem is that the first half is all Aaron Copland, and it may not be *loud* enough. I mean, if they were playing Gershwin, or Wagner, even the people in the next *box* couldn't hear us. I'm going to ask Andrew if he wants to come. He's probably got nothing to do tomorrow afternoon. Isn't that great?"

Alison giggled. "I didn't even tell you the best part. They're finishing with *Bolero*, and then the *1812 Overture*. Isn't that *hysterical*?"

"Would you do me a favor?" asked Corinne, who had heard enough.

"Sure, anything. What?"

"If you're going to make love with Andrew Barnes in a box in Carnegie Hall, would you mind not telling *me* about it?"

The comment surprised Alison, and she was about to lash out at Corinne for her lack of—well, for her lack of *something*. Compassion, maybe, or adequate interest in Alison's affairs. Alison knew Corinne lived vicariously through her conquests. Corinne's lack of interest confused Alison. Suddenly Alison caught on. She put the tickets back in the envelope and the envelope back in her purse. "Were you involved with him in the conservatory?" she asked. "Is that it?"

Corinne looked away.

"You were, weren't you?" Alison asked. She felt awful. "That explains everything. Oh, I can't believe I said all that stuff about wanting to sleep with him. Oh, Corinne, I'm so sorry."

"It's okay," said Corinne. "Forget it."

"No, it's not okay," Alison insisted. "I'm so embarrassed. Really, I'm sorry. If I'd only known—"

Alison's sincerity touched Corinne. "It's okay, girl," Corinne said. "No harm done. No real harm, anyway."

Alison was still shaking her head. "I was thoughtless," she said. "I really apologize."

Corinne had to laugh. "Okay, already. You apologized. Let's forget it."

"Did you love him?" Alison asked. As thoughtless as the question might have been, she had to know the entire story.

Corinne nodded slightly.

"What happened?" Alison asked.

Corinne thought it over. "I guess Elizabeth happened," she said.

"Who's Elizabeth? Oh, is that his wife?"

Corinne looked around the crowded restaurant, uncomfortable with the idea of discussing her private life in a public place. She sipped her coffee and spoke so softly that Alison had to strain to hear.

"I don't know how she did it," Corinne began. "All I knew was that one day Andy and I were 'engaged to be engaged,' and then the next day we weren't."

"*You* were engaged to be engaged to Andrew Barnes?" Alison asked, amazed.

Corinne shrugged. "Well, maybe not exactly," she admitted. "Maybe I was reading too much into things. But he said that he cared about me and that he hated to hurt me, but that there were certain aspects of his career that he had to try out before he made any commitments."

"Like what?" asked Alison. "What was he talking about?"

"Conducting, basically."

"That's crazy," said Alison, shaking her head. "I

thought he wanted to conduct from the time he was six. That's what it says in the program notes.'' Alison had already seen the program. Chorus and orchestra members sometimes receive copies of the program early on the day of the concert. The arrival of the programs from the printer triggers a stampede of performers who check first to see that their names have been included and spelled correctly. Alison's was.

"That'll teach you to believe program notes,'' said Corinne. "Elizabeth probably wrote it. All he wanted to do was teach music in his high school and coach wrestling.''

"I've seen his wrestling moves,'' said Alison, thinking back to his moves in bed the day before. "But a high school music teacher? Wasn't he a little overqualified?''

"Not Andy. He was a wonderful man in a lot of ways, but back then, there wasn't a single job in music that he would have been overqualified for. What do you mean, you've seen his wrestling moves?''

"Forget I even said anything,'' said Alison, who wanted to keep Corinne from getting upset again.

"There's something I want to ask you,'' said Corinne, looking serious. "As long as we're talking about Andrew. Doesn't it *bother* you, even a little bit, sleeping with someone just to get ahead in your career?''

Alison detected no malice in Corinne's question. Corinne simply wanted to know.

"You're not going to be judgmental, are you?'' Alison asked. To her mind, there was nothing worse than people who were judgmental. Alison liked the bumper stickers on people's cars that said "Live and Let Live'' and she told herself that she would get one if she ever owned a car.

Corinne shook her head. "I just want to know if you think it's moral. Using sex to advance your career.''

"What does sex have to do with morality?'' Alison asked, sounding innocent. Then she grinned. "Just kidding. Look. There are thousands of sopranos trying to make a living in New York, right? You know how they support themselves? Word processing.''

"Really?'' asked Corinne. "I thought all the starving sopranos waited table.''

"You're not taking me seriously. You asked a question and I'm trying to give you an answer."

"Sorry," said Corinne.

"They probably used to be waitresses, but if they can type, they become word processors and work as temps. It pays more."

"So?"

"So I think if you're a really excellent singer," said Alison, "word processing is *demeaning*. You know my friend Carla?"

"The soprano?" asked Corinne. "The one who lives way downtown?"

Alison nodded. "Her boyfriend's a choral conductor. She sings in one of his choruses. They both had their Carnegie Hall debuts the same night. He conducted the Fauré *Requiem* and she was the soloist. The next night, she was back at her word processing job, working from three to eleven. Typing wills. And *he* was back at this Italian restaurant where he works, waiting tables. The night after their Carnegie Hall debuts! That's humiliating! I'm not going through something like that. The night after *my* Carnegie Hall debut, I'll go—" She paused. "Someplace nice."

"And if you sleep with a conductor just once," said Corinne, "you can avoid all that typing? Is that it?"

Alison shrugged. "You know how much Carla pays for her voice lessons? A hundred and fifty bucks an *hour*. Plus airfare on the shuttle, because her teacher's down in Washington. She practically has to work for a whole week to pay for one lesson. You think I want to do that? Support some vocal teacher's mortgage payments with my word processing?"

"But what if it doesn't work?" Corinne asked. "I mean, what if Andy just forgets about you? Maybe a lot of women come on to him."

Alison's first reaction was to say that he could not possibly forget her, not after yesterday afternoon and last night. She had been good—and she knew it. Then it occurred to her that she might not be the only soprano in Manhattan trying to sleep her way out of the typing pool.

"He won't forget," Alison said, summoning false courage. Now her career and her vanity were on the line.

"Stranger things have happened," said Corinne. "Are you prepared to sleep with *every* conductor until you get a break?"

Alison thought it over. "No," she said solemnly.

"Good," said Corinne, finally studying the menu. "I'm glad to hear that."

Then Alison grinned. "I'll only sleep with the cute ones. I mean, you might as well be sleeping with *somebody*, right?"

"You're hopeless," Corinne said, but she had to laugh. She looked again at the hordes of police outside the window. They were all over Fifty-seventh Street. "I wonder what *that's* all about."

TWENTY-EIGHT

Andrew turned off his CD player, stood up, and headed south, out of Central Park and back to his hotel. It was six o'clock. He did not know how he was going to explain to Officer Caruso where he had been for the past two and a half hours. Then he decided that he was a world-famous conductor and did not have to explain *anything*.

He saw the first of the dozens of police officers when he rounded the corner of Sixth Avenue and Fifty-seventh Street. *I wonder what* that's *all about,* he thought.

And then, all of a sudden, he had a sinking feeling in his stomach. "Oh no," he said, as he approached the hotel.

"You can't go in there," said a policeman, a twenty-year veteran of the force with a bristle haircut and a prodigious stomach.

"Why not?" Andrew asked, surprised. He looked at

the officer's stomach and wondered whether he ever had to chase suspects down the street. He hoped not.

"One of the guests was kidnapped," said the policeman. "A conductor."

Oh, Christ, thought Andrew. "Andrew Barnes?" he asked.

The policeman nodded. "That's the guy."

"But *I'm* Andrew Barnes!"

"Yeah, and I'm Mantovani," said the cop. "Move along."

"I'm Andrew Barnes," Andrew repeated. "And I wasn't kidnapped, I was in the park!"

"Look, pal—" the policeman began. "If you're Andrew Barnes, what were you doing there?" asked the policeman. Andrew looked at his name badge. His name was Officer Moscowitz.

"I was listening to a CD," said Andrew, showing Officer Moscowitz his portable CD player.

"Of what?"

"Of Gershwin," said Andrew, trying to imagine why the policeman should care. *"Rhapsody in Blue."*

"You're full of it," said the policeman, making a dismissive motion with his hand. "Andrew Barnes would never listen to Gershwin. He doesn't conduct anything twentieth century."

"What are you talking about?" Andrew asked, bewildered. "How would you know that?"

"Look," said Officer Moscowitz, both hands on his hips, "just 'cause I'm a cop doesn't mean I don't know about classical music, okay?"

"But how would you know that Barnes doesn't conduct Gershwin?"

"Look, pal," said Officer Moscowitz, becoming annoyed, "my wife works for a travel agency, okay? Last year we went to London. We went to a concert every night. And I'm telling you. *Barnes doesn't do modern,* okay? He stops at Brahms. So do I, incidentally," Officer Moscowitz added, his tone suddenly more conversational than confrontational. "My wife likes the early-twentieth-century stuff. You know, your Stravinsky, your Bartók. I go along with Hindemith and Fauré, two creative geniuses, in my opinion, but I can't handle Bartók. Especially his chamber music. It really does nothing for me."

"I know what you mean," Andrew murmured sympathetically. "Bartók *is* pretty heavy."

"Exactly," the policeman said, looking approvingly at Andrew. He was happy to have someone to whom he could display his knowledge of great music. Some of the other policemen present noticed that Officer Moscowitz was talking about music again. He had been carrying on incessantly about music ever since they had been assigned to the hotel where Barnes was staying. They rolled their eyes and smiled and gave each other knowing glances.

"*These* clowns," said Officer Moscowitz, motioning with contempt toward his colleagues. "My wife and me— we both like the opera. We went to something every night. We had a very nice trip."

"I'm so pleased," said Andrew, always glad to meet a patron of the arts. Andrew was hoping that after Officer Moscowitz finished reciting his opinions about music, he might allow Andrew to enter the hotel. Andrew therefore thought it best to humor him and his opinions, which, so far at least, were not radically different from his own.

"Oh yeah," said Officer Moscowitz, taking off his cap and scratching his bristly hair. "We heard all the orchestras in London. It was very pleasant."

"*All* the orchestras?" Andrew asked, his vanity rising. "Did you get to the Royal Symphonic?"

"Sure," said the policeman, putting his cap on his head. He hitched his belt up over the beginning of his belly. "We saw Barnes. All-Beethoven concert. The Seventh Symphony and the Violin Concerto. Some eighteen-year-old girl soloist."

"What did you think?" Andrew asked, unable to resist. The concert had been a triumph for him: the orchestra received great reviews and he got the soloist's phone number.

"Huh?" asked Officer Moscowitz. "Not bad. Not great. Kind of a showman, know what I mean? He thinks he's Leonard Bernstein up there. He gets a little carried away with himself. You know, on the podium."

"That's not true!" Andrew said indignantly. "He does not!"

"Oh, I don't know," said Officer Moscowitz, convinced of his opinions. "We had good seats, right down close, and I think he was hamming it up for the crowd. Hey, they love him over there. But I think he's a showboat."

"Of course they love him over there!" Andrew exclaimed. "He sells more tickets than any other conductor!"

"That's what I mean," said Officer Moscowitz, his point proven. "It's the showboating."

"It's not showboating!" Andrew was practically shouting now. "He happens to love the music!"

The policeman made a face. "You're wrong. He loves the *applause*. They all do." He laughed. "Hey, while I was in London I heard a story about Barnes. You want to hear it?"

"I don't know," said Andrew, his feelings hurt.

"Come on, it'll make you laugh," said Officer Moscowitz. It was not every day that he could air all of his opinions about music. He was enjoying himself. "You know," he began, "at the end of the concert? If this guy Barnes doesn't hear people yelling *bravo*—you know what he does?"

"What?" Andrew asked, not sure that he wanted to find out.

The policeman nodded knowingly. "He takes a *big* bow and bends his face into his body like this—" he demonstrated for Andrew. "And then *he* starts yelling *bravo*. So no one can see him doing it. It only takes one guy to get it started. It's like doing the Wave at a ballpark. Pretty soon everybody's yelling *bravo*. And then Barnes gets this real surprised look on his face—you know, 'Aw, you shouldn't have,' that kind of look? You believe that?"

"I've never done that in my life!" said Andrew, appalled by the story.

"I'm not talking about *you*," said Officer Moscowitz. "I'm talking about Alvin Barnes."

"Alvin? Andrew! And *I'm* Andrew Barnes!"

The policeman studied Andrew carefully. "No, you're

not," he concluded. "Barnes is a lot taller than you are. I've *seen* him."

"It's the podium," said Andrew, his desperation mounting. "It makes you *look* taller."

"Really?" asked Officer Moscowitz, impressed. "I never knew that."

"Sure," said Andrew. "It gives you four to six inches extra in most people's minds. I read a study on it once. A lot of conductors are tiny."

"I never knew that," said Officer Moscowitz, rubbing his large chin. "My wife will find that very interesting. She likes conductors. She introduced me to classical music. She's a flutist."

"Flautist," Andrew corrected absentmindedly.

"Flautist," repeated Officer Moscowitz. "Thank you. I always forget that word." By now, though, he had grown weary of the conversation and was conscious now that the whole contingent of police was laughing at him and his opinions. "It's been very nice talking to you about music," he added. "I happen to know a lot about it for a policeman."

"You know quite a lot for anyone," said Andrew. "But I happen to be Andrew Barnes, and I don't think I've made clear to you how important it is for you *to let me in that hotel*."

Officer Moscowitz crossed his arms. The conversation was over.

"If I weren't Andrew Barnes," Andrew began, trying to employ logic to convince Officer Moscowitz that he was not lying, "then how would I know the name of the conductor who's staying here?"

"What are you, a wise guy?" asked Officer Moscowitz, getting provoked. "Hey, give me that," he told another cop who was carrying a copy of the afternoon edition of the *New York Post*. He showed it to Andrew. The massive front-page headline read "CONDUCTOR KIDNAPPED—Andrew Barnes Taken From Hotel Room At Gunpoint."

Andrew nearly fainted. "But I'm telling you," he said, *"I'm Andrew Barnes!* I've got *identification*!"

Before Andrew could take his wallet out of his back pocket, Officer Moscowitz shoved a finger in his chest.

"I've had it with you, pal. Now move along. If you don't quit bothering me, I'm gonna run you in!"

"Okay, okay," said Andrew, backing away from the policeman. "I'm going." He was secretly delighted by the policeman's words, because he had not been sure whether cops really used the expression "I'm going to run you in." Andrew always used it when he told his story about the trumpeter in the bushes in Central Park. More to the point, though, Andrew was anxious to get into the hotel because his formal wear, his baton, and his conductor's score were all in his hotel room.

Andrew decided to try the back entrance to the hotel. He rounded the block only to find the service entrance equally full of policemen. He did not want to become embroiled in debate with another musically trained policeman, so he continued up Fifty-sixth Street toward the stage entrance of Carnegie Hall. Still more police blocked the way. An enormous crowd had gathered. Andrew could not even get near the hall.

"This is crazy," Andrew told himself, looking at his watch. Six-fifteen. The concert would begin in less than two hours. He saw a pay telephone at the corner of Seventh Avenue and Fifty-sixth Street. He waited until it was free and tried the number for Carnegie Hall. It was busy. He tried it again. Still busy. Several people were lined up waiting for the phone. Andrew tried the number for his hotel. Still busy.

"This is unbelievable," he said, looking around. He saw a formal shop across Seventh Avenue. Formals By Max. He had an idea. He ran across Seventh Avenue and into the store.

"I'd like to buy a tux," he said.

"We don't sell, we only rent," said the clerk, a man in his fifties. He had the largest ears that Andrew had ever seen and wore a little button that said "Kiss me, I'm in the garment business."

"I'd like to *rent* a tux, in that case," he said.

The clerk looked Andrew over, shook his head, and sighed.

"I've got nothing that'll fit. Why don't you come back Monday?"

Andrew began to panic. "What do you mean, you've got nothing that'll fit?"

"You're a forty-two regular, right?"

Andrew nodded quickly.

"I just rented everything from thirty-six to forty-four. Sixty Japanese guys. You should have got here before they did. Then I would have had something nice for you."

"Sixty Japanese guys?" Andrew repeated. "Where were they going?"

"Carnegie Hall," said the clerk. "Some kind of big concert."

"Don't you have anything at all?" Andrew was becoming frantic. "It's an emergency—I've *got* to have something for tonight!"

The clerk looked Andrew over again and frowned.

"The closest thing I have to your size is a forty-six. But I don't think you're going to like it."

"Of course I'll like it," said Andrew. "Where is it?"

"I'm just not sure it's *you*," said the clerk, shaking his head. "The style, I mean. It's for a wedding on Sunday. If you *promise* to get it back tomorrow morning—"

"I promise," Andrew said quickly.

The clerk sighed. "Okay," he said. "But don't say I didn't warn you."

Twenty minutes later, Andrew emerged from the shop in a mint green tuxedo two sizes too big for him. The clerk, whose name, Andrew noticed, was Max, pinned the trousers, but the jacket flapped in the breeze. Andrew bought a ruffled shirt in his own size. He had to use cardboard cuff links and studs, though. Max did not rent shoes. Andrew was still wearing his high-tops. He figured that he could borrow shoes once he got into Carnegie Hall. He left the rest of his street clothes in the shop.

It was six forty-five. The concert would begin in an hour and fifteen minutes.

Andrew, oblivious to the stares of the passers-by, ran to the pay phone again and tried the hotel and Carnegie Hall. Both numbers were still busy. *This is terrible,* he thought to himself. *And I look terrible, too.* On top of everything else, he was hungry again. He went to another hot dog vendor, bought himself a hot dog, and ate it, trying to keep the mustard and sauerkraut off his rented tuxedo. He tried to think of what to do next.

TWENTY-NINE

The rehearsal room of an orchestra chorus usually jumps in the hour before a concert. Newer members mill around, asking each other if their formal wear looks right. Veteran campaigners take things more calmly, sitting as comfortably as is possible on the metal folding chairs, sipping their coffee or tea. If the upcoming performance is the second time through a given piece, chorus members will tell each other in grave tones what went wrong the night before, even if nothing went wrong. To say, "I thought we sounded pretty good last night" is to admit that your ear is not keen enough to notice all the subtle mistakes the group made. Such statements usually win not agreement but dirty looks.

Tonight, though, the usual rules were suspended. The chorus members were too frightened by what had happened to Andrew to worry about their bow ties or their makeup. None of them could ever remember a conductor being kidnapped before. Donald Bright, a Styrofoam cup of coffee in his hand, perched on the edge of his conductor's stool and gazed at his chorus with an expression of impending doom. All but some latecomers were seated. Corinne and Alison were in their proper seats. The singers looked straight at Donald, giving him anxious looks.

Everyone except Donald was worried about Andrew. Though it was five minutes after seven, less than an hour before the concert, Donald remained certain that Andrew somehow would escape his captors and deny Donald the chance to conduct the Mass. That everyone else believed

Andrew to be bound and gagged in a basement in Saddle River, New Jersey, was of no consequence to Donald. His firm belief in Andrew's safety and in the likelihood of his reappearance was his mechanism for coping with stage fright. His fear of performing had begun to overwhelm him.

Donald decided to ease the tension with a joke. In a voice loud enough to be heard throughout the rehearsal room, Donald asked James, who was seated at the piano: "James, is this a Steinway or a Baldwin?"

The room became silent as the chorus waited for James's reply.

"It's a Baldwin," James said, not sure why Donald should care right now.

"Well, in *that* case," Donald said with a grin, and he set his coffee cup down on the piano, to the laughter of the chorus members.

"I'm excited," he said, and he smiled, and the chorus, relieved, laughed again. "Why shouldn't I be excited?" he asked them. "You're going to be *marvelous*. You're going to be partners with Mozart."

The chorus practically shivered with anticipation.

"I know that you're all very concerned about what's happened to Andrew. I share your concerns. But I'll tell you something. I'm just *convinced* he's going to show up and conduct the concert tonight. I just can't believe anything bad has happened to him. You'll see."

The chorus members looked at each other nervously. They thought Donald's optimism was misplaced.

"You're going to make wonderful music," said Donald, "and you're going to make history at the same time. Leonard Bernstein's here. My conducting professor, Albert Nouse, is here. My high school music teacher, LouCelle Fertik, came up all the way from Florida. My *mother* is here, God bless her little heart, and she *despises* Mozart."

The chorus responded with laughter.

"I don't know what more I can tell you about the Mass. You know how I found it. You know how much this night means to me."

An edge crept into his voice.

"You know how little I think of the man who's going

to lead you. But I won't get started. Not tonight. I promise.''

Halting laughter from the chorus.

''How can Donald make fun of Andrew when he's been kidnapped?'' Alison whispered to Corinne.

''He must really think Andrew's going to show up,'' Corinne whispered back.

''Just a few notes on the dress rehearsal this morning,'' Donald said, getting down to business. He glanced in the direction of Corinne and Alison, as intolerant as ever of people speaking while he was addressing the group. ''Watch your cutoffs. Especially your final s's and t's. Those t's in particular. You sounded more like a machine gun in a gangster movie than a Mozart chorus. I know you aren't getting clear cutoffs from Barnes, but there's nothing I can do about that. I've asked him to be clearer, believe me.

''Look, the most important thing I can tell you is this: during the fugue in the Credo, when you see Barnes conducting with his big, broad, meaningless sweeps through the air—'' Bright mimicked him perfectly—''I want you to *translate* that in your own heads to this—'' And he conducted for a moment in his own precise, staccato style. ''Do you follow me?''

The chorus burst into laughter, but they wondered how Donald could be so sure that Andrew was all right. There was something eerie about Donald explaining how to sing for Andrew when Andrew had disappeared.

''All right. Be wonderful tonight. I'll be out there watching and wishing I was with you. Announcements.''

Donald Bright stepped off the podium to a rousing ovation from his chorus. He looked at them in surprise. He felt tears forming and he blinked them away. The applause lasted long after he had left the rehearsal room.

Gretchen Hemenway, the administrative assistant, stepped forward. ''Line up rows one and three stage right,'' she began, ''and rows two and four left. Jay Gregory will lead rows one and three and Tim McKenna two and four. Line up at ten minutes to eight *exactly*. That gives you fifty minutes, five-oh. Please be on time. Once you're onstage remain standing until you get the signal to sit. Keep your music in your right hand when you're coming out onstage. If you don't have a black folder for your score see me *now*. Any questions about the lineup?''

Silence.

''Good. Please. No talking onstage. *Quiet* page turns. It sounds awful unless you all turn your pages quietly. Also, no excessive aftershave or perfume, if it's not too late. Please be considerate of your fellow performers. Also, if this is your first concert, please don't *wave* to anyone in the house. Just nod your head or smile. They'll see you. And that's about it.'' Then she smiled. No one had ever seen her smile before. ''Oh,'' she added. ''And remember to have a good time.''

The chorus stood up with much scraping of metal chairs on the linoleum floor. The room filled with excited conversation. Some of the tenors heard that Alvin Reischel was offering thirty to one on Andrew and three to one against on Donald. The way the bets were running, if Donald conducted, Alvin would be up about four thousand dollars. If Andrew turned up, Alvin would be out close to sixteen thousand dollars. A number of singers headed over to the musicians' lounge to find an increasingly anxious Reischel to place their bets.

THIRTY

At seven-thirty, as Carnegie Hall's doors opened to admit the audience, Andrew Barnes was standing on West Fifty-seventh Street amid sixty tuxedo-clad Japanese men, scratching his head and trying to figure out how to get into the hall. The street was crowded with concertgoers and police officers, except for two adjacent, empty expanses of sidewalk across the street from the hall. These spots, marked off with blue-and-white police sawhorses, were to have been holding areas for the two religious groups that the police expected in large numbers, picketing Barnes's appearance. Barnes's absence, or perhaps a general lethargy on the part of the protesters, now that he had been kidnapped, resulted in large numbers of policemen surrounding two empty holding areas.

Andrew, unaware of this limitation on his detractors' civil liberties, hoped he might find someone with an extra ticket to sell. He was not the only one, though. The many favorable newspaper stories and television news features on Barnes and the Mass, results of the sodden press conference, brought a flood of ticket seekers to the hall. They could be distinguished from the ticket holders by their unhappy expressions and by the twenty-dollar bills they held in their hands, signals that they were in the market for tickets. The concert was long sold out. No one seemed to have tickets to sell.

Andrew took two twenty-dollar bills out of his pocket, held them up in his hand, and went through the crowd, shouting, "Who's got one ticket? Who's got one for tonight?" He felt ridiculous and he knew he looked ridiculous, but he could think of no alternative. No one had an extra ticket for the nervous man in the mint green tuxedo. After a few minutes of working the crowd, Andrew, nearly exhausted, went and leaned against the entrance to the building. The concert poster with his picture was right behind him; no one seemed to notice the resemblance.

Then Andrew spotted a young man standing near the curb and holding a ticket. Andrew fought his way through the crowd and ran over to him. The left cuff of his trousers had come undone and Andrew nearly tripped over it.

"How much do you want?" he asked, out of breath.

The young man looked him over. "Two hundred dollars," he told Andrew. "Take it or leave it."

"*Two hundred dollars?*" Andrew repeated. "That's robbery!"

"You want to get in there or don't you?" asked the young man.

Andrew examined the ticket. "But it's a balcony seat!"

he exclaimed. "You want two hundred dollars for a balcony seat?"

"Two hundred bucks," the young man insisted. "If you don't pay it someone else will. I don't have all day."

Andrew sighed. He opened his wallet and removed another hundred and sixty dollars. *I'm glad I'm rich,* he told himself.

The young man stashed the money in his pants pocket and handed Andrew the ticket. "See you inside," he said. "I'm sitting next to you."

"Like hell you are," said Andrew, looking at the ticket to make sure it was for tonight's concert. It was.

"I was supposed to go with my father," the young man explained. "But he just had heart-valve surgery and—"

"Tell your father I hope he feels better," said Andrew. "You, on the other hand, can drop dead."

"Is that any way to thank me?" asked the young man, stung by Andrew's words. "When I just made it possible for you to attend a very important concert?"

Unreal, Andrew thought, as he turned his back on the young man and headed toward the hall. *Scalped at my own concert.*

Now, though, everything would be easy, Andrew told himself, as he pushed through the crowd. He would enter the hall, passing through the metal detectors installed to protect him from terrorists. Then he would race down the parquet, as the orchestra seats in Carnegie Hall are called, and climb up onstage. Then he would find Kevin and George, explain everything to them, and everything would be all right.

Andrew, bristling with tension, handed his ticket to the usher and waited impatiently for him to tear the ticket and hand him the stub.

"Other entrance," said the usher.

"What?" Andrew asked.

"Other entrance. This ticket's for the balcony. Go in over there."

"But I have to be downstairs—" Andrew said, alarmed.

"Your ticket says balcony. You go in over there," and the usher pointed to the separate entrance for the balcony seats.

"But—"

"Come on, you're holding up the line."

"Oh, Christ," said Andrew, and he pushed past the surprised concertgoers and ran for the balcony entrance.

Onstage, all the orchestra members were in place and were warming up. Gretchen Hemenway carried a clipboard and stood in front of the chorus, making sure that the singers were spaced evenly on the long wooden risers. Then she gave the chorus members their cue to sit and she went offstage. Watching from the side were Kevin, George, Donald, James, and Elizabeth. George had taken a number of sedatives. Donald, resplendent in white tie and tails, mopped his brow. Kevin was looking at his watch. Seven fifty-four P.M. James was biting his nails. Elizabeth showed no emotion at all. The house-to-house search in Saddle River had turned up a large number of illegal immigrants working as housekeepers, but there was still no sign of Andrew Barnes.

"He's going to turn up," said Donald, ever the fatalist. "I just know it."

"Don't be stupid, Donald," said Elizabeth. "We'll never seen him alive again. I think we all know *that* by now."

"He *is* running out of time," said Kevin, alarmed at how calmly Elizabeth accepted the thought of the loss of her husband. "Donald, *you're* our conductor tonight, and you're gonna do a great job. I can tell."

Donald looked morose. "Andy'll show up. He's screwed me out of everything else I've ever wanted. He'll screw me out of this, too. He'll find a way. You'll see."

"I respect you, Donald," George said suddenly. "I really do. Do you respect me?"

Donald looked at George and then at Kevin.

"Tell him you respect him," Kevin whispered in Donald's ear. "Please. He's not well."

Donald looked questioningly at Kevin, who raised his eyebrows and nodded.

"Of course I respect you," said Donald, trying to sound genuine. "George, I respect you very much."

George only looked sadder. "You're just saying that

because you want to make me feel better," he told Donald.

Donald turned to Kevin. "Do I need this?" he asked.

James, standing next to Donald, was too scared to speak. He was trying not to think of all the terrible things that would happen to him once the police learned that he was the source of the threats. He was convinced that he had already been identified and would be arrested at the end of the concert.

"Five minutes," shouted a stagehand. "You're on in five, Maestro."

"No doubt in my mind," Donald said quietly. "I *know* he's going to show up. You'll see."

The concertgoers making the long climb to the balcony were surprised to see a man in a pale green tuxedo and black high-top sneakers shoot past them. Andrew nearly knocked over an elderly couple, apologized profusely, turned quickly, and bumped into an usher. It was Eric, the young man who had spoken to Donald the previous morning. He recognized Andrew.

"Maestro Barnes," he said, eyes open wide, a hand over his mouth, "what are *you* doing up here? And what are you *wearing*?"

Andrew did not respond. He looked down to the stage, which seemed very far away. He found himself thinking of the Gershwin concert, which he had watched from the same balcony view. Then he spied a fire exit, dodged some more concertgoers, and ran out the door.

"Not that one!" yelled the usher. "That doesn't go backstage—that just takes you outside again! The *other* door takes you backstage!"

It was too late—Andrew hadn't heard. He ran down the fire escape at top speed and found himself in an alley near the stage door on Fifty-sixth Street. He was winded from running up and down all those stairs, and now he wasn't even inside the hall any more. He was disgusted with himself.

The first oboist emerged from a door at the side of the stage and blew an unusually emotional A. She took the news of Andrew's disappearance the hardest of anyone in the orchestra. If only she had been a little more forward, she told herself, Barnes would have been in her apartment on the West Side and the PLO could never have kidnapped him. Then it occurred to her that the PLO might have kidnapped both of them, so maybe it was all right that nothing had happened between herself and Barnes. The other orchestra members responded to her A with a final burst of tuning and were still. The house lights dimmed.

The audience was silent, save a few rattling programs, some clearing of throats, and the unwrapping of candy and cough drops. All eyes were on the doorway from which the oboist had stepped. At any moment Donald Bright, followed by the two soloists, would start through the doorway to great applause. The three would acknowledge the audience with small bows. Donald would give an encouraging smile to the orchestra and chorus, look about to make sure that all were ready, raise his baton, and begin the Mass.

But there was no Donald.

"These things never start on time," Corinne whispered to Alison. They were seated in the first row of singers, near the tympani. They would have preferred to be anywhere else, because you can get an enormous headache from the tympani, but those were the breaks.

"Oh, of course they don't," Alison answered knowledgeably. "Everyone knows that."

"Donald," said Kevin, out of patience, "I'm going to make the announcement that you're filling in. When I get done, I want you out onstage. Andrew is *not* coming. *You* are going to conduct."

"Don't even bother," said Donald, sadly shaking his head. "He's on his way. I know it."

"You're as crazy as George," said Kevin, and he ran to the sound booth.

Andrew approached the Fifty-sixth Street entrance for one last try. The crowd had thinned considerably. The orchestra and chorus members had long entered the hall, and only a few latecoming ticket holders were going through the metal detectors next to Tommy's booth. Several dozen police officers remained, though.

Tommy, thought Andrew, and he started yelling. "Tommy! Tommy, it's me! Andrew!"

Tommy looked up at the sound of his name. He squinted into the crowd and saw Andrew.

"Hiya, Maestro!" said Tommy. "What are you doing out there? You're gonna be late!"

"Oh, thank God!" Andrew exclaimed. He pushed through the crowd. A policeman, standing next to Tommy, stopped him.

"Where's your ticket, pal?"

"I don't have a ticket, I'm the conductor!" Andrew shouted, hoarse and out of breath. "Ask him!" he added, pointing to Tommy. "Tell them, Tommy! Tell him who I am!"

"This guy?" Tommy said to the cop, pointing to Andrew. "Don't you recognize him? That's Leonard Bernstein!"

The policeman took off his hat. "Oh gee, Mr. Bernstein," he said, contrite. "I didn't recognize you! Right this way!"

Andrew, dumbfounded, looked at Tommy and then at the cop. Then he ran into the hall.

"Have a nice concert," Tommy called after him.

In the hall, the orchestra and chorus began to whisper among themselves. The whispering spread to the audience and gave way to muffled conversation. A minute or two went by.

"You think Donald has another case of stage fright?" Alison whispered to Corinne.

"Beats me," she replied, and then she grasped Alison's arm. "All of a sudden," she said slowly, "I have a funny feeling."

Alison shot her a concerned glance.

Just then Kevin Riordan's voice echoed over a loudspeaker.

"Ladies and gentlemen, may I have your attention, please."

His pause was met by silence.

"Due to the sudden indisposition of Maestro Andrew

Baker Barnes,'' Kevin's voice intoned, ''tonight's premiere of Mozart's Mass in F Major will be conducted by
Donald Bright.''

Electricity shot through the audience and through the
orchestra and chorus. It meant that Andrew really had
been kidnapped.

''Donald was wrong,'' Corinne whispered to Alison.
''Andy didn't make it.''

''I hope he's okay,'' Alison whispered back.

In the brass section, Alvin Reischel was so relieved
that he fainted.

All eyes turned to the stage door.

''Hello, everybody,'' said Andrew, out of breath but
smiling as though nothing were wrong. ''Am I late?''

Donald did not appear at all surprised. He looked at
Andrew's outfit. Andrew had lost all of his shirt studs
and his bow tie was undone. His mint green tuxedo and
basketball sneakers were smeared with grease from the
fire stairs.

''Well, if it isn't the Good Humor man,'' Donald said
archly.

''Look at your tuxedo,'' said George, shaking his head
sadly. ''They'll blame me for that, too.''

''After the concert, I'm going to kill you,'' said Elizabeth. In truth, she was relieved to see him. Without
Andrew to dominate, her life would have been immea-
surably duller.

''Darling, it's very kind of you to wait until then,'' said
Andrew, still breathing heavily. ''Um, Donald, do you
mind terribly if I—''

Donald sighed. ''Conduct? No, go right ahead. I knew
this would happen. I just knew it.''

''Actually,'' said Andrew, catching his breath, ''I was
wondering if I could borrow your baton.''

Donald shook his head and handed over the baton.

''And your score?'' Andrew asked sheepishly. ''Mine's
still at the hotel.''

Reluctantly, Donald handed over his score.

''And would it be too much trouble if I were to borrow
your jacket? Mine's sort of a mess.''

Donald sighed audibly, took off his jacket, and handed

it over. Donald was still wearing his white tie and tails, not the black tie formal wear traditionally favored by conductors, so sure was he that Andrew would return.

"You're a prince, Donald," said Andrew, putting the score and baton between his legs and trading jackets with Donald. In his baggy mint green pants and his snug-fitting white jacket, he looked even sillier. He looked longingly at Donald's shoes.

"They won't fit," said Donald. "They're not your size. I just figured out what you look like."

"What?" Andrew asked warily.

"Something from the *Sergeant Pepper* cover."

"Well, this isn't my usual concert attire," said Andrew. Just then Kevin rushed over.

"What the hell's the delay—*Andrew!*" he shouted. "I thought you were in Saddle River! And what the hell are you wearing?"

"Saddle River?" Andrew repeated. "Why would you think that? Where *is* Saddle River?"

"Will somebody please tell me who's conducting tonight?" Kevin asked.

Donald pointed at Andrew. "He is," Donald said sadly.

"Then get out there!" Kevin told Andrew. "It's time!" Kevin hoped George didn't go through all the Gelusil. He could have used one just now.

Kevin ran back to the sound booth. A few moments later, his voice boomed throughout the hall.

"Ladies and gentlemen," he intoned, "due to the sudden, um, *reappearance* of our scheduled conductor, tonight's premiere of the Mozart Mass in F Major will be performed by Andrew Baker Barnes."

Backstage, Andrew was wiping the grease from his trouser legs.

"Andy," said Donald.

Andrew straightened and looked at Donald. He expected Donald to say something cutting and nasty, reflecting Donald's understandable disappointment.

"In the fugue, in the Credo," said Donald, to Andrew's enormous surprise, "just conduct the basses. Everything else will fall into place."

Andrew looked with surprise at Donald. "Thank you,"

he said. Kevin reappeared. "*Now*, damn it!" he shouted to Andrew.

Moments later, a red-faced Andrew Barnes stepped out, to the surprise—and laughter and tumultuous applause—of the audience. Behind him trailed Janet Ikovic and Paul Martland, the soloists, who bowed to the audience and seated themselves in folding chairs to the left of the conductor's podium. In the Green Room, where soloists wait prior to the concert, Paul and Janet had been making plans to go out for dinner after the performance. Paul was about to call his agent and ask him to cancel his appearances next weekend in an opera festival in San Francisco, due to illness, in case Janet could join him at his summer house in Maine, when an usher appeared and told them to proceed to the edge of the stage.

"What the hell—" said Corinne, staring at Andrew's strange attire.

"Did you ever—" said Alison.

Andrew acknowledged the audience's applause. He looked quickly around the hall. The television cameras rolled. Charlie Churchill, in an enormous tuxedo and all alone in a first-tier box near the stage, was describing the scene into a microphone held by one of his technicians. "Good," he said, when he saw Barnes. "I never liked that other guy anyway. Gee, what a nice suit he's wearing."

Onstage, Andrew opened Donald's Mozart score to the first page of the Mass. He was surprised to see that it was covered with pencil marks of all kinds. He flipped through the score and saw Donald's markings on every page. *So that's what real conductors do,* Andrew told himself. *They make all these funny little marks. Maybe I should do that.*

He glanced around the orchestra and chorus to make sure that everyone was ready. The string players were still laughing at his clothes. Andrew grew concerned when he looked at the brass section, where the other trombone players were busily reviving Alvin, mostly by the method of slapping his face. Alvin came to for a moment, saw Andrew and not Donald, calculated how much money he had just lost, blinked, and passed out again.

Andrew waited patiently while the brass section revived Alvin, who remained conscious this time, if somewhat confused. Alvin finally signaled that he was ready to play. Andrew then motioned for the chorus to rise, and they did so, shuffling their Mozart scores, hidden in black folders, open to their first entrance. He looked for Alison, found her, and winked. Then he saw Corinne standing next to Alison, and he winked at Corinne, too, for good measure.

Andrew next smiled to Paul Martland and Janet Ikovic and invited Janet to rise. He looked around the bewildered orchestra and chorus one last time, and then he lifted his baton and held it for a long moment between his hands, which were, as always, clasped penitentially before him. At length he drew his hands apart, and with a graceful upward and downward motion of baton and right hand he commanded the orchestra to begin.

The strings played the first notes of the Kyrie Eleison, the first movement of the Mass. The chorus made its entrances cleanly and confidently. Janet sang her solo part in the Christe Eleison as if she were in the best of health. Chorus, orchestra, soloists, and audience forgot about what Andrew was wearing and concentrated on the music. The world premiere of Mozart's Mass in F Major, Andrew Baker Barnes conducting, was on its way.

THIRTY-ONE

Carnegie Hall shook with applause and cries of *bravo* for nine long minutes at the conclusion of the Mass. First Andrew, completely wrung out, took a solo bow. Then he turned to his right, clasped hands with the first violinist. Then he pointed to the various orchestra members

who had particularly difficult parts to play, inviting them
to rise and accept the audience's applause. Andrew barely
heard the applause. He was still thinking about the fugue
in the Credo movement. Andrew had followed Donald's
advice, concentrated on the basses, and watched the other
parts make all of their entrances cleanly and uniformly.
Andrew still could not believe that the fugue had worked.
Good old Donald, he thought.

He pointed first to the oboist, who had played to per-
fection her obbligato. She stood and bowed and gave Andrew a look confirming that the attraction between them
was mutual. *I'm in New York for two more days,* Andrew
thought, as he watched her bow again. Andrew liked the
way she bowed. *Maybe I can call a special rehearsal just
for oboes. And send home all of them except her.* Smiling
even more broadly now, Andrew pointed to the rest of
the woodwinds, who rose and smiled. Then he acknowledged the tympani, the viola section, and finally the entire orchestra. They could not believe how well they had
played. Andrew turned next to the soloists, kissed Janet
Ikovic, who was about to pass out from the excitement,
and shook hands with the stoic Paul Martland, perhaps
the only person onstage not to get caught up in the almost
religious fervor surrounding the performance.

Andrew linked arms with the soloists and they bowed
on his cue. Then Andrew turned to the chorus, gave them
a broad smile and a salute, and with a brisk wave of his
hand he invited them to stand. The effect on the audience
of the chorus rising was like some unseen hand turning
up the level of electricity in the hall. The audience dou-
bled and redoubled its applause for the chorus, which,
thanks to Donald's stern tutelage and Andrew's expressive conducting, was virtually flawless tonight.

Andrew smiled at them, raised his hands over his head
like a prizefighter, acknowledged the swelling applause,
and led the soloists offstage. The orchestra members,
laughing and chatting, resumed their seats. The string
players tapped their bows against their music stands, the
highest honor string players can bestow on a fellow musician.

Donald and James stood at the stage door, applauding
Andrew and the soloists. For the first time in his life,

Andrew saw a look of genuine admiration on Donald's face. Neither Donald nor James could deny that Andrew's conducting had been anything less than triumphant. "Let's go," said Andrew, hoarse and out of breath, grabbing Donald and propelling him onstage. "And you were right about the fugue." Donald, still without his jacket, went willingly.

After a few steps Donald turned back to say something to Andrew and he suddenly realized that Andrew had not followed him out onstage. Donald looked back to the stage door, not sure whether to stop or go forward. Andrew motioned quickly for him to keep going, and then smiled and folded his arms to indicate that he was not going out with him. Donald took a deep breath and made his way through the cello players and their music stands. When the chorus members saw him, they began to scream and shriek and whistle. They jumped up and down on the risers, pounding them and making them sound like an oncoming subway train. It was utterly unprofessional and no one cared.

The orchestra and the audience followed their cue. Most people in the house did not know who Donald was, but they reasoned that if he was taking a bow all by himself he must have played some important role behind the scenes. Donald turned and faced the chorus, blew them a kiss, turned back to the audience, and pointed to the chorus. Tears formed in his eyes. Andrew waited for what seemed like ages to Donald before he led the soloists back onstage. Andrew followed them. The audience and even the orchestra members rose to their feet. The applause was deafening. Donald thought it would never end.

THIRTY-TWO

What happened to you?'' Kevin shouted into Andrew's ear. The musicians' lounge was jammed with postconcert revelers of every sort, including orchestra and chorus members, their friends and spouses, ushers, technicians, security people, and members of the audience who had no connection with the performers but who wanted to see what went on after a performance.

Virtually everyone strained for a glimpse of Andrew, who was surrounded by well-wishers. Elizabeth, playing the good wife, a forced smile on her face, listened to four or five strangers giving their impressions of the concert. Paul Martland, the tenor soloist, was pushing through the crowd, looking for Janet. Janet was avoiding him for the moment—she wanted to savor her triumph. Romance could wait.

Champagne was spilling all over the furniture. Those present quickly overwhelmed a long buffet table set up by the Friends of the Symphony. Leaders of the Friends were making frantic telephone calls to caterers, trying to find more food. Outside the lounge, at the coffee table, people were lined up six and eight deep to collect their bets from Alvin and Leo. To the bettors' deep disappointment, all they received were IOUs.

"I can't hear you!" Andrew shouted back to Kevin. Well-wishers surrounded the conductor, all talking at once. Everyone seemed to have something important to say to everyone else, and no one could hear a thing.

"What the hell happened to you?" Kevin repeated. "Where did you disappear to?"

"To the park," Andrew shouted back. "Where did you *think* I was?"

"Speech! Speech!" someone yelled, and soon the entire room took up the chant. "Speech! We want Barnes!"

Andrew smiled and shook his head. He took a long pull on a glass of champagne that someone thoughtfully had placed in his hand.

"Come on, Maestro! Give us a speech!" yelled one of the violinists, already on his third glass of champagne. Applause and cries of "Let's go!" and "Speech!" filled the room.

"Okay, okay," said Andrew. He brushed back his hair and wiped the perspiration from his forehead. His clothing, needless to say, was soaked through with sweat. "I just want to thank—"

"Louder!" and "Can't hear!" came from the back of the lounge. More people were trying to push their way in, but there was not enough room. Andrew stood on a low table and addressed the crowd, which rapidly quieted down.

"What a night!" Andrew said, smiling broadly, raising his glass to the crowd. They responded with applause and cheers.

"I've never been through anything like this in my *life*!" he continued. "What an orchestra, what a hall, what a chorus—you all should be very, very proud of yourselves!"

More applause and cheering.

"But especially," Andrew said, putting a hand up to stop the applause, "you should be very, very proud of the man who found this piece, who edited it, who prepared the chorus, and who very nearly *conducted* the damned thing—Donald Bright!"

Donald, who had been standing in a corner with James Carver and Gretchen Hemenway, turned at the sound of his name. The chorus members present led the others in clapping and shouting for Donald.

"I told you Andy was a good guy," Alison shouted over the din to Corinne, who was standing next to her.

"*You* told *me*?" Corinne shouted back, surprised.

"Honey, I knew Andy was a good guy when you were still in grade school."

"I can imagine," Andrew continued, but only after the acclaim for Donald had run its course, "I can imagine that a few of you wonder what happened just before the concert. And no, this is not the normal way I dress for concerts."

The listeners reacted with laughter.

"You'd never believe me if I told you," said Andrew, grinning broadly. "*I* don't believe it, and I *lived* through it!"

More nervous laughter. Those present themselves had been through an ordeal, waiting for news of the missing conductor.

Andrew continued. "So don't ask me to explain. All of you were *so* great tonight. I love my orchestra back home, but you really spoiled me tonight." The listeners interrupted with delighted applause. Andrew smiled.

"While I'm up here, I just want to say thank you to my lovely wife Elizabeth, who in many ways is responsible for my being here tonight. I love you, darling."

Elizabeth, the good wife, smiled and blew him a kiss. *She wants to kill me even more than the terrorists ever did,* Andrew thought.

"All right," said Andrew, sensing the restlessness of a crowd silent too long. "I'll stop. I just want to say that I thank each and every one of you, and we'll try to do it again tomorrow night and Sunday afternoon! Okay?"

The listeners responded with more applause and cheers for Andrew. Then they seemed to forget all about him and returned to their own conversations.

George appeared at Andrew's side. He had just taken another sedative and was feeling better. "Good job," he said. "I knew you weren't really in Saddle River."

"What are you talking about?" Andrew asked, confused. "Why does everybody keep talking about Saddle River?" He had not heard that he was supposed to have been held there.

"*Ugo* lives in Saddle River," George explained. "He would never have permitted it. Ugo respects you very much."

"Thank you," said Andrew, even more confused.

"I respect you, too," said George. "I respect everybody."

Across the room, Donald, James, and Janet were standing together. Each held a glass of champagne.

"You were great," James told Janet. "I knew you'd be. How's your throat?"

Janet smiled wearily. "Not so good," she said, her voice as hoarse as it had been the night before. "I feel like Cinderella back from the ball."

"You were just wonderful," said Donald. "Where have you been hiding that beautiful voice of yours?"

"At every audition in New York City," Janet said. She had gone for the cortisone shot just before the concert, and while she sang beautifully in concert, now she could barely speak. "I figured nobody would notice me there."

Donald and James laughed. Donald turned toward James. "Well, we came pretty close," he said. "I'm wrung out. I'm just beat."

"That was nice of Andrew, to give you that curtain call," said James.

"Andy isn't all bad," said Donald. "He just caught a few breaks."

"I'd rather be lucky than talented," said James, relieved to see Andrew alive and well, even if it meant that Donald did not get his concert. When the concert ended and no one stepped forward to arrest him, James began to feel much better.

"I know what you mean," said Donald. "No question."

Near the doorway, Tommy the doorman, champagne glass in hand, was lecturing the stagehands on the role he played in the evening's festivities. "And the cop says, 'Who is this guy?' So I say, who does he look like? It's Leonard Bernstein!"

"Don't you mean *Barnes*?" asked a stagehand.

"Huh?" said Tommy.

"It wasn't Bernstein, it was Andrew Barnes. Bernstein's much older than Barnes."

Tommy stopped and thought about it. "You know,

maybe you're right,'' he said, shaking his head. ''I thought nobody but Lennie would have the balls to dress like that. You should have *seen* the guy.''

THE
FOLLOWING
TUESDAY
EVENING

THIRTY-THREE

Donald Bright sat in his office watching the special on the Mass on a portable television set. He kept hoping to catch a glimpse of himself, but the aggrieved Charlie Churchill had managed to keep Donald almost completely off the screen. So far, Donald had seen himself only for a moment, sitting next to Andrew at the press conference. Churchill had not even mentioned Donald's role in finding the score of the Mass.

On the screen at that moment, Andrew was conducting chorus and orchestra in the Credo movement of the Mass. A postconcert interview with Andrew had been dubbed in. "All through the performance," he was saying, as the orchestra played and the chorus and soloists sang, "I kept thinking of this Leonard Bernstein concert. I saw him here at Carnegie Hall, conducting *Rhapsody in Blue* from the keyboard. I'd never seen anyone play and conduct at the same time before. I guess it made a big impression on me. I was sitting up in the last row of the balcony—but I could tell that he just kept making *mistakes*."

Donald sat up, offended by Andrew's criticism of Leonard Bernstein. "How the hell would *he* know?" he asked aloud.

"There was nothing wrong with his conducting," Andrew said. "It was his *piano playing*. He just hit a lot of wrong notes. The thing is, people *loved* it. Nobody minded the mistakes. It wasn't a flawless performance but it was a *great* performance. Bernstein caught the exuberance of the music—he caught the *spirit* of the piece, and he just swept the audience along with him.

"I bought a recording of Bernstein playing *Rhapsody in Blue* the other day, and believe me, on the recording, his playing was perfect. Every single note was right. In my wildest dreams, I could never hope to master the 'grammar of conducting' like Bernstein. But that *Rhapsody in Blue* performance showed me that most listeners aren't interested in technical precision. I mean, you can't get away with conducting badly. Believe me, I did enough of that early in my career. But the most important thing for me is doing what Bernstein did that night in Carnegie Hall—capturing the intent of the composer, and sweeping the audience up in the spirit of the piece. I don't know if that makes any sense, but that's what I try to do."

Donald nodded in agreement.

"A conductor doesn't just keep time or study the score. He's a messenger from the composer to the audience. An advocate for the composer, to use Erich Leinsdorf's phrase. Leinsdorf's another great conductor. And that's what I tried to be with the Mozart Mass in F Major."

"How come he gets to talk about Leinsdorf and I can't talk about Robert Shaw?" Donald asked. He wanted to turn the set off.

He did not, though. He watched the program until the end, waiting to see himself again. He did not see himself at all. He acknowledged to himself, though, that Andrew's conducting had been as brilliant as he had thought it was during the concert.

Millions of Americans also watched the program until the end. Among them were numerous administrators of American orchestras. In London, the next morning, at the offices of the Royal Symphonic Society, requests to book Andrew poured in from all over the United States. Andrew was invited to guest-conduct, to lead concerts at summer festivals, to become part-time chief conductor in a few cities, even to conduct opera (which he hated, although he never told Officer Caruso). Andrew could have given up his Royal Symphonic post to become a full-time guest conductor on the basis of the offers that arrived in London Wednesday morning. Suddenly Andrew Barnes was the hottest classical musical property in America.

The fact that Andrew was a good conductor did not matter. What mattered was that ninety-five reporters had recovered from their hangovers and written favorable stories about him and that Charlie Churchill had thrown his arm around him on the PBS special. In the weeks to come, over Elizabeth's strenuous objections, Andrew would politely decline each of the guest-conducting offers. There were no guarantees, after all, that an Officer Caruso would materialize before each rehearsal to tell him what to say to the orchestra. Retire from guest conducting batting a thousand, Andrew decided: one for one.

Guest conducting, Andrew concluded, was like being a substitute schoolteacher. You could never hope to make a mark on someone else's orchestra, or someone else's classroom. The most you could hope for, unless you were a conducting genius who knew more about music than anyone in the orchestra, was to escape with your dignity intact. In refusing the guest-conducting offers, Andrew once again would show the world that he knew his limits. If anything, it would only increase his stature.

Elizabeth would not see it that way. She would view his rejections of the offers as a personal snub, a rejection of all her hard work. To Elizabeth's mind, Andrew simply did not want to become any more indebted to her than he was already. Elizabeth was not entirely wrong.

THE
FOLLOWING
WEDNESDAY
EVENING

THIRTY-FOUR

Wednesday evening at seven-thirty, the members of the New York Symphony Chorus were settling into their folding chairs in the chorus room. They were waiting for Donald to arrive and lead the first rehearsal for the next piece the chorus was scheduled to perform, a concert version of Verdi's opera *Rigoletto*. The singers flipped absentmindedly through the new scores that Gretchen Hemenway had given them as they entered the rehearsal room. They sipped coffee or tea from Styrofoam cups and talked quietly about the Mass.

The chorus members felt quite good about themselves. The reviews of Friday night's performance singled the chorus out for the precision of its attacks, its clear diction, and its emotional involvement with the music. Chorus members always love it when their group rates a mention in a concert review. The reviewers had little to say that was negative about any of the participants. There were unusually kind words about the orchestra and both soloists. Andrew himself won raves.

The Saturday night and Sunday afternoon concerts were equally successful, although they lacked the color and drama of Friday night. Also, a substitute soprano sang in place of Janet Ikovic, who, Symphony management was informed Saturday morning, was unable to sing the final two concerts because of the sudden development of a sore throat. She enjoyed her drinks with Paul Martland, though, and would spend the next weekend with him at his summer place in Maine.

Officer Louis Caruso of the Midtown South bureau finally admitted that he had not seen anyone from the PLO, or from any other organization, abduct Maestro Barnes. In light of the fact that Andrew turned up unharmed, Officer Caruso was let off with only a departmental warning. He considered himself a very lucky policeman.

George was resting comfortably at Ugo Barelli's home in Saddle River. To Kevin's deep disappointment, George was giving no thought to the possibility of retiring. This prospect scared Kevin beyond words. One Ugo was enough. In that respect, he was becoming more and more like Ugo. Ugo, still in Sardinia, had yet to hear about the events surrounding the performance of the Mass. He would not arrive in New York for a few more weeks.

Alison and Corinne, friends again, sat side by side in the soprano section, waiting, along with the rest of the chorus, for Donald's arrival.

Donald, sitting in his Carnegie Hall office, had begun only this afternoon to sort through all the mail that had arrived in the week leading up to the performance of the Mass. A few minutes before the rehearsal was to begin, he opened a letter from the London Philharmonic Orchestra, one he had assumed to be a concert announcement. When he read the letter, he received a shock.

Maestro Bright [the letter began]:

As you may be aware, the Music Director of the London Philharmonic Orchestra, John Leipzin, has announced his retirement effective two seasons from now.

"No, I wasn't aware of that," Donald said aloud. He looked at his watch. He did not want to be late for the rehearsal. "Why should I care about him?" he asked. He read on:

For the past six months, the Trustees of this Orchestra, under my direction, have sought a suitable candidate to replace Maestro Leipzin, one who will continue the great traditions upon which this Orchestra was founded.
We confess that we were unfamiliar with your work until Maestro Andrew Barnes of the Royal Symphonic Society, a member of our search committee and a dis-

tinguished conductor here in London, advocated forcefully on your behalf.

At the urging of Maestro Barnes, we undertook a careful study of your career. We spoke at great length with conductors in Britain and the United States for whom you have prepared choruses. The reaction that we encountered was unanimous. Every conductor whom we contacted spoke of your musicianship, your vision, and your conducting abilities, in only the most glowing of terms.

Donald was puzzled. He wondered what the point of this letter was. He read on.

We at the London Philharmonic remain in Maestro Barnes's debt for calling you to our attention. It is now my extreme pleasure to offer you the position of Music Director and Chief Conductor of this Orchestra upon the retirement of Maestro Leipzin. We invite you to visit the Orchestra at your earliest convenience.

It is our fervent hope that the challenge of running your own orchestra, as well as the financial terms (including relocation costs and the provision of suitable lodgings for you, both in London and in the country), will be sufficient to draw you away from your current post with the New York Symphony Chorus.

We certainly hope that you will give serious consideration to our offer, and we look forward to hearing from you.

> *Yours very truly,*
>
> *Lord Richard Potts,*
> *Chairman,*
> *London Philharmonic Orchestra*

Donald's heart raced as he read the letter. It made no sense. He had finally been offered what he had always wanted. This letter that he had nearly thrown out promised to change his life. But what if he screwed up his first concert? Or every concert? *Why me*, he thought. And then he thought: *why not me?*

Donald put both hands on his desk, closed his eyes, and took several deep breaths. He wanted to call everyone he knew to tell them about the letter, but not before he could reread it, but there was no time now.

The most surprising words of all leapt out from the letter: *At the urging of Maestro Barnes. Why would Andrew do this for me,* Donald wondered. *I don't even like him.* He thought about calling Andrew to thank him, but he calculated quickly that it would be the middle of the night in London. He wondered why Andrew had not mentioned anything about the job offer. *Maybe Andrew didn't know,* he concluded. *Or maybe he did.* Donald could not sit and speculate, though. His chorus was waiting. He pulled the letter from his pocket, read it again, stuffed it back in, and practically ran from his office down a flight of steps and into the chorus room.

He perched himself on his conductor's chair and looked from face to face in the chorus. His Verdi score rested unopened on his music stand. James, seated at the piano, was quietly going over some of the trickier chords in the piano part. Gretchen Hemenway, serious as ever, leaned against the back wall, marking attendance in a notebook. Alison and Corinne sat side by side, as usual. Finally Donald looked around the room and cleared his throat, and there was silence, save a few people still whispering or turning pages in their scores.

"All right, all right, let's get started, folks," he said. His attitude was all business but his face was shining with excitement. He tried to control his emotions. "This is an enormous piece, and we may have to do it from memory."

Groans from the chorus. Occasionally, Ugo demanded that the chorus memorize its part and perform onstage without their musical scores. Ugo did this most often in concert productions of operas. Conductors like the dramatic effect of a chorus singing from memory. Choruses have mixed emotions about singing without scores. The singer really learns the piece, but the work involved is increased exponentially. So are the chances of making an enormous and embarrassing mistake.

"We won't really know until Ugo gets back from Sardinia," said Donald, not surprised by their dismay.

"Whenever *that* is. Let's take it from your first entrance. Page eleven of your scores. We'll talk more about what the opera's all about, but what's happening here is, um—"

Donald flipped through some notes. " 'The Duke spies the beautiful Countess Ceprano and leads her away under the very nose of her husband.' Typical opera nonsense. Okay, find the page quickly, please—no talking—James, do you have the place?"

James nodded. No one suspected him of making the threats. As far as he was concerned, the matter was closed. He saw quite plainly that something was up with Donald, but he could not tell what it was. He wished that he could stop the rehearsal so that he could ask Donald to explain.

"Here we go," said Donald. He stood. Standing was a small psychological ploy conductors used to capture their musicians' attention. "Five measures before we come in," he said, his baton in his right hand, which he held out before him at shoulder height. He looked quickly around the room. The singers sat up in their chairs, found the right page, and looked back and forth between Donald and their scores.

"Ready?" Donald asked, his baton poised. He glanced in the direction of the soprano section, his eyes asking for silence. "Okay, let's do it." His hands moved together, apart, up, and down as he commanded, "Two, three, four—AND!"

The singers sang haltingly if spiritedly through their part, ignoring Donald's expressive direction in favor of keeping their heads buried in their scores. Singing Verdi reminded the chorus members that their role in the Mass really had come to an end. The feeling was bittersweet. It meant expunging from their memories all the tricky spots of the Mozart score and preparing to learn—and perhaps to memorize—the intricacies of the new piece.

Donald was not concerned just now with the psychological adjustment his chorus faced. His mind was on the letter from London. *At the urging of Maestro Barnes,* he kept thinking. He could not get that phrase out of his mind. He thought it odd that an orchestra would turn to a rival conductor to solicit names for a new music director, but maybe that was how they did things in England. He wanted to reread the letter, just to make sure that he had not dreamed its contents. Instead, as the chorus sang, he stepped down from the podium, took out the letter, placed it on the piano for James to see, and went back to the podium.

"Okay," he said, stopping the chorus with a deft motion of his baton. James read the letter and nearly fell off the piano bench. Donald glanced at him but did not say anything.

"What I need here from the tenors," Donald said, "is a little less vibrato and a little more, you know, *bounce*. TEE-ta-ta, TEE-ta-ta, know what I mean? Gentle? Delicate? This isn't World War III, folks. It's just Verdi. Okay, let's take it again. Ready?"

For the first time in several years, Donald almost felt like contacting his parents and his brother Sam. Then he decided that they would hear about his appointment in due course. The three had been running a small talent agency ever since Sam's retirement from the world of performing. Let *them* call *me*, he told himself.

At the urging of Maestro Barnes, Donald thought. The irony of Andrew's involvement in the search committee was not wasted on him. He wished that he could have won the job without Andrew's help. Then he remembered that Leonard Bernstein had gotten help from other conductors, when *he* was getting started. Donald felt better and better.

AUTHOR'S NOTE

Novels mixing fact with fiction often leave readers wondering which was which. This novel is intended as a farcical, if accurate, portrait of the world of classical music performance. The following things, though, were invented for the sake of the story: the New York Symphony Orchestra and Chorus, Philip Popham and his prostitutes, the Royal Symphonic Society of London, the Manhattan Conservatory of Music, the letters from Mozart to his publisher and from Beatrice Hofsteder to her friend, and the "long-lost" Mozart Mass in F.

If you liked this book, you have my brilliant and demanding editor, Robert Asahina, to thank. In addition, many musicians and nonmusicians gave generously of their time. Their contributions should be acknowledged here. Michael Flood, the noted Livonian musicologist, did his usual outstanding job. The soon-to-be-famous conductor Andrea Goodman read through several drafts of the manuscript to check the musical references, and I am in her debt for her comments and corrections. Errors and biases in the text, of course, remain strictly those of the author.

For their individual and collective wisdom, comments, patience, and advice, my thanks to: Ashley Adams, Jennifer Bates, Joel Berkovitz, Don Bishop, Judy Bradt, Deborah Cole, Pamela Coravos, Reg Didham, Dorre Fox, J. J. Gertler, Susan Goforth, Rocky Goodman, Judi and Richard Hannes, Kristen Hornlien, Julie Howard, Jennifer Jewison, Stephanie Jonah, Brad Justus, David and Melanie Katzner, Stephen and Nancy Petchek Kohn, Francis Leger, Audrey Levin, Wendy Levin, Andrew and

Marina Lewin, Bertrand Lipworth, Attilo Poto, Connie Petropolous, Maggie Riley, Marion Shaw, Janet Snow, and David Snyder. Special thanks are due to my many friends among the students, faculty, and staff of the Boston Conservatory of Music, and to the members of the Aspen Chamber Choir of the Aspen Music Festival.

The following excellent, highly readable books offer considerable insight into the art of conducting: Elizabeth A. H. Green, *The Dynamic Orchestra*, Prentice-Hall, 1987; Erich Leinsdorf, *The Composer's Advocate*, Yale University Press, 1981; Max Rudolf, *The Grammar of Conducting*, Schirmer Books, 1980; and Harold C. Schoenberg, *The Great Conductors*, Simon and Schuster, 1967.

Finally, three teachers of music deserve special mention—Anthony Taglino, LouCelle Golden Fertik, and Henry Mishkin. This book owes its existence to them.

M.L.
Marblehead, Massachusetts
July 1988

About the Author

Michael Levin studied Ancient Greek and English at Amherst College and is a graduate of Columbia Law School. He is the author of two critically acclaimed books: a comic novel about law school, *The Socratic Method* (1987), and a nonfiction study of Judaism, *Journey to Tradition* (1986). Levin has written for *The New York Times*, CBS News, and the *Jerusalem Post*, and he is currently at work on his next novel.

through ti   ectors next to Tommy's booth. Ser-
                  at remains